## SNOWLINE

'Where in El Salvador do you want me to take the money?'

'Nowhere you've ever heard of. Guazatan. It's a small place north of the capital, not far from the border with Honduras. Not easy to get to.'

'Well, if I physically take the money into El Salvador, can't a bank transfer it to Guazatan?'

He shook his head. 'The place isn't on any map. It's just a dirt-street village. It's got no bank. There probably isn't even a store. It's got nothing.'

I noted that *probably* it meant he hadn't been there himself.

'And it's dangerous in Guazatan?'

'There's a bloody war going on. Sometimes the army controls Guazatan, sometimes the guerrillas. I'll be frank: the danger is that either side could think you're spying for the other.'

The door opened and his eyes went from my face to check the newcomer. Then, as if it was part of the same movement, on to the bar: 'Another whiskey, please.'

**Also by the same author,
and available from Coronet:**

Skorpion's Death

**About the Author**

David Brierley was born in 1936 and spent his
childhood in South Africa, Canada and
England. He attended Oxford University, and
later taught English in a French *lycée* before
working in advertising for fifteen years. He
took up writing full-time in 1975 and his
previous novels include COLD WAR, BLOOD
GROUP O, BIG BEAR, LITTLE BEAR,
SHOOTING STAR, CZECHMATE and
SKORPION'S DEATH.

Mr Brierley lives with his wife and daughter in
England, apart from the time spent abroad each
year researching locations for his books.

# Snowline

# David Brierley

**CORONET BOOKS**
Hodder and Stoughton

Copyright © David Brierley 1986

First published in Great Britain in 1986
by William Collins Sons & Co. Ltd.

Coronet edition 1987

**British Library C.I.P.**

Brierley, David
  Snowline.
  I. Title
  823'.914[F]        PR6052.R4432
  ISBN 0-340-40569-4

---

Printed and bound in Great Britain for
Hodder and Stoughton Paperbacks, a
division of Hodder and Stoughton Ltd.,
Mill Road, Dunton Green, Sevenoaks,
Kent (Editorial Office: 47 Bedford
Square, London WC1B 3DP) by
Richard Clay Ltd., Bungay, Suffolk

This is for Ann
First Lady of Madison
With my love

# 1

He'd made love to me a dozen times. It had been in the dark with a silvery light flickering in my eyes. His lips had brushed my lips. His hands had rested on my shoulders and then slipped under my sweater to unhook my bra. Strong arms had gathered me up to lay me on the bed. His fingers had stroked my body. I had scarcely breathed at their touch. I had felt their caress on my skin, almost felt it, ached to feel it.

Now I waited for him in the Café Charlot. I sat at a table by the window so I could have that unguarded first sight of him before he arranged his face in greeting. The place had steamed up as good Paris cafés do in winter and I'd wiped away a patch of condensation on the glass.

Jules Debilly came from the direction of place St-Michel. He appeared suddenly from behind a group of students. He was hurrying though he wasn't late for our meeting. I was early. I'd been impatient to see him in the flesh.

It was Debilly, no doubt of that. But he was shorter and balder and more careworn than I expected. He was on the far side of the road and he hesitated at the edge of the pavement. He knew the kerb drill: left, right, left, though rue St-André-des-Arts is supposed to be traffic-free. I'd been fifteen years old when I'd first seen Debilly and he'd been vivid and vital, a passion that filled my fantasies. It's a shock to discover your teenage crush is middle-aged and cautious.

Debilly opened the door and brought February into the café with him. He wore a dark topcoat with the velvet collar turned up against the wind. Raindrops glistened on his shoulders. He wore no gloves. His hands were raw from the weather. In his left hand he carried a briefcase. On his right hand he wore a signet ring with a diamond that winked out a message in morse: I'm rich.

It was the dead time of afternoon: half a dozen in the café. François behind the counter, a couple of businessmen over another last cognac, men from the market, me. 'How do I recognize you?' Debilly had asked on the phone. 'No problem,' I replied, 'I know you.' 'Ah, of course,' he said, a degree of satisfaction in his voice.

I recognized him. No one else did. You can't be nine years without making a film and still have star quality. Not in Paris.

He came over when I beckoned. 'You're Cody?'

'Yes,' I said.

'Thank you for seeing me so promptly.'

That much of the legend was still intact: the courtesy, the smile, the voice like the sea drawing back across shingle. That voice had seduced me and every teenage girl who'd ever heard it. I'd sat in the local Odeon and felt a prickle come in the palms of my hands, and my stomach had tensed so much it ached. Just his voice had done that to me. I'd sat forward on the edge of my seat to watch. He'd had the mannerism – it was the signature of a Debilly love scene – of hesitating just before his mouth closed on the leading lady's mouth, his tongue sliding out like a promise of what was to come. And in those seconds I had held my breath, waiting for the touch of the lips.

'Will you have another coffee?'

'No, thank you.'

'Something else?'

I shook my head.

'Give me a whisky,' Debilly said to François. 'Make it a double.' To me he said: 'After all it is February, and it's been one of those days.'

He smiled and I noticed the lines that bit into his cheeks and the pinched white nostrils. When his whisky came he drank half of it in one gulp, neat. And I noticed the pale half-moons under his eyes and the twin furrows between his eyebrows. I didn't think he was a drunk. I thought there was tension in his face. *Drôle de Guerre* was his last movie and if you missed it you were in good company. The script was puerile, the direction uninspired, and Debilly's magic had gone, as if he no longer cared. Late seventies that had been and he hadn't made another film since. That diamond in his signet ring might only be a rhinestone. Perhaps money was a problem. The millions rolled in and you never imagined the millions could roll out. Like love floods in and love ebbs out.

*Stop*. I mustn't think about it, mustn't long for Philippe, mustn't hate *her*.

Debilly smiled again and I smiled back and said: 'You'll be glad of the whisky. They say there's a storm coming. Personally I could do without more snow.'

He paused like an actor who's forgotten his next line. He stared at me with the smile draining out of his face. It left his eyes and his cheeks and his mouth. Did I say something stupid? It was nothing more than a bit of social icebreaking between strangers meeting for the first time. But Debilly was on edge. He knocked back the rest of his drink and put the glass down on the table with exaggerated care. He shook his head as one does to clear it of unruly thoughts.

'You do certain jobs for a consideration,' he said. He came straight to the point. There was to be no chitchat first. 'That's right, isn't it?'

We'd already established that when he telephoned in the morning. I just nodded.

'In fact, you do for real what I only did on film. In which case you are worth every franc of what you are paid.'

I remembered him as a pilot struggling with the controls of a burning plane, a resistance hero being tortured by the Gestapo, a crusading journalist up against the mob. If that's how he saw me . . . I made a face. I wasn't contributing much but what could I say? Debilly had no Anglo-Saxon shyness about discussing money. He asked straight out: 'Do you operate on a fixed scale of charges? You know, so much a day?'

'No. It depends what I'm asked to do.'

'The difficulties?' he suggested.

9

'The difficulties,' I agreed. And we both knew we were talking about the dangers.

'Let me explain what I'm expecting of you.' He offered me a cigarette and lighted one for himself. Normally a man lights a cigarette and goes about his business while he's doing it. Debilly took his time, arranging things in his mind. He glanced at me once before he began. There was a look in his eyes: worry? More than that. I would swear he was scared of something. Fear shadowed his eyes and then it was gone. The actor had his lines off perfectly.

'A hundred thousand dollars is still a pot of money,' he said. 'It's not worth anything like it used to be in the United States or here in France. But there are places where it's a fortune. In certain Third World countries a whole town hardly earns that in a year. A hundred thousand can buy a lot: water supplies, agricultural equipment, a school, roads, housing, even a cottage hospital. Sometimes, in these Third World countries, the problem is getting the hundred thousand dollars to the place where it's most useful. If the money goes through official channels there is corruption all along the way and the hundred thousand is slimmed down to seventy, sixty, fifty, even twenty thousand. The trick is in avoiding the official channels.'

He gave me a smile, as if to disarm my doubts.

'That is what I want you to do: deliver a hundred thousand dollars to a poor place in a desperate country.'

He spread his hands on the table. They were palms up, a beggar's hands. Had his acting always been like this? He'd stopped talking as if he believed he'd given me all the information I needed. But he'd told me nothing. Now a man who tells you nothing is in fact giving something away. He's signalling that the job is dangerous or dirty or illegal. Why else hide the facts?

And yet, it was Jules Debilly who sat across the little table from me. It was Jules Debilly, star of a couple of dozen films, tough and tender actor, heart-throb of my youth, my very first sex object. Not that it would do me any good. He had no use for women. The passionate love scenes had been the best part of his acting. I knew that now. The whole world knew for the newspapers had been full of it when Debilly had been beaten up in a gay bar in Berlin. He'd tried to take some American soldier into a back room.

He was waiting for me to respond so I said: 'What's the name of this desperate country?'

'El Salvador.'

Jesus.

They'd been having a civil war there for years. I couldn't remember when it began. Perhaps it had been going on for ever, rebellion breaking out like boils erupting on a body with an unhealthy bloodstream. There were images in my memory of soldiers and corpses and screaming mothers. I'd seen press photos and newsreel clips. The whole of Central America was a cocktail of death, poverty and destruction. But the war in El Salvador, people said, had a special quality. Vietnam, Cambodia, Uganda, the Congo, all have had that special quality at some time or another.

'Where in El Salvador do you want me to take the money?'

'Nowhere you've ever heard of. Guazatan. It's a small place north of the capital, not far from the border with Honduras. Not easy to get to.'

'Well, if I physically take the money into El Salvador, can't a bank transfer it to Guazatan?'

He shook his head. 'The place isn't on any map. It's just a dirt-street village. It's got no bank. There probably isn't even a store. It's got nothing.'

I noted that *probably*. It meant he hadn't been there himself.

'And it's dangerous in Guazatan?'

'There's a bloody war going on. Sometimes the army controls Guazatan, sometimes the guerrillas. I'll be frank: the danger is that either side could think you're a spy for the other.'

The door opened and his eyes went from my face to check the newcomer. Then, as if it was part of the same movement, on to the bar: 'Another whisky, please.'

11

'This hundred thousand dollars,' I said. 'I must ask you what it's for.'

He swung back and leaned across the table. His face was close to mine. Normally you only let a lover that close. How had he felt, I wondered, about kissing all those women? How had Philippe felt kissing me and then kissing *her*, going from my bed to . . . *Stop.*

'Of course,' he said. 'You're careful about the jobs you do. That's good.' He smiled again, an actor's smile. 'Do you know much about the situation in that part of the world?'

'There are forty or fifty countries in the world right now where there's fighting going on. Salvador is one of the bad ones. I don't know anything in particular.'

Debilly paused a moment while François brought over his drink. He held it to his nose to smell the whisky. You only ever see a Frenchman do that.

'They've been fighting there for half a dozen years,' he said. 'There is talk of peace, negotiations, a truce. Then a few killings and the bloodbath starts again. The army gets its weapons from the United States and the guerrillas get their weapons from the army. It's a war where both sides are funded by the American taxpayer. The areas to the east and the north are the main combat zones, and that's where Guazatan is. A lot of the peasants have moved out. If they stay, the army conscripts the young men and rapes the women. The guerrillas are no better. The guerrillas have destroyed the big estates so there's no work. The army has killed the peasant leaders so there are no cooperative farms. It's a terrible life and who gives a damn about it? A few priests, a few doctors, a handful of teachers, nobody else cares.'

Philippe was a teacher and I thought he'd cared. About me. He'd cared about *her* too. When I found the bra and panties they were so small she could have been a girl he taught at school. He wouldn't talk. Not about *her*. Not about us. Typical man, he got angry as if it was my fault. *C'est foutu*, he'd shouted, and walked out of my life.

Debilly was staring. Had he stopped talking long ago?

Come on, stupid woman, stop pining. Concentrate. This is important, this is a job, this is your life.

'What's special about Guazatan?' I asked.

'There's a medical mission. It's been going for ten years. The biggest killer in Salvador is dysentry, so the doctor has been educating them about hygiene, clean water supply, sewage disposal. It's basic stuff. It's no good sending sulfa drugs and bodyscanners if the peasant kids play in pig dirt. But the mission is faced with closure for lack of money. That's what the hundred thousand is for. To keep the mission going.'

'You're a generous man.'

'It's not just me. I haven't made a film for some years but I have good friends in the business. I made a few phone calls. You'd be surprised how open-handed people can be. Or perhaps I twisted a few arms. I feel strongly about the place. I want to help. Oh, the doctor's name is Burchell.'

'American?'

'No, English.'

As I was. And Burchell was a doctor, as my father had been. Burchell lived in the middle of a civil war and would never be wholly trusted by either side. But he was a *gringo* and that would be a certain protection.

I looked away through the patch I'd cleared on the window. It was still raining, nothing heavy, just a drizzle that found its way into your soul. There were people about, men with umbrellas, kids with coat collars turned up, women with plastic bonnets and shopping bags, a man sheltering in a doorway. Debilly wasn't saying more. I had the essentials; he was waiting for my decision.

There was a little coffee in the bottom of my cup and I sipped it. It was cold. Outside, evening seemed to have come down half way through the afternoon. In my private life there was emptiness. Paris in February had nothing to hold me.

'Okay,' I said.

'Wonderful,' he said. He put his hand on mine and gave it a squeeze. It was like a Hollywood handshake: warm and sincere, but read the small print of the contract. 'There are a lot of poor people who'll owe their lives to you.'

'Do you have the money with you?' I nodded at his briefcase.

'I don't carry sums like that round Paris streets.'

'How do I get it?'

'Collect it from my apartment.' He gave me a visiting card from his wallet. I don't normally mix with people who have visiting cards. 'Come this evening about seven. But first there's the matter of your fee to settle.'

I nodded and thought of a lot of things and said: 'Five thousand.'

'Dollars?' he asked, very sharp.

'Yes, five thousand dollars.'

'You realize that's five per cent of what we're sending to keep the medical mission going.'

Air fares, hotels, car hire. The army and the guerrillas as enemies. Carrying a lot of cash to Central America when he was scared to bring it half way across Paris. A week out of my life. Five thousand didn't seem a lot to me. Couldn't he see that?

In his films Debilly had been fearless. He'd fought half an army bare-handed. Also he'd been a great lover, irresistible to women. And generous and warmhearted. Now even his courtesy had leaked away. I was seeing a long-ago idol crumble in front of me. I should have got up and walked away. If he wanted someone cheaper I could give him a name or two. There were people in Paris like Badacsonyi and Verderet who would do a cut-price job. That was the problem though. Put a hundred thousand dollars in their hands all at once and you might never hear of them again.

'The figure I had in mind . . .' he began and stopped. He sat up straight. I could see him physically gathering up his tattered dignity. 'You're right,' he said. 'It's not like sending someone to buy a kilo of sugar. Five thousand. Yes, I agree. You shall have that tonight as well. *Monsieur*.' He turned round to find François.

Debilly paid for his two whiskies. He even paid for my

coffee. He shook hands with me and murmured: '*A ce soir.*' There was a time when that gravelly promise would have sent electric shivers through me. I cleaned my little patch of window again to watch as he turned out of the café door.

I saw him go just as I'd seen him come. And then abruptly I was on my feet and struggling with my coat.

'What's the rush?' François called out. 'He's too old for you.'

I hadn't time to swap jokes. There had been this man sheltering in a doorway from the rain. He'd been motionless for twenty minutes or more. He could have been a statue in a niche in a cathedral wall. As Debilly turned left and walked towards carrefour Buci, the man stepped out to follow. Debilly had his head hunched down against the weather and saw nothing. The man was a dozen steps behind him. It was too far to be a bodyguard, too close to be a professional tail.

Why?

Before I could reach it, the door swung open and Guy came in. He was cussing the weather and shouting out greetings and gathering me up in his arms all at once. Guy is on the evening shift behind the bar at the Café Charlot. He was born in Martinique and would see eye to eye with most of the Harlem Globetrotters. When Guy picks you up you don't lash out because it's a long way down if he drops you.

'Idiot! Pygmy! Put me down.'

'What's the big rush?'

'She's after an old-timer with a fat briefcase.' That was François.

'Hey, after him. Go get him, Co.'

Guy let me down and slapped me on the rump and I was out of the door into the street. Guy would never have done that to a man. I'd lost thirty seconds just because I was a woman. Everything that happened in the whole of the next seventy-two hours you can put down to my being a woman and the turmoil that Philippe's treachery had thrown me into. If I'd got out of the café in time and caught up with Debilly, I would have demanded a reason for the man who

15

had waited in the doorway. If he'd told me the truth, I'd never have touched the job. If he'd refused to tell me or got shifty with lies, I'd have backed off. But now, as I dodged between shoppers and students, events were running ahead of me. I became committed.

Debilly and his shadow had already crossed the road and headed towards the market in rue Buci. On this winter afternoon the lights were on early and the stalls glowed like a promise of paradise. Clementines and oranges were a golden sunrise. Avocados made a soft green hill. Bananas lifted up yellow hands. The man at Debilly's back lifted up his hand and called something out. He must have done because Debilly swung round to face him. I couldn't hear any words. I was too far away. But I heard the other sound.

Don't believe that old tale about a gunshot sounding like a car backfiring. This didn't. It could have been someone clapping, a single clap to shoo away a bird. For a moment nothing was altered. The sound of traffic and voices continued. I tried to run but the crowd was thicker here. I'd pushed four or five steps forward when the scream came. It wasn't Debilly. It was a woman's scream. There were no words to it. It went on and on, bubbling out her fear and horror.

# 2

There was a sea of people. Debilly had vanished but I could tell where he was. He'd tumbled to the pavement and the spot was marked by emptiness. People pushed back from the act of violence and the empty space grew. It was like a stone tossed in the water, the ripples spreading wider.

'They should ship them all home,' a woman called out. She seemed to be shouting at me.

'Who?'

'The Arabs,' she said. 'Libyans, Algerians. Send the whole lot packing.'

'What are you talking about?'

My eyes were on the move, searching for the man who'd fired the shot.

'Shooting in the streets, murdering, raping. You take care, mademoiselle, it's not safe to go out after dark.'

'Was he Arab?' To me the man had looked Mediterranean, a mobster from Marseille or Corsica. My eyes were checking faces and finding nothing.

'They're all terrorists. Send them back. Let them eat their oil.'

She was a dumpy woman, dressed in black, with a mouth that snapped shut like a mousetrap. There are ten million like her in France: against the Jews, the Arabs, the blacks, the Americans, the English.

'Where is your horse, madame?'

'What do you mean?'

'If they don't send us their oil . . .'

'Traitor,' she hissed. 'Communist.'

Hated them too.

Where had the gunman got to? I pushed forward from the

woman in black. I could hear her muttering: 'Hitler wasn't such a fool, you know.'

When Debilly had fallen, he'd crashed into a stall selling flowers. Buckets of irises and roses had been knocked over, their blooms scattering round him. It could have been a funeral, except the corpse was writhing and moaning.

'Oh God, someone help me. Do something. It's unbearable.'

Except Debilly would have to bear it. He had no choice.

Blood ran through the flowers, darkening their petals. In this strange light the blood showed black. Later it would be hosed away, leaving no stain on the pavement. Only a passing dog would swerve to sniff.

The man from the flowerstall blocked my way. I made to go round him and he took hold of my arm.

'Are you a nurse?'

Because I'm a woman, you understand. If I'd been a man, he'd have asked whether I was a doctor. The hell with him. I shook his hand off and knelt beside Debilly.

'Don't touch him. You must wait for the ambulance.'

'Is unbuttoning his collar going to shorten his life?'

The flower-seller went on grumbling behind my back. The hell with him again. I fiddled with the knot of Debilly's tie and bent down closer.

'It's me.'

He was in shock. He didn't recognize me. The bullet had wiped his memory clean. I was simply a face looming close to his own.

'Oh God, help me.'

'There's an ambulance coming. Debilly, do you know who I am?'

'The pain. You've no idea. It's terrible.'

I should have felt sorry for him. He was a man, suffering badly, and I should have been a ministering angel. Instead I felt a hint of anger. He was a teenage crush and then he'd been noble and heroic and now he was revealed as timid and tearful. I felt cross. At myself really for expecting adolescent

18

dreams to last. So I stroked his cheek and tried to soothe away the shock.

'You musn't worry. There's no danger. You've been wounded in the upper leg. It's well away from the artery and the bone. It's a flesh wound. Boys get hurt worse playing football.'

'The agony.'

'I know it hurts. Be brave. You'll be all right. Who was the man? He was waiting for you outside the Café Charlot.'

Debilly focused on my face. He was frowning as memory came back.

'Cody?'

'Yes.'

'Where's he gone?'

'I don't know. I can't see him. Who was he? Do you know him?'

There were some decidedly odd things about this incident.

'Was he alone?' Debilly asked.

'I didn't see anyone with him. How long has he been following you?'

'I don't know.'

'Who was he?'

'I don't know. I've never seen him before.'

He looked away as he said this. In the distance was the sobbing of a police siren. The ambulance would come later. In Paris the cops always get there first.

'*Le fric*,' Debilly whispered.

'What?' His voice had been so soft.

'*Cherchez le fric.*'

'What's he saying?' It was that fool of a flower-seller again.

'Get the cops,' I said.

'They're coming. Have you gone deaf?'

But no, Debilly hadn't said *flics*, he'd said *fric*. He'd said it twice. There was no mistaking it. He was insistent that I collect the cash.

'Come closer,' Debilly whispered. 'Get the cash from my

19

apartment. Use what is necessary for your expenses. I'll pay the rest of your fee when you get back. You mustn't waste time.'

'Now hold on,' I began. There were things that were nagging at me. My brain had been muzzy before: the shock of breaking with Philippe, the eagerness to meet a celluloid hero. But there's nothing like a gunshot to clear the mind. 'I need to know –'

'There's no time for questions,' he said. 'It's urgent.'

'You haven't even given me directions –'

'Blum,' he said.

Was he delirious? Blum?

'When you get to San Salvador, go and see Blum. He'll help you. Ernesto Blum. Have you got that?'

'But if you already know somebody there –' I broke off.

There's a police station not far away in rue Bonaparte. The squad car sounded quite close now. Debilly turned his head a fraction and then back to me.

'I trust you,' he said.

Trusted me? I stared at his face. There was something childlike about him. He'd been gunned down in the street and now he depended on me.

'What's Blum's address?'

'I don't remember.'

'Doesn't matter. I'll find him.'

I stood upright and faced a ring of faces: the tired, the hopeless, the cynical, the shocked, the excited. They were Paris faces, winter faces.

'He needs air,' I said and tried to ease myself into the crowd. 'Poor man, he's in great pain. Have you seen how much blood he's lost?' And people stopped staring at me and looked at the blood.

I thought I knew where the gunman had gone. There was a supermarket on the corner and he'd dived in the entrance while everyone's eyes were rivetted on the fallen figure. He'd have scuttled out of the exit in rue de l'Echaudé long ago. He'd taken Debilly's briefcase with him, which was another of the oddities. First the gunman had shot Debilly, not to

20

kill him, not even to wound him badly, but to cause him pain. Odd. It was like a very forceful warning. Then the gunman had run off with the briefcase. You can see a hundred thousand briefcases in Paris every day, in the métro, on the streets, at restaurants. But the gunman had singled Debilly out and waited for him. It was as if he had reason to believe there was money in it.

And when he discovered the briefcase was bare, would he hunt down the person Debilly had seen last? Would he come gunning for me?

It took two men to carry and when they got it outside the taxi-driver refused to take it.

'Too big,' he said.

'It'll fit in the boot.'

'I'm not having any mess,' he said.

'It won't melt – that's the whole point.'

'I won't have it stinking the car out,' he said.

'Doesn't smell either. Come and see for yourself.'

He reared back. I got it now. There was nothing rational about his objections. The driver had a simple dread of the thing.

The two men from Fauchon stood with the carton between them. They could have been waxworks. Only the rich shop at Fauchon and the rich demand their servants stand and wait.

'They'll never allow that on board a plane,' he said.

'Monsieur, who said anything about the airport? I simply want to go three or four kilometres in your taxi. Of course if you don't want the money . . .'

I took a note out. I even rubbed it between finger and thumb. You can always buy a taxi-driver. I watched his face, seeing the battle of emotions there. He was an old man and I saw old memories stir. His eyes jumped from the money in my hand to the box. Vapour was leaking out and it hung in the air.

He swallowed and it looked as if it was painful. 'Listen, my father got a lungful at Clocher. Even now, if there's a

21

fog in winter, I lock the door and won't go out. I tell myself it's crazy to be on the road when visibility is so bad, but it's not that. You understand?'

'Perfectly.' The vapour drifted like mist. It must have been like this when his father was in the trenches seventy years ago. This wasn't poison gas, just the vapour given off by dry ice. But the horror had gripped him anyway.

The two men from Fauchon tried but the carton was too tall for the boot of the car to close. In the end it rode on the back seat beside me. I held the box steady as we raced from one traffic jam to the next.

'All the same,' he admitted, 'it is beautiful.'

'They are artists there.'

You can buy anything at Fauchon. All you need is unlimited money. The foods make Fortnum and Mason look like a village grocery. What I'd bought was a swan carved in ice. It sat in a nest of dry ice, serene, mute as any swan, lovely. I wondered whether they had a swan-shaped mould they put in the freezer or whether some sculptor carved it from a solid block of ice. It was ephemeral art, taking pride of place in a buffet, reduced to water when the night was over.

'Is this the street?' he asked.

Paris taxi-drivers are lost once they get past rue de Rivoli. We were close to place des Vosges, the sort of area people maintained was 'a good investment'. This meant they crossed their fingers it was about to be gentrified.

'Yes,' I said. 'Go slowly.'

Because I had to be careful now. If you weren't sharp you could get shot in the leg. There might be a cop on duty outside Debilly's building. Or they might have sent a couple of plain-clothes men to sniff round his apartment while the doctors patched him up. But it was the gunman who was the worry. He'd have found nothing in the briefcase and might have come to check the apartment. I was positive he'd known about those dollars. Debilly had been phoning round his old *copains* to raise money for the medical mission in Salvador. Old friends or not, there are damn funny people on the fringes of the film world in Paris. Also, though the gunman had been on his own, he didn't look the type who could plan things himself; which meant he'd have reported back to some boss.

'Over there,' I said.

The building had hopeful fresh paint and no sign of a watcher. Nobody stood in a doorway. Nobody sat in a car. There was no café close by. There were people about but they were trudging from a day's work or hurrying to an evening's fun. I tipped the taxi-driver enough so that he helped me carry the ice-swan into the apartment building. The carton rested on a table, leaking fumes. It could have been a special delivery for Count Dracula.

The concierge peered through a hatch in the wall and then came out to look closer. She had the kind of figure that is called motherly. Her hair was yellowish with grey streaks. She wiped wet hands on an apron and stared with her head thrust forward.

'What is it?'

'It's a swan, madame.'

'A swan, it's a swan.' It was a word new to her. She tried it again and said a word in some other language. I couldn't place the accent but she had the look of a Slav. Most concierges nowadays come from Portugal or North Africa or Jugoslavia. Their work permits are never in order and the police lean on them to spy.

'Why is the swan smoking?'

'It's packed round with dry ice to stop it melting.'

'Dry ice?' It was something else new to her. She frowned.

'It's for Monsieur Debilly's surprise party,' I continued. 'I'm from Filmagique. Have the others arrived yet?'

She raised her eyebrows. 'What others?'

'To help set up the party.'

She shook her head.

'They'll be here soon. It's marvellous news, isn't it? I mean about Monsieur Debilly making another movie.'

She looked puzzled.

'Hasn't he told you?'

23

The expression on her face changed to massive doubt. She would have been a great actress in the days of silent movies.

'Oh, he is a man of mystery, our Monsieur Debilly. Isn't he just! But the secret's out now and that's why Filmagique is throwing this wonderful party.'

She was looking confused.

'You've heard about us, of course. I mean, you do know about Filmagique?'

'Oh certainly,' she said. She had her pride, hated to confess ignorance.

'The film is going to be called *Le feu rouge* and it's going to be big. That's why we've planned this celebration tonight. It's so exciting. Imagine all those mega-stars coming through here – Resnais and Bowie and Streisand and Hoffman . . .' I took a breath while she gawped at me. 'And Brando and Bardot and Stallone and Delon and –'

'Alain Delon is coming?'

'One hundred big names have been invited. There'll be reporters and press photographers and television cameras.'

It took us two full minutes to get the swan upstairs, through the door into Debilly's apartment and onto a hall table.

'Is there time to get my hair done?' she asked.

'Madame, it is imperative you stay on duty downstairs. There'll be deliveries of champagne and lobsters and smoked salmon and glasses and you'll be responsible for directing them to the right apartment. First there will be the other people from Filmagique arriving. Warn me on the phone when they've come.'

She went down to wait. She saw camera flashlights and mink coats and black ties and silk and satin. She was going to be a star. And I was left alone in Debilly's home.

Some home! They'd taken Debilly to the wrong sort of hospital. It wasn't his body that needed patching up. The apartment was amazing. Only a disturbed person could feel at home. If you weren't already disturbed, living here would nudge you over the edge. It was as if he'd had a succession of art directors for lovers and each had been given one room to design.

*Look for the cash.* That had been Debilly's whisper. He hadn't told me where to look so I started in the living room.

I've been to Berlin a couple of times, both sides of the Wall. On the East side I came across a dead reporter in a car and a French Security cop called Crevecoeur tried to turn me in to the East Germans. Another time I was in the Western sector and a financier was pushing me to do an assassination. He was American, the kind of man they call a superpatriot, believes Reagan is soft on commies and Thatcher should have nuked Buenos Aires. He would have felt at ease in this living room. The chairs were stretched hide. The tables were glass and steel. Wolf skins served as rugs. An illuminated aquarium had an anchor on the sand and a gaudy tropical fish, only one, because it was a fighting fish that would kill anything else. There was a video player and a shelf of tapes and the titles on the spines were of Debilly's own films. The ceiling light was a huge crystal globe and it shone like a harvest moon. When I closed the venetian blinds they formed a blown-up photo of the Manhattan skyline at dusk. An American flag flowed across one wall but with the fifty stars replaced by fifty nuclear mushroom clouds. There was a cocktail bar and on the wall at the rear a blue neon display said '1986', in case you got so smashed you forgot what year you were in. The shelves held every drink I'd ever heard of. I searched among the bottles and under and behind and inside everything I could think of and drew a blank. No hundred thousand dollars.

The kitchen was done in Farmhouse Breton. It had an antique wood-burning stove converted to gas. There were shelves of blue and white crockery. Breakfast coffee bowls were deep enough to sink your nose in. There were *terrines* and *marmites* and *daubières*. Onions and garlic hung in pretty ropes. The store cupboard held basics: coffee and tea and jam. The fridge contained nothing but milk and Dutch cheese, but it did boast an automatic ice cube dispenser. The kitchen was for show. Debilly wasn't domesticated. He would entertain in restaurants. And there was no hundred thousand.

A cough, stifled. It had come from the corridor outside the apartment. It was a man's cough and a hand had cut it short. I crept to the front door. Footsteps were coming closer. My ear was against the panel. Jesus, there were two pairs of feet and the low tone of a man's voice. It could be the people who'd shot Debilly and they wouldn't let the concierge phone. They were right outside and my eyes were searching for a place to hide and finding nowhere. Or something hefty enough to stop them as they came through the door and all I could think of was the ice-swan. My brain had rusted up. A swan is no defence against a pistol. Then the footsteps faded. I eased open the door and saw nobody. Down the corridor were doors to two other apartments and that was enough for me.

I checked a cloakroom with a collage of posters for Fassbinder films above the basin. I tried a guest bedroom. This was Star Trek stuff. Walls, ceiling and floorboards were painted midnight blue. Stars were scattered like confetti and winked with little lights. A crescent moon glowed. Damned if I knew what the control panel by the bed did. No money. Why hadn't Debilly whispered where I'd find it? Scared of being overheard?

The master bedroom was Sheik of Araby. I had the feeling of walking into a harem. Purple and gold silk fell in folds from ceiling to floor. Bokhara rugs were thrown on top of deep pile carpeting. There were low tables and the lamps on them were mock oil lanterns. The bed was roomy enough for a threesome. I was searching everywhere now because only a bathroom remained after this. The money could be a thin packet – say in one thousand dollar bills, new and unused. That wouldn't be bulky. Or it could be a suitcase stuffed with grubby singles, though there was no logic in that. But was there logic in a bedroom like a fantasy? In a closet with sober suits ranged on the left, *djellabas* on the right? Or in a whip propped up in a corner like a fishing rod? Or in a *narghile* standing on the floor between two cushions? One of the cushions showed the imprint of a body. I knelt beside the *narghile* and put my nose to the upper container.

There was a lingering aroma of marijuana, not recent. On the other hand, that cushion showed that someone had sat by the *narghile* recently. Sometimes it's called a hubble-bubble because smoke is drawn through a lower vessel of water which cools it. The first *narghiles* used coconut shells. This one was of brass. I separated the two parts and the lower container held no water. It was crammed with money.

These were bills with the portrait of Franklin Delano Roosevelt. I counted two hundred. I was checking just to be sure. All correct, a hundred thousand in the folding money they welcome in any country in the world. It was destined for a medical mission in Central America. And it was jammed into a water pipe in the bedroom of a faded movie star with exotic tastes.

I was thinking about all this when the phone began ringing. It was beside the bed but I couldn't see it at first. A low cupboard stood next to the bed and I opened the door and there the phone was, in among the bedtime toys.

'Hello.'

'Mademoiselle, is it you?'

What answer do you give to a question like that?

I said: 'Yes, it's me.'

'This is the concierge speaking. Your colleagues are on the way up.'

'All twenty of them?'

Her laugh was a surprise, as if I'd told a dirty joke. 'Only two.'

Two was enough. Even one. He hadn't been shy about putting a bullet in Debilly's leg in the middle of a busy street.

They'd been quicker than I expected. Or I'd been slower searching. Very few seconds were left to me. I didn't know how prompt the concierge had been with her phone call. But she would have told them: Your colleague has already gone up and can let you in. And once out of her sight they would race for the stairs.

The only way out was through the front door and I couldn't risk that because I could run into the pair of them in the corridor. Living room, cloakroom, bathroom, guest room –

27

I slammed from one to another and there was no back door. The kitchen didn't even have a garbage chute. Damn it, there *must* be another way out. There *must* be a fire exit. Back to the master bedroom. Doors out onto a balcony with a table and chairs in plasticized white and tubs of yuccas and rain dripping from a broken gutter and the sound of distant traffic and a different sound from the front door. I wheeled round. Not a knock or a ring but a scratching. It came again and then a third time, the rasping of metal on metal. Skeleton keys, a whole ring of them. Then a click. I could see right down the hall with the light coming through the open door from the corridor. The concierge was right. There were two of them. I didn't see the men. I saw the shadows they cast as they stepped into the apartment.

It was all in dumbshow. They didn't speak. For a moment they stood still, listening. The shadows they threw on the wall were huge and full of menace. I was frozen, unable to think of any move. I hated the way they wore hats indoors. Even more I hated the way they both drew pistols from their pockets.

One of them shut the door to the corridor and the shadows were wiped out and my brain unblocked. These weren't police; these had the brutal directness of the man who'd shot Debilly this afternoon. They knew about his money and had come to lift it. The concierge had told them I was here and they'd assume I was after the money too. Surprise parties? They'd sneer at fairy tales like that.

Their first action was going to be to find me. There was nowhere in the apartment I could hide for long and the only way out was through the front door. But they didn't know that. I had automatically closed the door onto the balcony when I heard them trying skeleton keys. Now I opened it. I went to the closet and made myself a hiding place behind the *djellabas*.

It was a matter of psychology, that's all. They had the guns but suggestion can outgun anything.

The act of opening the balcony door had set up a draught and a trickle of cold air drifted into the hallway.

28

'Jo-Jo,' a voice said with sudden urgency, 'come on, through there.'

'You go first. I'll cover you.'

'*Ne fais pas le con.* She's getting away.'

A sound of footsteps hurrying into the bedroom.

'*Nom de Dieu,*' the one called Jo-Jo said.

'The balcony,' the other man said.

They had eyes for nothing else. I heard the crunch of shoes on cement and when I stepped out of the closet I saw two figures bending over the wall. There was a garden of sorts below with those dismal box hedges the Parisians think smart. They're evergreen and provide perfect cover and that is what they were peering down at. I went on hands and knees. I had to. I passed in front of one of the low table-lamps, my shadow humping beside me.

'There,' Jo-Jo called out. 'Moving towards the corner.'

A moment of panic. I almost blundered to my feet and ran. Twisting my head I could make out Jo-Jo with his pistol raised, aiming down into the garden.

'Idiot,' the other said. 'It's a bugger of a shadow. It's nothing.'

'Look. It's moving. She's crawling –'

'Your imagination is crawling. You drink too much.'

My knees across the nap of the carpet sounded like sand-paper. It took forever to reach the bedroom door.

'What about the roof?' Jo-Jo suggested.

'Look for a drainpipe.'

Hurry. The balcony couldn't hold their interest long. I rose to my feet and tiptoed through the hall. I got the door open and turned to check they weren't following out of the bedroom. I stepped into the corridor and pulled the door shut. Be gentle, be infinitely cautious so the lock doesn't click. Remember you heard the scratching of the skeleton keys out on the balcony. Easy, careful, bend to it.

At my back the voice said: 'Are you looking for someone?'

I kept still for a moment. He was behind me and I couldn't see his face or the way he held himself and we rely so much on how people look. All I had to go on was his voice. It wasn't enough. I could feel the sweat start on me. He could be another of them.

'Here,' he went on, 'you should try the bell.'

My hand was on the doorknob. He moved to my side and reached over to press the bell.

'It's no good,' I said. I turned so I blocked the bell. I turned very quickly indeed. The last thing I wanted was a ring fetching someone to the door. This man wasn't one of them. He looked like a lawyer or a middle-ranking bureaucrat. 'It must be broken. Or Monsieur Debilly isn't home. It's no good knocking either. I've tried that.'

'The concierge shouldn't have let you up if no one's at home.'

Definitely a lawyer with sharp eyes on the witness in the stand, alert for any stumble. I couldn't spare the time for cross-examination.

'I agree absolutely. Firstly, it's a waste of my time. Secondly, she could have let anybody up – burglars, terrorists . . .'

I walked quickly towards the stairs. I felt his eyes on me every step of the way. I didn't give a damn what he thought as long as he didn't ring the bell and bring the men with guns to the door. I'd not seen their faces but I was certain their eyes would have that blank stare, the killer stare.

I reached the bottom of the stairs when two things happened at once: I heard a door slamming somewhere above and the concierge waved through her hatch. I crossed towards her. She'd taken off the apron and tidied her hair under a snood and put on pearldrop earrings. She was going to be a star for fifteen minutes.

'Your colleagues were in such a hurry,' she said.

'It's all rush-rush-rush in the film world.'

Footsteps began echoing from the stairs. I played my last card.

'Madame,' I said, 'is there a high class florist in the quarter?'

'What you do,' she said, 'is go out and turn right and walk down to rue St-Antoine –'

'Thanks,' I interrupted. 'Must rush.'

The footsteps were clattering closer. I got out of the building and turned left. I ran. A hundred thousand dollars under your shirt gives a whole lot of power to your legs.

# 3

There must be fifty hospitals in Paris and I tried the Laënnec and the Hôtel-Dieu because they were close to where he had been shot. Debilly had not been admitted as a patient, or there was no record of him, or they weren't telling. Could be the last because when I said he was an emergency case, victim of a shooting, I was both times put through to a man who began asking questions and I gently put the phone back.

The thing is, it was the same man both times. My calls were being rerouted and it seemed pointless to try any more hospitals.

So, Monsieur Debilly, I have known you for four hours and twenty minutes and I have one hundred thousand dollars of yours and gangsters have broken into your apartment and mention of you at hospitals puts me through to someone in authority and you have vanished and I would very much like to ask you one or two questions.

Most important was this: because I'd known Debilly from his films, I'd never asked him how he'd heard my name. Call it carelessness. Put it down to the emotional upheaval of the split with Philippe. I hadn't been thinking straight. Debilly had been famous a few years back and that had been enough for me. Now I wanted to know who'd put him onto me because it's a kind of reference. Who told him to go and see Cody?

I waited for the Green Man and crossed over to the fountain in place St-Michel. Nothing looks more forlorn than a dead fountain in winter.

I don't advertise in the *Herald-Trib*. There are people who know about me – lawyers, cops, minor diplomats, fixers, journalists, politicians. When I first lived in Paris it seemed the only people who knew my name were British Intelligence

– who'd recruited me once upon a time – and the CIA –
who'd trained me until I could stomach no more and got out.
Now I'm on business terms with a lot more. Some I trust.
Others I run from. Which kind had given my name to
Debilly?

I crossed from the fountain and went through the gateway
and down the steps to rue de l'Hirondelle. On one side of
the road was the sort of hotel where no one sleeps much
during the night. On the other side was a Club Folklorique.
It was here when I was new in Paris that my life had dwindled
away almost to nothing. A man had sighted at me from the
corner. The streetlight had glinted on the barrel. He was
only fifty metres away. You don't miss with a rifle at that
distance. Not if you're a professional.

I am still alive. But it was a close run thing that evening.
I had made a mistake in not heeding the warning signs. Right
now I was hesitant because a number of little things didn't
seem quite right.

So, Monsieur Debilly, I have your *fric* but I cannot ask
you more questions. So do I sit tight in my apartment and
wait for you to surface? Or do I go straight to El Salvador
as you hired me to?

The decision was made for me.

At its east end rue St-André-des-Arts has become an Arab
*souk*. You can buy couscous and Tunisian sandwiches and
violently coloured pastries and the windows flood brilliance
onto the street. As you approach the Café Charlot, the street
grows more subdued. Look up and the walls have darkened
with dirt. At street level you glance into the windows of a
stationer's, a chemist, a hardware shop. There's a whole
window crammed with bidets. Anastasia brightens the world
with young fashion. Like every boutique it's always a season
ahead. Summer had already arrived. This year the beautiful
young things in St Trop will be wearing swimsuit bottoms
made of clear polythene. Unless they steam up, you'll be
able to see every hair.

My apartment is close by Anastasia.

The street was closed to ordinary traffic some years ago.

But the car that came from behind me was no ordinary car. Well, a Renault 9 is nothing special but it passed me slowly, engine idling, tyres swishing on the wet. A man in uniform was driving. I could see that. It was the man in the passenger seat I couldn't make out.

I was wearing a bomber jacket with the collar turned up against the weather and I was in the dark patch just before the Café Charlot when the car pulled into the kerb ahead. The passenger got out and the car drove away. The man stood a moment, his head lifting up to the second floor of my apartment building.

I died.

If the heart stops beating, the blood stops circulating. Starved of oxygen, your brain dies. For one beat of my heart I was dead. The street dissolved in rivers of light and the buildings swayed. Then the world came right as my heart began to pump again.

He was tall and thin-chested and wore a dirty fawn raincoat. It was too dark to see if it really was dirty but Crevecoeur's raincoat always had been. He ducked his head down and disappeared inside my apartment building, the coat flapping round his knees.

I stayed in my bit of shadow with my heartbeats for company. Is there a word 'policist' like 'racist' or 'sexist'? I'm not policist, or no more than anyone else in France. I can imagine having a Chief Inspector of the Sûreté Nationale as a friend, just about. But not Crevecoeur. The thing is personal. I cannot stomach the man. He's used me, fooled me, abandoned me, tried to throw me to the dogs. He stands close, as if he was a lover. He lets himself into my apartment, also as a lover does. He's ruthless and acknowledges no law. He has his own reason for what he does: the security of France he calls it. That justifies any trickery.

I kept very still, concentrating on the building, watching the windows of my apartment. They stayed dark. It was possible Crevecoeur had gone to slip Madame Boyer a thousand francs. She spies on me for him. They should get married. They deserve each other.

Five minutes. People walked past. A man asked me a question and shrugged and went away. I could hear traffic on boulevard St-Germain and a cello, far off, playing old Beatles songs, the soulful McCartney ones. Crevecoeur didn't come out. I didn't expect him to or he wouldn't have sent his car and driver away. But I kept the hope alive for ten minutes. By now Madame Boyer would have puffed up the steps ahead of him and unlocked the door to my apartment. The curtains were open and I'd seen no flicker of light. But Crevecoeur was happy to wait in the dark. It suits him, the dark. He'd wait and wait and if I went in and found him and got angry he would listen, lips parted, a shine to his eyes. He imagines he owns me, body and soul. Perhaps he had shut himself in the bathroom with a clutch of my letters to read. Or was in my bedroom, burying his face in the pyjamas from under the pillow.

I *knew* he was up there. He's done it to me before. This time I wasn't going to let myself get trapped. He would want to question me, threaten me, blackmail me. But I'd been quiet since the beginning of winter. He had no hold over me. It was nothing I had done and it certainly wasn't a social call. It could only be connected with this afternoon's events. At the hospital Debilly would be questioned about the shooting. What were you doing in that quarter? Who were you seeing? Or a cop could have ransacked his pockets and turned up a scrap of paper with my name and phone number on it.

Why should that interest Crevecoeur? He was no ordinary cop.

The young man was over towards the wall, sitting astride a kitchen chair. At his side was his personal bit of jungle, a swiss cheese plant. Seeing me he frowned a moment, puzzling what to do. His hair looked bleached out of a bottle. His legs and shoulders and chest were well muscled. He was naked.

Erica followed me into the room. 'This is Heinz,' she said, speaking English.

'Franz,' he corrected, a small frown troubling his face.

They were all Heinz to her. She picked them up in bars, brought them back to her *atelier*, kept them a couple of nights and threw them out. She made no effort to give my name.

I walked over to the easel and looked at the painting. She'd given the young man a vacant stare. She always did that. That's how she saw men: strong, slightly stupid, all the same, all of them Heinz. In the background she'd put daubs of carmine and purple. It wasn't painted from the wall of the studio but from her imagination. The paint had been put on with a palette knife in thick whorls. It was like bruised flesh. It looked as if she'd laid it on in anger. She'd given his feet jackboots and by them sketched a child's doll with a smashed face.

'Erica, can I sleep here tonight?'

'Darling.' She had an intense face and she tilted it to one side to look at me. 'Well yes, bloody right you can.' She was tall and almost beautiful, with dark hair and dark eyes. At a guess her mother was Jewish. The men she picked up and used and kicked out always seemed to be virile Aryans from Germany. Freud would have made a meal of that. Speaking over her shoulder to the man she said: 'On yer bike.'

'Please?'

'You're out of luck tonight.' She still held my eyes while she spoke to him.

'What is the matter?'

'Put your clothes on and piss off.'

From the state of the painting and her disdainful treatment of him, I guessed the German had been here a couple of nights. He was just about due for the boot even if I hadn't arrived. *Men are animals.* That was her philosophy. She didn't condemn them for it, just treated them accordingly. *They're a bundle of animal instincts. They're driven to sniff out a new woman and once they've done it with her they lose interest. It's kindness, wouldn't you agree, to push them out afterwards. Set them free for the chase.*

I caught a movement and looked at the German. He'd got up and stood staring at us. There was colour in his cheeks.

36

He wasn't wanted as a model and he wasn't wanted in Erica's bed. You could see the thought strike him that he was a naked man in the presence of two women. He turned his back and searched for his jeans among the pile of discarded clothes.

Erica rested her hands on my shoulders. Her eyes opened very wide, a hunter's eyes. There seemed to be movement at the back of them. It was extraordinary, as if a trap door had been lifted and you glimpsed nameless things seething in the darkness.

'Erica, I love you very much, but not in that way,' I said. 'You in bed, me on the floor.'

For a moment she went on eating me with her intense eyes. Then the trap door at the back slammed shut. Her lids drooped a fraction. In an even tone she said: 'Heinz, get your clothes off again.'

'You mean me?'

'Yes.' She turned away from me at last and found a pack of cigarettes and puffed smoke up into the air.

'Erica,' I said and waited until she looked at me. 'I need your help. That's why I asked if I could spend the night here. But I can't tell you in front of him.'

A smile tucked up the corners of her mouth as if she found me interesting after all.

'Heinz, get your pants on again.'

Heinz-Franz said quite a lot as he got dressed. He spoke German. Everything in German sounds like swearing to me.

Erica let him out and came back into the studio. 'As bad as bloody Feydeau,' she muttered. The cigarette was in the corner of her mouth and her head was tipped to one side so the smoke didn't go in her eyes. 'In trouble, are you? Going to tell me about it?'

It's why I was here, but I hesitated. This was work and I'd always kept work separate from my private life. It's the only way to survive.

'Not up the spout, are you?' she asked. 'Bloody men.' She took a puff from her cigarette and blew the smoke towards the ceiling. It was always hazy in her studio, like a bad day in Los Angeles. 'I blame the pill. Back in the Dark Ages men used to put on their little balloons and a woman knew where she was. When the pill came, it was men who were liberated. Three cheers, they said, it's not our chore any more. Now they go one further and all of them claim they've had the snip-snip. Lying ratbags, that's what they are, darling.'

Her attention wandered to the painting on the easel. She moved to look at it from another angle and said: 'Not bad. But as a person he was as dull as cabbage. Bloody midnight express in bed. Into the tunnel and out again in two minutes.' She shrugged. 'What the hell. It's cheaper than paying a professional model.'

'You can afford it.'

'All right,' Erica said. 'But it's more interesting my way.'

Also more dangerous. One day one of the young men would wander over to see how she had painted him and something would snap inside his head. Not everyone appreciated her paintings. A good dozen were stacked against a wall. I'd seen them before. They were all of men: lying in bed, lolling in chairs, in the shower, on a tigerskin rug, crouching on a window ledge, biting an apple, stepping out of underpants, a couple dancing together. All the men were naked. Erica said men had painted nude women long enough and she was going to redress the balance.

She stubbed out the cigarette and came over to me. She was smiling, an invitation. 'Don't waste the night on the floor. Men are only for fucking. Women are for love.'

'I find the two things go together.'

I smiled back at her. But my mind went to Philippe and keeping that smile lit up was a struggle. Erica's gaze was moving round my face as if his betrayal showed there. Perhaps it did.

'Tsk, tsk. We're sisters under the sheets.' She was silent a few moments and made a face. 'So what's happened?'

She lived off rue Mouffetard, an attic room with sloping ceilings. Only one wall was suitable for paintings. There were two there that interested me. Erica gave her pictures jokey titles on white cards pinned underneath. One canvas was called 'Sydney – Homo Australis'. It showed a sneering youth standing on his head. Of course you might think the painting was hung upside down but if you inverted it you noticed the genitals flopped the wrong way. The other painting was of a blond god on which she'd added a curious black cowlick of hair and a Hitler moustache. He was naked apart from a military cap. This was called 'Private Partz of the Wehrmacht'. I took the painting off the wall.

'I want to buy it.'

'I'd give it to you, you know.'

I suppose she meant if I went to bed with her.

'I'll buy it on one condition: that you hang it for me.'

Then I told her about Crevecoeur.

Erica was gone so long I began to wonder about her and Crevecoeur. When she came back her hair was slicked down with rain and there was colour in her cheeks. She must have walked the whole way. She worked her boots off and tossed them in a corner.

'Your cop is marvellous,' she said. 'Not a single redeeming feature.'

She clasped me in a brief hug. My cheek and shirt were wet. It was like a dog coming out of the water and shaking itself over you.

'How did it go?'

'Fanbloodytastic.'

She took off her coat and there were damp patches on her sweater where the rain had come through. She pulled the sweater over her head and unhooked her bra for good measure.

'We must have been very wicked,' she said, 'the angels are weeing all over us. *Mama mia* I'm cold. Just feel where the rain wet me.'

She came and stood in front of me and hunched first one shoulder towards me and then the other. It made her breasts shake. Shadows from the lamps danced over her skin and played tricks with her nipples. She cocked an eyebrow at me and sighed.

'Prude.'

'No, Erica, just different tastes.'

She went into the bathroom and came back with a towel.

'At least you can rub me to get the circulation going.'

I took the towel and dried her shoulders and rubbed her back and draped the towel round her.

'Did you run into Madame Boyer?'

'Of course. She scuttled out of her hutch.'

'Did she recognize you?'

'She didn't use my name. She sniffed.'

'She recognized you. That's how she greets my friends.'

'She wouldn't let me go up,' Erica said. 'Told me you weren't in. That's all right, I said, I've only come to hang a picture. I showed it to her.'

I took a deep breath. I could imagine Madame Boyer's reaction: lips pinched tight, hands up to repel the filth, but eyes open wide to feast on every detail.

Erica had bluffed her way up, said she knew the man in my apartment and he could help her hang the picture. Crevecoeur opened the door and she pushed past while he was still telling her she couldn't come in.

'So I said to him: "Why? It's not your apartment, ducky, unless you've had a sex change operation." I spoke English like you said.'

Crevecoeur spoke almost perfect English. But I doubted whether the men with guns did. Speaking English was a minor check that Erica could make without needing to know why.

She'd moved into the living room. Crevecoeur had followed, flapping a hand, unbalanced by the irruption of this wild spirit. She unwrapped the painting again and showed it to Crevecoeur.

'He gawped at it like a goldfish.'

The first time you see an Erica Fawcett painting is something of an eye-opener. 'Private Partz of the Wehrmacht' was no exception. She had leant the canvas against my desk and gone over to unhook the Klymchuk from the wall.

40

'What sort of weirdo paints something like that?' Creve-coeur had demanded.

'This sort of weirdo,' Erica had retorted, tapping her chest. 'Isn't it to your liking? Are you shy of men's bodies? Afraid of your feelings? Something stirring down in the forest?'

The thing about the painting of the nude man was that the cowlick and Hitler moustache were added like graffiti but not to the face. They were done in bold black strokes on the man's genitals. You wouldn't think it possible to embarrass Crevecoeur. Erica succeeded. He muttered about making coffee and took himself off to the kitchen. Which gave her the chance of going to the shelf of records. She found Stockhausen's *Stimmung* – I'd loved Canuck even though he'd given me that for my birthday. She slipped out the passport, driving licence and run-money. It was the perfect hiding place. Who plays Stockhausen for choice?

'Why do you keep your passport hidden away like that? And money?'

'Haven't you heard of burglars?'

'And why are you running away?'

'It's just a cop being a nuisance.'

'Been a bit naughty have you?'

She slipped the towel off her shoulders and wiped her face and peeped out at me. There was a hint of something in her eyes, a certain speculation. She looked like someone who was going to chance a kiss but wasn't certain how it would be received.

'Why don't you paint him?' I asked.

'Crevecoeur? You're some comedian.' She balled the towel up to chuck it aside and stopped. Her look went inward. You could see the birth of an idea showing on her face. She tipped her head to one side. 'Well, why not? Make a change from fifty-seven varieties of Heinz. You know him better – would he strip for me? You know what I'll call it? "A Cop's Truncheon".'

At Charles de Gaulle it was raining. At JFK it was snowing. At Miami the air conditioning was on. At El Salvador

41

International Airport the sun struck hammer blows on my head.

Passengers tend to cheer up after a flight. The plane hasn't crashed, the journey's over, there are friends to see. But I couldn't make out a smile anywhere. Over by the glass and concrete building soldiers crooked automatic rifles in their arms and watched as we walked towards them.

Welcome to El Salvador.

# 4

'So,' Blum said, 'you've come from Paris. Jules Debilly sent you. You're a friend of Jules?'

'No,' I said. 'I've met him. He asked me to come.'

'*Asked* you? And he gave you my name and address?'

'He gave me your name. The telephone directory gave me your address.'

He nodded for some time, looking me over.

'Do you want breakfast?'

'I've eaten.'

'Some coffee then. Fetch the lady a cup, sweets.'

'Ring for the maid and –'

'You don't understand, sweets. I want you to go and fetch a cup. And then I want you to go and shampoo your hair and dry it. And then I want you to take a shower. And then I want you to paint your nails. In other words, beat it. I've got things to discuss.'

She got to her feet. She wasn't his wife. Blum didn't treat her like that. Nor was she American like Blum. She was Salvadorian, with high cheekbones, black hair and cinnamon skin. She wore lounging pyjamas and as she left the dining room you could see her body moving underneath. She made sure of that, knowing that Blum's eyes would be on her.

'Sit down,' Blum said. 'It makes me uneasy seeing a lady stand.'

I took the chair across the table from him. He began eating again. The plate in front of him had bacon, sausages and fried plantain.

He said: 'You don't mind if I finish breakfast?'

My opinion would make no difference. He was an eater. As a young man I imagined him hard and muscled. In middle age his body had padded out. Hair was thick on his arms but

43

sparse on his head. He had a bull neck, like a Nazi officer in a wartime film. He put more food in his mouth before he'd finished chewing the last forkful. When a small space was cleared on his plate, he served himself a fried egg with *ranchero* sauce. Neither of us talked. He looked at his food and across at me and back to his food. The woman returned with a cup and leant across Blum to put it on the table. Under the lounging pyjamas there was only her body. Blum's eyes followed the outline of her breasts. I think in the kitchen she'd rubbed the nipples to make them stand out.

'Now beat it, sweets. *Hasta luego.*'

She gave me a look as she left. She hated me. It showed in her eyes. She was thirty years younger than Blum and all she had to offer was that body and when Blum lost interest she would be finished. I wanted to reassure her: Don't worry, I'm not next in line, I'd rather kiss a toad.

That is how Blum looked with his well fed cheeks and eyes peeping over hillocks of flesh. He had high blood pressure and an honest doctor would warn him he'd be dead before a couple of years were up. Then two or three ex-wives would fly down from the States. Sweets or whatever her name was would do battle with them over the inheritance. And the lawyers would grow sleek.

'All right,' Blum said. 'You're not Debilly's girlfriend?'

'No.'

'No kind of friend.'

'No.'

'Not an associate, a business associate?'

'What business is this?'

Blum just stared at me.

'Is he paying you?'

'Yes.'

'To do what?'

'To take money to a medical mission that's desperate for it. Hasn't he told you any of this?'

But it wasn't Ernesto Blum's style to answer questions. He put a hand inside his shirt and scratched his chest

44

and stared. He was a great man for staring. I detested him.

'So what is my part in this?' Blum asked.

'Debilly said you would help me get to the village Guazatan.'

'And get my ass shot off? Ha! The guy has finally gone soft in the head.'

From the front garden there was the sound of barking, the deep hollow bark that Dobermans and Alsatians and Labradors have. There were two dogs from the sound of it. Blum listened and someone said something and the dogs went quiet.

'You mean you're not going to help me?'

'I ain't driving you there, sweets.'

'Don't call me "sweets". I'm not. My name is Cody and I'm here doing a job and not trying for your favours.'

I couldn't stand the man, that was all. He got a cigarette out and tapped it on his thumbnail, staring at me. The colour in his face darkened. Ease off, someone should tell him, that coronary is just around the corner. Finally he lit the cigarette and smiled.

'You're quite something, ain't you?'

At least I suppose you'd call it a smile. There was no friendship or good humour in it. It was just something to do with his mouth when he wasn't eating. I knew what he was like: one of the hard men who worked with Jimmy Hoffa in the Teamsters' Union. He'd milk his union members and do a deal with the bosses at the same time. He'd live off the fat of the land. And if a coronary didn't get him, concrete boots would. I wondered what he was doing here.

'How do you know Debilly?' I couldn't see anything in common between them.

'From my time in LA. Jules was over in Hollywood shooting a movie.'

'Are you in films?'

'Movies in Salvador? You're a joker. Ha! I'm the agent for the Tropicana Line. We ship coffee, cotton and sugar north, and anything that pays on the way back. I tell you, it doesn't matter a damn whether the Congress votes dollars for military aid or not. The weapons come in. They're killing Sallies like it was pogrom time for Jews in Poland.'

He gave a shout of a laugh at his own wit and slapped his hand on the table. He could have been swatting a fly or crushing a Pole. There are some things you don't make a joke about. If my name was Blum, I wouldn't make a funny about killing Jews.

'What were you doing in Los Angeles?'

'Bit of this, bit of that. Is this a Federal court? What gives with all the questions?'

'I'm feeling my way. I don't really know Debilly and I don't know El Salvador. It's certainly not Paris.'

'Paris I wouldn't give two bucks for. Went there once on a contract. Fairies and know-it-alls, that's Paris. New York with garlic on its breath. Debilly's another fairy. Jesus, what does a lady like you do for it in Paris?'

Blum had stared at me before. I stared at him now.

'Okay,' he said, 'so you're new here and you want my help. The best advice I can give is tell you to keep your nose clean. Don't ask questions in this town. Don't talk politics with the barman. Don't give opinions to the cab-driver or he'll flash his lights at an army patrol and they'll haul you in. Don't stare. Don't run. Don't walk too slow. Don't look over your shoulder. There's a war going on. There are guerrillas and army and secret police and they don't specially care who they kill. Then there are the *escuadrones de la muerte*. They're cops and soldiers out of uniform. A night on the town for the boys. They're tough guys, sweets. Nobody taught them manners. They don't know how to say "please" and "thank you". None of them do.'

The dogs were sounding again. Then there was a woman's voice, rising shrilly above the barking. The woman screamed. Blum's thickset body shifted in the chair towards the noise, but he made no effort to get up. A man shouted and the dogs quietened.

'I'll tell you a story, right?' Blum said. 'Not a fairy tale, true. Had a kid down here from San Francisco last summer. Heard about him from a guy at the embassy who had to pick up the pieces. The kid was bumming his way south. Going to Peru to stare at his navel or something. I guess nobody warned him what it was like here. Just a kid, nineteen years of age, long hair and spots. The Guardia Nacional picked him up near San Vicente. That's just down the road from here. They threw him in a cell and roughed him up a bit even though he was a *gringo*. They didn't seem to believe the answers he gave so they beat him up again. Rifle butts, blowtorches, that kind of thing. They had him for a week. In the end they didn't know what to do so they shot him and dumped the body in a field. The thing is, they thought the kid was on his way to join the guerrillas. You know why? He was wearing a pair of army surplus boots. Ha!'

Blum stopped and waited for my reaction. He wanted me to cry out in amazement, horror, disgust. I didn't. I believed the story. I felt for the kid. But I wouldn't show my feelings in front of this man. He'd think of another story if I did. I picked up my cup and sipped some coffee. It was cold.

'Have something else,' he said. 'The beer's good. Or have a scotch. Helps you see things straight in this country.'

It wasn't yet nine in the morning. 'Coke if you've got it.'

He made no move to ring for the maid. He simply stared and his eyes showed no expression. I was aware of his breathing. His mouth was open and his breath came roughly. He seemed to be thinking about something. I never got the Coke.

'This money,' he said. 'It's a large sum?' When I didn't answer he went on: 'Large enough, I guess, or Jules wouldn't have sent you. How is he, by the way?'

'Somebody shot him two days ago.'

'Happens all over,' Blum said. 'You can be out walking the dog and some crazed Arab comes along and looses off his machine gun and says it's to liberate some lousy oasis nobody's ever heard of.'

'He was shot by a man who was following him. It wasn't an Arab. His apartment was raided and they weren't Arabs either. My guess is they were looking for the money I was

47

to bring out here. So if it's all the same to you, I'll deliver that money and get out. I seem to have involved myself in something I don't understand and I'm not sure I'd like it if I did. How do I get to Guazatan? You don't have to take me, just tell me. It's not on my map.'

'It's not on any map,' Blum said. 'It's the biggest asshole in the world. You got the money on you?'

His eyes were wandering all over my body. I felt I needed a bath just with his eyes on me.

'How do I get there?'

'You've got a problem, sweets. Brought your map along?'

The map was in my shoulder-bag. I cleared a space for it on the dining table. Blum got up and walked round and stood just over my shoulder. He wore shoes with elevator heels. The smell of cologne was heady. When he leant forward to the map it was for the same reason the Salvadorian girlfriend had leant across him: to make a physical impact. He was disgusting. I stood up.

'I've rented a car,' I said. 'Just show me where the place is.'

'You'd do better with a jeep. This is why.' He traced a route with his finger. 'You head straight up the main road here. It goes due north, over the Lempa river, and eventually crosses into Honduras. About twenty kilometres before the border you take a turning off to the right. About here. The road's not marked to Guazatan. It's signposted to Puente de los Negritos, which is over some unnamed river. It's got big black rocks on either side of the river. Thing is, they've blown the bridge up and only the rocks are left.'

'Who blew the bridge up?'

'Who do you think?'

'In Vietnam –' I began.

'The commies blew the bridge up, sweets.'

'So how do I get across?'

'You ford the river. That's why I said a jeep would be best. But a car will do this time of year. It's the dry season and the river will be mostly empty.'

'And then?'

'And then you go right on.'

'To Guazatan?'

'You betcha.'

'How do I know when I've got there?'

'That's where the road goes. It's the end of the line.'

'You've been there?'

'I know the area. But it's on the edge of one of the *bolcones*. Heard of them?'

'No.'

'*Bolcones* are little pockets of land between Honduras and Salvador. Kind of contentious issue whose land it is. Jesus, they had a war over a football match a while back so you can imagine what a border dispute is like. The army are in and out and don't stay long enough to pacify the region, which suits the terrorists just fine.'

'Do you know where the medical mission is? Run by an Englishman called Burchell. How will I find that?'

He raised his eyebrows. I was being a dumb broad.

'They'll find you, sweets. You'll be the event of the year in Guazatan, believe me. They'll put on a welcome parade for you. Three men and a mule.'

I folded up the map and put it away.

The dogs were behind wire mesh fencing. There were two of them, black Alsatians. They were trying to get at me, voicing their eagerness. The servant who was letting me out shouted at them and they went quiet. But their mouths stayed open, tongues running over their teeth. The man unlocked a gate set in a high wall and let me through. We didn't speak.

Outside the gate was a private security guard. He wore dark blue trousers and a light blue shirt. The badge on his cap read La Linea Tropicana. Strapped to his shoulder was an automatic rifle. This was in Colonia Escalon, the posh district of the capital where there is something worth protecting.

As I walked away a bell started ringing. The security guard

shouted out to me and I turned. There was a phone in a box on the wall. The guard was holding the receiver for me.

I went back and spoke into the phone. 'Yes?'

'Come and see me when you get back, sweets.' It was Blum. He clicked off before I could choose my words.

# 5

The bus began to overtake me and I slowed. Boys waved from the windows as it slipped past. There was a blind curve in the road ahead. I waved back, goodbye. Vivid stripes were painted down the side of the bus: yellow, green, orange, blue, red. It was like a rainbow painted by a child. The bus pulled ahead. On its back was the bold slogan: *Confort y Seguridad.*

I crossed the Lempa river. There was a roadblock but the soldiers peered through the window and waved me on. I was a *gringa* on my own and I wasn't wearing army surplus boots. After the turn-off to Chalatenango the traffic thinned. There were farm trucks and the odd motorbike, a bus and an army jeep with rifles threatening the fields. The road was narrow but tarred.

'Puente de los Negritos' the sign said. I turned onto a dirt road. The land on both sides was poor and scrubby. Gulches would flood in the rainy season but were dry now. The hills were tiny with steep slopes. They looked violent, as if just made. Once I passed cattle and a couple of cowboys gazing over their shoulders at my car. Crows circled, looking for carrion.

I rounded a corner and two women were walking at the side of the road. They carried bundles on their heads. I would have offered them a lift but for the men who walked in front. I kidded myself four was too many for the car. The men held machetes in their hands.

I drove through a place called Pulapeque. Blum hadn't told me about it. He considered it of no importance. It was squalid beyond imagining. The buildings were of breeze blocks and tiles. A lot of the windows were smashed and bullet holes peppered the front of a café. A market was in full swing and I supposed this was what the people on the road were making for. There were half a dozen stalls; mainly it was just sheets laid on the ground. It was a mammoth jumble sale. There were plastic combs, chewing gum, tee shirts, belts, crucifixes, comic books, clothes pegs, sandals, knives, ball pens, dried fish, plates, slices of mango and watermelon in plastic bags. I drove slowly because of the children. I noticed the children and the old people and the women. There were no young men. They'd been conscripted. Or they'd fled over the border into Honduras to escape army service. Or they'd joined the guerrillas.

The village was a single street. It swelled into a square, then petered out along the dirt road and I was back in the country again. I went over the brow of a hill and braked hard. There were half a dozen women and some small children and an old man in a group. In the centre of the group was the first young man I'd seen. He was on the ground and he was dead.

The women were wailing, their voices rising and falling. It was a primitive sound. It was a primitive death. One woman was silent. She knelt by the corpse and had twisted the hem of her skirt up and was biting it. No sound came from her but her chest convulsed. It was as if the sobs couldn't find the way out of her body.

I remembered what Blum had said about the young American: *In the end they didn't know what to do so they shot him and dumped the body.* I've seen violent death, more than I want to. I've never seen anything like this. My eyes closed while I fought to stop my stomach rising. It was unbelievable, horrific. His body was a battleground. His trousers were stained and wet. He wore no shirt. There were cuts and bruises and scorch marks all over his chest. His navel was burnt as if someone had used it for an ashtray, stubbing out a cigar. Patches of his hair had gone. Blood had dried black on his lips. Something had been inserted in his nose and a nostril burst open. Finally he had been shot in the temple. There was scarcely any blood on the ground. The man had been killed elsewhere and brought to this place.

I sat with my hands gripping the wheel. The engine was still running. I could turn the car and drive straight back to San Salvador. I could drive right through the capital and on to the airport and be in time for the afternoon flight to Miami. I could be back in Paris tomorrow. I could go and dump the hundred thousand dollars in Debilly's apartment and leave a note saying I'd changed my mind. What was I doing driving into the no-man's-land of a civil war? What business was it of mine?

I tried to work up anger. It was to cover my nausea.

The children stared at the body. They were too young to understand.

How could anyone understand?

I switched off the engine and got out of the car. 'Who was he?' I asked the old man.

'Of this place. Of Pulapeque. Armando, the son of that woman.'

She was the woman kneeling by the corpse. Her head rocked from side to side. Her face was made ugly by the sobs that couldn't escape.

'He's been tortured,' I said. Sometimes you say the most obvious things because you don't know what else to say.

The old man was short and thin. He turned away from the body to speak to me. 'His cousin has been denounced as a guerrilla. Or as a helper of the guerrillas. Or an admirer of the guerrillas.'

'Not that dead man? Not Armando himself?'

'No, his cousin.'

In El Salvador, it seemed, it was necessary to choose your relatives with care. I stared at the old man's face. It was brown and wrinkled, like a dry date.

'I don't understand,' I said. 'Armando's cousin is a guerrilla sympathizer –'

'Maybe, maybe not,' the old man interrupted. 'His cousin hasn't been seen for more than a month.'

'What's happened to *him*? Is he dead too?'

The man didn't reply. He didn't even shrug. He simply

stared at me as if I came from a different world. Which I did.

'What will happen now?' I asked.

'We must take him to Pulapeque. Tomorrow he will be buried. There is no priest. Not any more.'

What had happened to the priest? I couldn't bring myself to ask.

'You will carry the body?'

'How else?'

I walked to where the woman knelt by her son. The others had kept a step or two away so her grief shouldn't be intruded on. I put a hand on her shoulder. Sometimes to touch a person is the best help you can give. To say you're sorry is meaningless. What did it matter to this mother whether a stranger pitied her? My hand shook to her sobs. The body was twisted, its legs at an awkward angle. The signs of warfare commanded my eyes to notice. The trick is to look but not to see. How can men do such things to another human being?

'Let us put the body of your son in my car. I will drive him to Pulapeque.'

Two of the other women stopped their wailing long enough to help me load the body onto the back seat. The mother rode in front, kneeling on the seat as she had on the ground, facing backwards towards her son. I drove a kilometre in first gear so the women and children could jog beside the car. I was directed to a shack on the outskirts of the village. We carried the body inside and laid it on a bed. I wiped blood from the car seat like any proud housewife clearing up after a party. Then I left. No one was interested in me.

I drove out on my route again. I slowed as I came over the brow of the hill and stopped where the body had been. The old man was there. Everybody else had accompanied the corpse to the village. A dog had appeared and was sniffing at the earth where a smear of blood had darkened. Its ribs almost burst its skin. If there was no food for people to eat, what was left over to feed a dog? The man picked up a stone and the dog scuttled away.

'I have taken Armando to his mother's house,' I said.

'There is nothing more you can do. Why should you help anyway?'

Because he was a young man, younger than me, with a whole life ahead. Because he left a grieving mother and maybe a girlfriend. Because he was tortured.

The old man began scuffing dirt over the bloodstain.

I asked: 'When was his body discovered?'

'Not long ago.'

'Who dumped it here?'

'Who?' He closed his eyes and shrugged.

'I came from the main road and I passed no vehicle. A few people on foot but no car or truck. Whoever brought the body must have gone the other way. They must have come from Puente de los Negritos.'

He didn't respond. He scuffed at the dirt.

'Perhaps someone there will be able to help. There's no traffic on this road. A car would be noticed. Who lives there?'

'There's only the army.'

'Well, the soldiers must have noticed.'

For a long time he was silent. He simply kicked at the earth with a shoe. Then he looked me full in the face. I felt about six years old, like those children who'd stood round the corpse, too young to understand. There's only the army, he'd said.

'Well, perhaps I should inform the police. Is –'

I broke off. There was something like anger in his eyes at my stupidity. I began to walk back to the car. The dog was sitting in the shade of a tree, waiting for the humans to leave so he could return to the bloodstain. I turned back. The old man was staring at me.

'Tell me,' I said. 'There was earth in Armando's mouth. Why was that?'

'His cousin Alonzo has been organizing peasants to take over the abandoned estates. So they made Armando eat a mouthful of earth before they killed him. It is a warning.'

I had driven about a kilometre down the road before

turning the car and going back again. I wanted to ask the old man about Guazatan and if he knew where I'd find Burchell. But the old man wasn't there. There was no house in sight. How could he have vanished? Perhaps he was hidden among the bushes on the hillside watching me. Perhaps half a dozen pairs of eyes watched me. Even the dog had gone.

The road began to drop. I passed a place too small for a signpost. Half a dozen shacks could have housed pigs or people, there was no telling which. The buildings had mud sides and tin roofs. Old advertising boards held the walls up. *Coca-Cola es asi*, it promised. And for the fashion-conscious: *Doberman Jeans – New York, Paris, London, San Salvador*. No smoke rose from the chimneys, no chickens scratched, no children stared. If the place had a name it must have been Puente de los Negritos. Round the next corner were a jumble of charcoal grey rocks, a shrunken river, a bombed bridge and the army.

To the left on a bluff overlooking the river was an old stone building. I guessed at one time it was a rancher's house. Stretching back from this were rows of tents disappearing among trees. I could see huts that held latrines or weapons. Smoke curled up from fires. Jeeps were on the move. Barbed wire wrapped up the camp. A firebreak had been cleared all round the perimeter fence.

The army was also in front. Three soldiers blocked the road. They'd heard the car before it turned the corner and had their rifles three-quarters up to the firing position. I slowed and crept forward and stopped where they could see inside the car. One of them said: 'Switch off your engine and throw your keys on the ground. Get out slowly.'

I got out. I made no sudden movements and kept my hands away from my body. A trickle of sweat ran down between my breasts and it was from more than the sun. The three young men were frightened and their fear was infectious. A scared soldier is closer to shooting than any person I know. Their fingers were inside the trigger guards. Their eyes were huge. There was no welcome in their faces.

'Where are you going?' the same soldier asked.

'To Guazatan.'

'Impossible, señorita. The bridge is closed.'

I wouldn't say it was closed; I would say it was blown right away. I kept my mouth shut. On the right, just a stumble away, a track had been created by vehicles going parallel with the road. The track led to the muddy stream. The riverbed was of gravel between isolated boulders. The water level was low. Blum had been right: a car could ford it. My eyes followed the track as it weaved between the boulders, disappeared under the stream, and emerged to join the road on the far side of the bridge.

'There is another way,' I said, raising my arm slowly and pointing. 'Cars get through.'

'Where are your papers?' the soldier asked. He seemed to be the leader, old enough to have a moustache. None of them had stripes on their sleeves.

'My passport is in my bag.'

I fetched the shoulder-bag and made sure the soldiers had a clear view of my hands as I opened it. I pulled out the passport Erica had brought from my apartment.

'British passport,' he read. 'You are English?'

'Yes.'

He licked a finger and turned the pages. He looked at every page, at the United States visa, the entry and exit stamps for Italy and Turkey and Greece, all the blank pages. He went back to the photo and compared it with my face.

'Why are you going to Guazatan?'

'To visit the hospital.'

'There is no hospital.'

I couldn't think of the translation for *medical mission*. I said: 'To see the doctor.'

'What doctor is this? There is no doctor in Guazatan. There is nothing.'

'There is an English doctor. His name is Doctor Burchell.'

There was talk among the soldiers. It was too quick and slangy for me to follow. My Spanish was picked up in the months I'd spent in Madrid, licking my wounds after splitting with M. Salvadorian speech was rougher and louder. It suited the country.

'It is not possible for an Englishman to live there.'

'Have you ever been there?' I asked.

They didn't answer my question.

One of the other soldiers said: 'I heard there was a *Yanqui* there once. But he left when things got bad.'

One *gringo* was much like another, I decided.

'That's him,' I said. 'He looks like a *Yanqui* but he is English. And he is still working there.'

'You see this doctor because you are ill?'

'I am well, thank you. I have come to pay my respects to a fellow countryman. He is in a position of some danger but he carries out his duties with honour. He is a good friend of your country and a man of courage.'

You can make a flowery speech in Spanish. It sounds right. There was a moment of uncertainty. They had no experience of dealing with a woman from another culture. The thing was to assume success so I said: 'The road stops at Guazatan.'

They agreed that.

'Therefore I must return along this same route. This afternoon when I come back I shall bring you a letter signed by Doctor Burchell himself. Then you will have proof this brave and good man exists.'

I was full of self-confidence, wasn't I? I turned my head and looked up the valley as if the matter was now settled. From up in the army camp came the sound of soldiers chanting as they double-marched.

'All right,' the one with the moustache said. 'Turn round and put your hands on the roof of the car.'

'Why?'

'It is necessary to see if you carry any weapons.'

'You wish to search my body?'

'It is the regulation. We must make certain you carry nothing that could be of use to the terrorists.'

'Look,' I said and held open the bag. 'Have a look inside. Comb, pen, lipstick, mirror, a little money – you can see there's nothing of use to terrorists. And look.' I held my arms away from my body. 'I'm wearing an ordinary shirt and slacks. There is no room for weapons. You can *see* that. Go on, look.'

You wouldn't think it was so hard to get three men to look at a woman's body. It was as if they suspected some trap. I wore a cotton shirt with narrow yellow and grey stripes and a ruffled collar, and dark blue slacks. I'd bought them at Miami airport while changing planes because I hadn't been able to collect my lightweight clothes in Paris. In the heat of midday I wore the shirt loose. I put my hands on my hips and swung my body first one way and then the other. Go on, look, I implored, but don't feel me until I'm yours.

'Nothing hidden. You can see that. I do not wish to be touched by strangers.'

They stared. It was time for a hint of authority. I put on my duchess's face and said firmly: 'A lady does not allow a man to handle her.'

The man I took to be the leader swallowed and his Adam's apple bobbed. They were used to dealing with peasant women. I was exotic. I was self-assured.

'Okay,' the leader said, 'you may pass. On your return you will show this letter signed by the English doctor to our sergeant.'

'Certainly,' I said.

I picked up the keys and got the engine started and nosed the car onto the track. It was stony and uneven and I took my time. It was more than the roughness that slowed me. I was quitting the area controlled by the forces of the government. I was on the frontier. Even the makeshift camp seemed an outpost. Did they mount sentries by the bridge at night or retreat behind the barbed wire? Daylight made them jumpy enough; the dark would be unbearable. In the mirror I could see a tail of dust, and through the dust three soldiers. They gazed after the car, rifles held across their chests. The thing is, I hadn't wanted their hands on me, feeling my body, asking: 'Señorita, why do you wear a moneybelt under your shirt? Why is it necessary to hide this fortune in dollars?'

*

59

Open a paper to the foreign news page. Under the headline is the byline: 'From our own correspondent'. Underneath that: 'Somewhere behind guerrilla lines'. That was now my position.

Except it's a lie. There were no guerrilla lines, no trenches, no command post, no sandbagged gun emplacements. It was the same damn countryside, the same toy hills, the same scrub. Nevertheless I had crossed a shadowy line. We are used to Iron Curtains; this had been three boys with uneasy eyes. There were the same shacks too. Some showed signs of people living in them. Others looked dead. A family was walking down the road ahead of me. As I drew closer they got off the road, scattering among trees. I looked back in the mirror and they were on the road again.

A rock was splashed with a slogan in white: VIVA FDR! Not, I decided, the same FDR whose portrait was on the dollar bills that thickened my waist. The rock was on a hillside and shouted its message. On the other side of the river the army would have scrubbed the words off. Or if that didn't work, they'd have painted the slogan over. Or if they'd run out of paint, they'd have blasted the rock to tiny pieces. But that was on the other side of the river. Here it was different.

The road twisted as it climbed. On the horizon was a range of hills. Sitting above was a layer of cloud. That was where Honduras began. I was driving with all the windows open. I wanted no reflections on the glass, no shadows inside the car. I went slowly. I wanted no mistakes. Eyes would be watching the road and must note that I was a woman, of foreign appearance, alone. I drove past fields of dead maize grazed off by cattle, a pocket size lake with a boy fishing, a dip and a curve and Guazatan.

That was how I arrived. There was no sign. The road simply spread into a broad empty space and stopped. There were a couple of dozen houses, a café, a boarded up shop. A two-storey building would have been a skyscraper. A breeze blew a scrap of paper across the ground. Nothing else stirred.

I switched off the engine and got out. A car insulates you from the sights and sounds and smells of a place. I could see nobody but the feel of the village wasn't empty. I heard a noise: the paper was flutting against railings. Then nothing. It was as if Guazatan was holding its breath while it watched what I did.

'Is anybody there?' I tried English first and repeated it in Spanish.

I felt a prickle at the back of my neck. The tip of a bayonet, a knife selecting a fatal spot, that sort of prickle. I took deep gentle breaths, braced my toes, flexed my knees, exploded in a forward roll across the earth and jumped up into a crouch, facing backwards. Nothing had been pricking my neck. Nerves. But I saw movement as a shadow changed in a doorway.

'Hullo,' I shouted. 'I want to speak to you.'

I began walking towards the shadow. An old person's footsteps I took. What the *hell* am I doing here? I was angry with myself. But I went on. Cody always goes on.

'I've come to see Dr Burchell. I have something for him.'

Anywhere in Europe this would have been the village square, the *piazza*, the *plateia*. It had a café (Cerveza Suprema promised the sign) and a general store (Pollo Indio it had, or used to have). But that was all. It was just an area of beaten earth. There was nowhere to sit, nothing to look at, no memorial or fountain or flowers, no friends to greet. I walked past a puddle. Had there been a storm recently? Accident with a water cart? In the mud were footprints. Some were small, some were smaller. The smallest had no shoes.

Nothing in sight could possibly be taken for a medical mission. I'd been on the move for two days. I was jet-lagged. I'd come a long way to deliver Debilly's money and I wanted to get back. But all I'd seen was the shadow of someone watching. Unease made my voice rise.

'The Englishman – you must know him. Where does he live?'

The shadow moved and formed itself into a boy. I saw him

in pieces. First the feet, which were bare. Legs grew up. Then the buckle of the belt that held up his shorts. His shirt had what looked like a stain on one shoulder. His head moved and the stain was lowered and I made out a rifle. I had walked half way from the car to this doorway in the sights of this boy's rifle.

He stepped out of the building. Perhaps he was twelve. He looked younger, apart from his face. The rifle was as tall as he was. Other movements caught my eye. I made a complete turn. They had all appeared, from doorways, from windows, from behind walls. They had rifles, pistols, a grenade in one hand. Half a dozen began moving forward. It was the start of a lynching. Or a pack of dogs moving in for the kill.

One of them came right up to me. A woman, about my own height. Like all Salvadorians she was *mestizo*, a mixture of Spanish and Indian. Perhaps there was more Spanish in her ancestry, more of the *conquistadores*, more pride, more melancholy, more ruthlessness.

'Who are you?'

'My name –'

'I mean *what* are you?' she cut in.

'I am English. My name is Cody. I am a teacher.'

All that is written in my passport. A teacher is a useful thing to be. A teacher has a certain social standing but doesn't draw any attention. Every country respects a teacher. There is only one other occupation that is universally accepted and that is being a doctor.

'What brings a teacher to Guazatan?'

'I've come to see Dr Burchell.'

'Who?'

'The English doctor.'

'What doctor? What Englishman? You're lying. There's only us. Tell me why you have come.'

'What business is it of yours?'

It's just that I don't like the arrogance of people with guns. Because they can put lead fillings in your teeth it makes them behave like commissars.

A man reversed his rifle so that it was butt forward and stepped towards me. The woman put a hand on his elbow to restrain him. She gave it a little squeeze. It was a curiously intimate gesture. I thought: those two are together but she is the dominant one.

'Cody is your name? All right, Señorita Cody, let me make things clear. You have come to Guazatan, which is in the *zona libra* of El Salvador. To get here in your car you must pass the army roadblock at los Negritos. That simply is not possible. They do not let people through. Do you understand? They call us terrorists and say we must be destroyed. They cut us off from the rest of our country, or try to. Tourists from England are strictly forbidden. So – perhaps you are a spy.'

'Soldiers stopped the car. They questioned me, looked at my papers. I was allowed through. That is what happened.'

'Well then, it is unfortunate for you. If you go back after being in Guazatan, they will shoot you. That is what they do. You have been in the *zona libra*, so they will kill you. You understand, it is they who are the terrorists, not us. We are the people.'

She raised a clenched fist in a salute. Che would have approved. She stared with dark eyes. Her gaze was intense, compelling. What made her even more striking was a shock of white that ran through her black hair.

'I will find a way back,' I said, 'after I have seen Dr Burchell.'

She shook her head. 'You have come to the wrong village.'

'This is Guazatan? I was told how to get here by a man in San Salvador.'

'Who were you talking to about this place?'

'A man called Blum.'

'Ernesto Blum?'

I nodded.

She suddenly smiled, not at me but at the man by her side. For the first time he spoke:

'There's no doctor here. It's *us* you want to see. We weren't expecting it to be an English woman. Where is the money?

63

Is it in dollars? We don't want English money. We demanded dollars.'

The sun boiled, the colour bleached from the sky, the buildings swayed. God almighty, these revolutionaries were expecting me. Debilly had tricked me. I'd been offered bullshit by an ageing actor and I'd swallowed it. A new feeling welled up inside me: self-disgust.

A second, two seconds, it couldn't have been longer before the giddy world righted itself, as much as it ever does. The man and woman were right in front of me and I saw the smile die on the woman's face.

'Where is it?' she screamed. 'Where's our money?'

She took a couple of steps back. It was to give herself room as she swung the rifle barrel up. It was aimed at my stomach. Her finger curled round the trigger and I could see the whiteness of her knuckles. I fixed my eyes on the woman's face but those white knuckles shone out at me from the edge of my vision.

'Where are our dollars?'

# 6

The Agency trained me. It took four years of my life. I had the whole feast, from soup to nuts. Nuts were terrorists and how to deal with them. Lesson one is to head for the exit at the first hint they're around. Terrorists are very bad news. They play a different game, change the rules, move the goal posts. But suppose you're caught up. Don't give in to their demands – bring the prisoners, hand over the ransom, whatever. Once you give in they have no further use for you. Since they despise you anyway as a tool of imperialism, they're likely to kill you. 'Never surrender your soul.' It was an Israeli Major on secondment to the CIA who urged us. 'Show them you have willpower. Make them respect you.'

The year before last Major Kahan was killed in Rome. He was confirming a reservation in the El Al office when four 'students' burst past the security guard. Afterwards they were identified as a Libyan-Bulgarian group calling themselves People's Fist. Kahan shouted in English: 'What do –' Those were his last words. The leader of People's Fist shot him at that point. He didn't respect Kahan.

These people would call themselves guerrillas, not terrorists. With the woman's rifle steady on me, the difference seemed small. I said: 'If you shoot me, you'll make a mess of the money.'

Show her I'm tough, show her I'm cool, and pay no heed to the mice scampering in my guts. I kept my eyes locked on hers. Some of the tension went out of her face as she took in that I was carrying the money. The rifle eased down to a point somewhere between my feet.

'All right,' she said. 'Good.' She sounded in better humour.

Nothing seemed good to me.

'Try to understand,' I said, 'I don't know Blum. I met him this morning for the first time. It was a man in Paris who asked me to bring the money.'

'We know nothing of that.'

A badge was sewn on her sleeve. *Brigada 24 de marzo* it said, and a star was done in red stitching. It was a five pointed star but the topmost point was replaced by an explosion. All the guerrillas had these red and white badges, like blood soaking through a bandage.

'His name is Debilly.'

'It means nothing.'

'The French film star.'

'Do you see a cinema?' She waved a hand at the shacks. 'Film stars are not significant here.'

'And Blum means nothing to me.'

'He is an American gangster. That is all. A criminal, an exploiter, another Reagan. But we knew about him and we made use of him. Lenin said you should make a pact with the devil if it brought the revolution closer.'

'I was told the money was to help a medical mission.'

'I don't care what lies you were told.' Suspicion clouded her face. 'It is the full amount you've brought? One hundred thousand dollars?'

It padded out my waist like middle-aged spread. I nodded.

'Hand it over.'

I tried one last time. 'Debilly said I should give it to Dr Bur –'

'There is no doctor.' She was screaming again. 'There is no hospital. The people die like flies because of disease and hunger and nobody does anything. Can't you see what sort of place it is? Nobody cares, the government, the army, nobody. The rich landowner who lived up there cared least of all. The men herded his cattle, the children picked his coffee beans, the women warmed his sons' beds. While the people lived, he exploited them. When the people died, we buried them. He's gone and there's nobody there now. Capitalism is dying and it's only the army's rifles that keep it alive.'

Her rifle had risen to my stomach again. She lowered it.

'All right,' she said, 'because you've brought the money, because you've come from Paris, because you are a woman, I'll show you the ruins of capitalism. Then you'll be convinced.' She snapped her head round to the man beside her. 'Search her car, Alonzo. Just in case. The boot, underneath the spare wheel, door panels. Make certain there are no weapons or radio transmitters. Be careful of booby traps.'

'Don't teach me my work,' the man said. He scowled. He didn't like being ordered around. 'I know what to do.'

She considered his sour look. Odd, I knew just what was going through her mind: Men, they don't change just because there's a revolution. They can't stand a woman being boss. 'I know you do. Otherwise I wouldn't ask you.' She reached out and touched his cheek and then she was on the move. After half a dozen steps she turned to look at me. 'Aren't you coming?'

The man who'd been tortured and dumped like a sack of garbage had a cousin called Alonzo. A guerrilla, organizer of peasants, disciple of land to the tiller. Should I tell him what I'd found along the road?

'Come on,' she said, very sharp.

I followed. There was a gap between two shacks of corrugated iron. The back of the village was a wilderness of beaten earth, rusting cans, broken bottles, orange peel and the plastic jetsam of the poor. Eucalyptus trees stood guard on either side of stone gateposts. I'd thought there was no way out of this village except the road I'd driven in on but this had been hidden. The gate was shut but not locked. There was a chain with a padlock but the padlock would never work again. It was shot out. I thought they only did that in Westerns when the action got a bit slow.

We walked along a dirt road. I like dirt better than the black stuff because it tells a story. There were recent tyre tracks but none, I thought, of cars. The tracks were heavily ridged. Off-road vehicles – jeeps for instance – have tyres like that. Horses had passed this way. A bicycle. The road climbed a rise, winding between grey rocks. One vehicle had

had to swing wide to take a corner: a big vehicle, broad tyre prints, wheels in pairs. Say a truck big enough to transport cattle or soldiers.

The road straightened and we were on a plateau. Ahead was a cluster of buildings – a *hacienda* – a world away from the hovels hidden below. The dirt road had given the skeleton of a story; there was flesh put on here. The main building had once been large. Even what remained was impressive. But one end had been blown up. Tiles lay smashed around it. Windows were shattered. Gaps showed in the stone walls. Beams that supported the roof had jagged ends, like so many butcher's bones.

'Do you see any medical mission?'

What does a medical mission look like? A hut with a red cross painted on it? A sign above the door? A line of patients waiting? A glimpse of a nurse? There was just this shattered house. Amazing that the whole place hadn't burned to the ground.

'The rancher was called Montalvo. He only stayed here three or four months of the year. The rest of the year he was in Florida – not Miami, that is for *peons* and Cubans, somewhere for rich people. Montalvo had a manager who lived in a small house at the back. One night last year we came when the manager was asleep and went to his bedside and asked if he would join the revolution. He said yes but in his eyes you could see he was lying. The next night our sentries found him escaping. So now he lies over there.'

She gestured at a line of trees. It seemed to mark the boundary between the gardens round the house and the farmland beyond. I could see a heap of earth, about the length of a man.

She said, as if it was an epitaph: 'He was a stupid man.'

'The manager's dead,' I said, 'the owner's in the United States, so no one farms here now.'

'Nobody picked the coffee this year. Montalvo got the cattle out before we could stop him. The horses – the army has taken them. We have the mules. We ate the pigs. Once a peasant owns a pig, he is half way to being a capitalist and is no longer interested in revolution. Better to eat the pigs therefore.'

Her attention was caught by a jeep at the far end of the house and her mood changed. At one time the jeep had belonged to the army. Two guerrillas took their ease in the front seats, one in a camouflage jacket, the other in a red and white tee shirt advertising Nissan. They were smoking.

'What the hell do you think you're playing at?' The woman was in a sudden fury. 'If you're fiddling with your matches and your cigarettes, your mind isn't on your job. You're meant to be watching the sky. Look! There! And there! And there!' She jab-jab-jabbed a finger up at the enemy blue. Her finger was as angry as her voice.

'If they come in helicopters,' the Nissan boy reasoned, 'we'll hear them before we see them. There's no danger, Beatriz.'

So she had a name: Beatriz. She still glowered. It wasn't the challenge to her authority; it was as if these boys lacked total commitment. She was a woman of action. Never lose momentum, keep busy, get things done. That's how I saw her. She could have been my sister, only wilder.

'If the wind is blowing the wrong way, you won't hear them.'

'There is no wind, Beatriz.'

'Do you mean if the wind gets up, you're going to throw away your cigarettes?'

Beatriz didn't wait for an answer but strode off. The two boys switched their gaze from her to me. Their high cheekbones stood out like small rocks. Dark eyes were four bullet holes.

'Come on.'

I caught up with Beatriz by a swimming pool. There was no water in it but you couldn't describe it as empty. There were discarded ammunition boxes, a smashed sub-machine-gun, ejected cases, a boot, odds and ends of plastic sheeting, a pile of earth, dead leaves, a great sweep of broken blue tiles. The pool had been used either to launch an attack on the house or as a forward defensive trench.

'Is this your base? Do you stay here all the time?'

She halted like a horse when you haul back on the reins. She swung round on me. 'Why do you want to know? Do you want to fetch the army to get your money back?'

'It looks as if the army has already been here.' I pointed to the litter of war in the swimming pool.

'We keep on the move. That is the essence of the liberation struggle. A few days here, a week beyond the hills. The army never knows where or when we will strike and they exhaust themselves looking for us. El Salvador is a small country but the army is smaller. They can't be everywhere. That is why we will win. Sometimes the army comes here, sometimes we do. They tremble so much they cannot shoot. They spent a couple of nights here last September and we heard they were here and Alonzo came to the trees and yelled out at them: "Hey little boys, we're going to cut off your *cojones* tomorrow. Your girlfriends won't know you." Then the soldiers shoot off a few hundred rounds into the darkness and none of them sleeps, waiting for tomorrow. You know what they are – *cojones*?'

I nodded. 'But this time you have settled down.'

The rifle was a barometer of her anger. It rose to my chest.

'Who told you?'

Did she believe I was so decadent my brain no longer worked? 'You had time to get a message to Blum, Blum got in touch with Paris, Debilly contacted me, I flew in yesterday, and you're still here today.'

She thought about it and the rifle lowered. 'Thursday last week. Because of the storm. Too long in one place. We had no choice.'

Suddenly Beatriz was in a tearing hurry again. She'd left a heap of urgent questions in my mind: What was the money for? Why was an ageing French film star so eager to fund guerrillas? Why did they have no choice but to stay here for nine days? What was her purpose in bringing me up here? Why was she racing ahead?

We passed between two long flowerbeds where weeds were choking the cannas. A lawn had grass that had grown long

70

in patches and browned off in the dry season – lions in a small circus have that same mangy look.

She twisted towards me. *Come on*, her fierce stare said. Her shock of white hair was urgent. It was like a migraine made visible, cutting her head in two. We walked along a terrace with broken stone slabs, a table with rust bleeding through white paint, chairs tumbled over, a pair of urns where agapanthus plants had withered. On this side of the house there were citrus trees with dark shiny leaves, lanky papayas with topknots of leaves and fruit, bananas that had been cropped but not cut down. Beyond this tropical orchard was something like a fenced paddock. Beyond that was grassland, cattle country. I could just make out maize cobs stacked in wire-sided silos on stilts to cheat the rats.

Every detail stood out sharp in the midday sun. We were the only living creatures. There were no cattle, no horses, no dogs, no chickens, no cats, no pigs. They had been wiped out of creation. There were no people either. And then we turned the corner of the house.

'I wanted you to see this,' Beatriz said, 'so you would understand us better.'

There was a row of shrubs that acted as a screen to the backyard. They were smashed to the ground: the army, the guerrillas, no telling. Squatting on the ground was a semi-circle of children, boys and girls mixed. They were kids, none of them above ten. Once they got into double figures, I guess they were old enough to tote a rifle, old enough to kill, old enough to die. A dozen or fifteen of them, and in the centre was a young woman, an older teenager, on her knees, and with her face tilting towards us.

'Beatriz!'

A boy had spotted her and then the whole lot of them were scrambling to their feet, whooping and rushing towards us like an Apache raid.

'Beatriz, Beatriz!'

The boy jumped up into her arms. The rest swarmed round.

'Is he your child?'

71

'They are all my children.'

She put the boy down and scooped half a dozen together in her arms. They laughed and shouted and tumbled. They were kittens. She was a stern mother cat.

'This is school,' she said. 'Aminta is the teacher. We have no books, no desks, no pens and paper, no blackboard. But we have the earth and Aminta has a stick to write with. Hey Felipe, what does two and two make? This lady has come all the way from Europe so just you tell her what two plus two is.'

Felipe was the one who'd jumped up in her arms. He said without hesitation: 'Eight.'

She cuffed his head in slow motion and he ducked away. 'Felipe has a sense of humour. Amazing when you consider everything that has happened to him.' She smiled at him a moment, the creases by her eyes making her look wary. 'These youngsters are the future. They are our hope. They are what the struggle is for. We must fight and fight so they can live in peace. We must destroy the oppressors so they can have dignity.'

She had spoken in a low even voice. Now she raised a clenched fist in the air and her voice rang out.

'The future is ours! The victory is ours!'

A dozen little fists punched the air: 'Victory!'

Beatriz looked round the young faces and then at me. Her eyes didn't trust me. I wasn't part of the family. 'The army is already defeated,' she said. 'Our greatest problem is convincing them they're dead.' She swung away to the young teacher. 'Aminta.'

'Yes, Beatriz.'

'We're moving out. Prepare the young comrades to march.'

'To the dormitory,' Aminta ordered. 'Military rules – no playing. Come on, Jorge.'

This teenager, the teacher, gathered up the hand of a five year old. They marched in step, the boy lengthening his stride to its very limits to keep pace. Watching them you wanted to laugh – it was like something out of an old Charlie Chaplin classic. Then remembering the command *Military*

72

*rules – no playing*, you wanted to cry. They aimed towards the house while Beatriz gazed after them. She watched without laughing. I think she watched without love. She was judging them as comrades in the struggle, as soldiers of the future. She turned to me.

'You smile,' she said. 'But they must learn discipline. They must become fighters. If they don't learn discipline, their lives will end very young.'

The smile had faded from my face. It left an ache in the muscles of my cheeks. The last of the revolutionary school class disappeared into the house.

'There is no medical mission here. Do you accept that now?'

'Yes,' I said.

'You were told to bring money to Guazatan. You must hand it over. Then you will have done what was intended all along.'

I undid the bottom two buttons of my yellow and grey shirt. The money was concealed in half a pillowcase I'd got from Erica. She'd gawped when she'd seen how much money I was sewing up and demanded to know if I'd become a high class tart. In a manner of speaking, I'd said, and sworn her to secrecy. I'd used a simple tacking stitch to keep the money secure and sewn on four lengths of string, which I used to tie the home-made moneybelt round my waist. I gave the moneybelt to Beatriz. I backed away a few paces. The simple act of handing over the money changed our relationship. She held a gun in one hand and a hundred thousand dollars in the other. I had neither. I was a pauper. But she wasn't going to shoot me. I was sure of that. I was to be allowed to return to Europe to spread the news of the strength and commitment of the guerrilla struggle. I could be useful to them.

She snapped the thread and looked inside at the notes.

'It's all there, isn't it?'

'One hundred thousand dollars,' I said. 'Count it if you want.'

'No,' she said, shaking her head. 'You have the typical bourgeois morality. You are honest in small everyday

73

matters, blind to the terrible dishonesty of the society you live in.'

I imagined I could see right inside her, to her very heart.

'You mean I haven't the guts to shoot some peasant boy who's been conscripted into the army.'

'They've all been conscripted but they don't have to stay in the army and fight us. They can steal away at night and join us. Some do. We welcome them.'

'And most of them don't. I wonder why not.'

We stared at each other in silence, each understanding the other. I am right-handed and she was like my left hand.

'You will be permitted to leave,' she said finally. 'But only after we have moved out. An elementary precaution in case you have after all some connection with the army. Then my advice to you is to leave quickly because the army will come to this place. If the army find you here after we've left, they will kill you. It is Major Portillo who will kill you personally. Each time you think you are dead, they will bring you back to life so Major Portillo can kill you again.'

'How can you be sure the army will come?'

'They will come. If you stay here you will see.'

I was eight thousand kilometres from home, on my own in a civil war, guerrillas all round and the army at my back. I had just delivered one hundred thousand dollars to the greater glory of the revolution. I understood nothing except I'd proved myself the most gullible fool since Adam accepted the apple.

Beatriz nodded a farewell and walked towards some outbuildings. She paused as the group of children filed out of the house, packs on their backs. The teacher lined them up in pairs, the oldest at the front, herself at the rear to sweep up the youngest.

'Victory is ours!' Beatriz shouted, raising her rifle high above her head.

'Victory! Victory!' they cried back.

The teacher gave the order and they began to march away.

'What is A for?' the teacher called out.

'A is for the army,' they shouted in unison. 'The army is

bad. The army steals our land. The army exploits the people. The army kills our families.'

'What shall we do with the army?'

'We shall kill the army,' they shouted back and stamped their feet.

'What is B for?' the teacher called.

'B is for the Brigada. The Brigada is good. The Brigada protects our farms. The Brigada loves the people. The Brigada fights for justice.'

'What shall we do with the Brigada?'

'We shall give our lives to the Brigada.'

'What is C for?'

'C is for Cuba. Cuba is good. Cuba sends us weapons to fight the army. Cuba loves peace. Cuba . . .'

They marched round the corner of the bombed *hacienda* and faded out of earshot.

# 7

C is for Cody.

D is for dimwit, dummy and dupe, all of them me.

E is for enemies, on every side.

F is for friends, none.

G is for guerrillas. Three of them came out of a barn at the rear of the house together with Beatriz. No, two guerrillas. The third was taller by a head and had a stomach big enough for two Salvadorians. He wore jeans and a tee shirt and carried a leather jacket over his arm. He wasn't handcuffed but he'd been kept prisoner. The signs were there. He looked up at the sky, the first action of any person who's been locked away against his will. He glanced round at the big house, the barn, the stables, laundry house, store rooms, me, gardens. I was only of passing interest. With my dark hair I could have been another guerrilla.

So this was what the hundred thousand dollars had bought: the release of this man. No, there was more to it than that.

Nobody cared that I was watching. Beatriz may even have felt I ought to watch, I ought to check I was getting my money's worth.

They set off away from the big house. Beatriz led the way with a kind of fury. Her stride lengthened until she'd drawn ahead of the others. She snapped a remark over her shoulder and hurried on again. The men came in a tight group. One guerrilla had a machine pistol half pointed at the prisoner. If they were setting him free, why keep him under guns? Because it was second nature to them, first nature even. They were men who wouldn't be able to eat a fried egg unless they had it in their gun sights.

I toyed with the idea that this was the famous Dr Burchell of the fairy tale Debilly had told me in Paris. No, Burchell

76

had never existed. Burchell was just the piece of cheese that had been put in the mousetrap.

It was early afternoon. The same day? The following week? I seemed already to have done too much, seen too many guns, travelled too roughly for one day. And my day was far from over. It was going to prove the longest day of my life.

The sun was high and burning on my head. The air was hot but dry, not that tropical steambath which soaks you in sweat and slows you to a saunter. With Beatriz leading the charge, the little group went in the direction of a paddock. And what should I do? Sit down and brown my face in the sun? Go and wait by the car until I had permission to leave?

I set off after them. It was a battlefield I went through. This last battle, the one before, half a dozen before that. The ground was chewed up as if by tanks. But tanks would have been useless here. Heavy trucks then, doing some crazy military manoeuvre. Tyre tracks were smoothed down by rain, puddles had formed and dried. Bits of metal glittered. Jewels they were, the gems of war. Horses or mules had also been here. Piles of dung were bleached by the sun. A gauze bandage had been discarded, a sock, greased paper. The guerrillas had been in the house, the army had been attacking. Or the other way round.

The others had vanished ahead of me. I edged through scrub that had dropped its leaves. I couldn't go silently. The leaves were hard and brittle and made a noise like dry spaghetti snapping underfoot. Had they gone straight on? Perhaps they were going to some distant place of execution to shoot him. No prisoners on the road to revolution. I went through spindly trees and came to a line of agaves. Some had flower spikes that had exploded up into the sky and now stood brown and dead. One agave looks romantic. A whole row of them is a Berlin Wall. The others couldn't have come this way.

I turned and followed the agaves and came to a track of sorts. Recent feet had scuffed the dirt. The track went through a gap in the agaves and I followed it and halted. The sun hammered my skull and my shirt was clammy with sweat. In front was a clear space and a hundred metres away was another line of agaves and thirsty shrubs. Further off twisted hills boiled up into the sky.

Then I grasped what it was: an airstrip. It was of brown grass, poor and shabby and grazed low by animals. In the centre was a track that had been kept free of vegetation. You could hardly call it a runway, just dirt. Not even the metal lattice strip that I had steered the Skyvan along and hauled up into the air at Borj Mechaab. That had been in the deep south of Tunisia. That had been last year, when I was young and in my prime.

Voices came from the left and there they were, the three men and Beatriz, by a plane. It was a twin-engine job I didn't recognize. Towards the tail was painted in bold red: AIR TODAY. The tail of the Y curled back under the name, emphasizing it. For a moment I felt the shadow of the CIA fall across me. That was the kind of name they chose for the bogus airlines that ran weapons to the tribesmen in Laos and Cambodia. No, not a CIA scenario. They wouldn't have just one player out on the airstrip doing business with revolutionaries. They'd have a bigger presence. They'd overorganize everything. There'd be smooth men murmuring into sleeve-mikes, iced water drinking fountains, air-conditioned limousines.

Navigation aids at this field would drive the International Airline Pilots Associations into convulsions. A windsock hung dead from a pole. There was no control tower, no radar, no anemometer, no radio aerial. Drums were stacked a short way from the plane.

Now what was going to happen? The *gringo* was going to climb into the aircraft and disappear into the wide blue yonder?

It was Beatriz who disappeared. She turned on her heel and walked at her brisk pace down the airstrip and vanished from sight. Perhaps there was a footpath. Otherwise she'd have a scramble getting down the hillside to the village. But she was used to that. The two *muchachos* who were left looked on while the pilot set about his preparations. This entailed climbing up folding steps into the payload section, walking through to the flight deck and doing whatever tasks were first on his check list. What had I done before I'd taken up the Skyvan for my first-ever flight? Look for the master switch, Antoine Nortier had commanded. Get the engines warming. Jesus, Nortier, they've heard us, they've seen us, they're shooting at us. And he so calm while he talked me up into the air.

Antoine, there are nights when the moon is full and I'm alone when I still mourn you.

The pilot was coming down the steps again and he spoke to the boys. Spanish I suspect, because English wouldn't get you far here. Nor did Spanish seem to because he swore – I heard the *hijo de puta* distinctly – and his voice grew louder with anger. There was more talk from the pilot and a lot of gestures: up in the sky, down at the ground, flinging both arms wide. It had the right effect because they laid down their guns at a safe distance and came to help. Together they manhandled a drum close to the plane. From behind the stack of drums a wicked monkey wrench was produced, which the pilot used to unbung the drum. A gangling machine was passed to him – he was standing on the drum – and he dropped a length of tube into the drum and a second hose through a flap on the wing. Then he set to work. It was a pump, for pity's sake. He laboured at this while I laboured with theories.

The man was American. His Spanish had an American broadness. He had a confidence about him, even when it was the guerrillas who had the guns. Also there was the matter of his clothes. He was the first man I'd seen wearing blue jeans. It must be the uniform of hippies and international terrorists and this was one country where you didn't want to acquire that reputation. But he was American and a pair of Levi's was almost guaranteed under the constitution.

The pilot had put his plane down here nine days ago. Because of the storm? Because he was low on fuel? No. He'd put down on the airstrip because he knew the fuel drums were here. How did he know? I'd think about that later. It had been his bad luck to run into the Brigada 24 de marzo and be taken prisoner.

The two boys had picked up their machine pistols to watch the *gringo* pump in fuel. Now they had to lay them down to help him again, roll the empty drum away, haul up another full one. The pilot was out of breath. His muscles were more attuned to pulling the ring on a beer can than pumping. A lot of argument had no effect. A little imperialist money did. One guerrilla got up on the drum and pumped. I half expected the American to pick up the spare machine pistol and mount guard over the operation. But the second guerrilla backed off, his arms cluttered with both weapons.

So the Brigada had captured the pilot and found out what he was doing and who his contacts were and sent word to the repulsive Blum: we'll let your pilot go free provided you pay us enough dollars. Blum wasn't risking his neck here. He had passed the demand to Paris and I had been hired. So it might be the freedom of the pilot that was being bought, or the recovery of the plane, or the release of what it carried. No passengers were in evidence; cargo therefore.

There was clamour out on the strip. The second barrel was empty and a third was rolled up. And yes, the other guerrilla was persuaded by the power of the dollar to pump fuel.

It wasn't one of those big cargo jets. But it could still pack in a handy payload and had an effective range of, say, twelve hundred kilometres. Come on, Cody, you're guessing at that. Pretending to know just to make yourself feel better. This was guerrilla country and if there's one thing guerrillas are always hungry for it's weapons. That was the most obvious cargo. He'd flown in nine days ago and there'd been a hitch about payment and I'd been hired to bring the cash. Dollars, naturally. *You mustn't waste time*, Debilly had said, *it's urgent*. Okay. That theory made a kind of crazy sense. But there was a big but. It simply did not hang together with the pilot being held prisoner. My bringing the money hadn't released the cargo. Nothing was being unloaded. The money had released the pilot and now he was . . .

I felt the prick at the back of my neck.

I'd felt it before in the dirt square in the village below and imagined knife or bayonet and had been wrong. This time it wasn't nerves. I'd been so busy exploring my theories, my brain had been closed to the real world around me. There would have been a noise, a foot grating against the earth, a breath, clothes rubbing against skin, the creak of a shoe. There'd been something but my theorizing brain had blocked out the primitive warning. I was too damn civilized and this was the jungle.

It felt like a stiletto, very sharp point, slim, the kind of knife only an expert uses because it needs precise knowledge of the vulnerable points. Such as the carotid artery. Or the central nervous column up the spine.

A voice said: 'Do not shout for help. Do not scream. Keep one hundred per cent still. Who are you?'

My brain had been asleep. Now it was working and I thought there was hope. He spoke English. Spoke it well. But there was no mistaking the accent. I've never met the Frenchman who is easy with the word *who*. But that wasn't why I had hope. It was what he'd said, the warnings he'd issued. He didn't want the guerrillas – or possibly the pilot – to be alerted. That was the weapon I could use against his knife.

'Who are you?' he asked again.

Down the airstrip the pumping of the third barrel was completed and a fourth barrel was being rolled forward. They were engrossed in the task. I think they had no interest in me anyway. If they bothered to look my way they mightn't even notice the man who'd become my shadow.

'Who are you?' He tried this time in French. His voice was low and urgent.

It was time to educate him in the facts of the situation. 'If you stab me,' I said, 'I'll scream. It'll be involuntary. Do you understand? Nothing you or I can do about it. Those men over there will hear the scream. You don't want that.'

'Why are you here?'

81

'Why are you here?' I retorted. 'Who are you? Why don't you want those people to know?'

I eased my shoulders. My muscles had locked solid. It was tension, the closeness of the knife. At that slight movement I felt the knife prick my skin. I think there was blood.

'If you use the knife,' I warned him again, 'I'll scream. It's automatic, a reflex. It's the body's reaction to pain. You might as well put away the knife. Are you from Paris?'

'How do you know? What are you doing here?'

The point was pricking again. Why couldn't he understand? Couldn't his brain grasp he had a weapon it would be suicide to use?

'Take that knife away. It's no use to you.'

We could have gone on this way until Christmas. But from the left came a whistle, three distinct notes, a recognition call. An answering whistle came from the boys out by the plane but I hardly heard it for by then I had made my move. At the first whistle, the knife's point had moved away from my neck as the man had jerked round in the direction of the sound. I moved at that instant, while he was distracted, before the point returned to prick my skin, before he decided to be done with it and plunged the knife in to the hilt and pig's squeals shrilled out from me.

I never saw him except as a blur as I ducked away to the right and exploded into a sprint like it was the hundred metres with Olympic gold at the end. My life was the prize, and there's nothing more golden than that. Second place got no prize.

'Stop,' he hissed.

Oh sure.

I was pounding down the agaves, feeling very naked on the airstrip, wanting a way through so I could lose myself among the shrubs and trees beyond. He's right behind me, arm raised to strike. He's not following at all, he's a knife artist and he's poised to let fly. Faster, faster.

My back felt huge. Nobody could miss such a vast target.

There was no gap between the agaves. I'd walked down the other side of the line and I knew it. Then scramble over them. But the agaves could stop a cavalry charge, cut the horses to shreds. Bloody get over them.

I turned the evolutionary clock back. I became a monkey again. I'd been so sophisticated before, theorizing to myself like the marvellous *homo sapiens* I was, that the instinct for self-preservation had been pushed under. Now I went back to the jungle. Like a monkey I ran up the sword leaf of a bent-down agave. It was broad and thick and armed with spikes. Not as murderous as the knife, just nature's barbed wire. I got a foot into the heart of the agave, reached for a flowering stalk built like a tree trunk, swung myself over and jumped clear of the bayonet ends of the leaves down to solid ground on the far side.

At my highest, while I gripped the stalk, I risked a glance back. The guerrillas had gone. The man who'd had the knife at my neck had gone. Only the American pilot remained, hands on hips, staring in my direction.

He must have wondered what the hell was happening. Made two of us.

A whistle came, those same three distinct notes. It sounded half way down to the village already. The Brigada must be in a tearing hurry to get out. The man with the knife – had he gone with them? Or was he out of sight, waiting for me to trip over his feet?

Five minutes I was in the sun before I heard him. He was crossing the belt of thick fallen leaves and they crackled underfoot. I had the tiniest glimpse of him, tan slacks and a black and white check shirt. He was passing through shrubs that hid his feet and head. In two seconds he had gone, heading towards the house.

I turned back to the agave. Pressing my cheek against a shark's fin of a leaf I could see a corner of the airstrip. Moving left I could make out the fuel drums, moving right I could see part of the plane. I couldn't see both together. I couldn't see the pilot either until he wandered in, zipping up his flies. Preparing for take-off, wasn't he. He hustled straight up the aircraft steps without looking round or waving goodbye. That's a pilot all over: eager to get his bum on the seat, his hands on the controls, his plane up into the blue. He hauled the steps up and closed the door.

For an age nothing happened. He was paranoid about doing his checks.

I wondered about radar. Not here; at the army camp. With or without radar they'd see this plane climbing up into the sky. The army would come to investigate. That's why the guerrillas were heading for the hills. That's why Beatriz had warned me to get out.

An engine turned over. It was an alien scene. There were hills like sleeping beasts, an azure sky, bleached grass, reddish-brown earth. There were no humans, just this machine. And it was coming to life. First the port engine, then the starboard engine. I brooded some more while the engines warmed.

Why hadn't the army come to investigate the plane's arrival? That was the smart thing to do. The storm must have hidden it. The pilot would have thanked whatever he held holy as he escaped the tropical thunderheads, then cursed his rotten luck that the guerrillas had chosen this place to shelter from the flood.

The plane began to move, turning on the strip as if one wingtip was nailed to the ground. There was no wind so the sock, out of my sight, wouldn't be stirring. The pilot gave the engines full throttle and the plane gathered speed, leaving a sandstorm in its wake. I saw it in flashes through the leaves. It came past surprisingly fast and was airborne half way down the strip, up, up, and curving round in an arc that pointed it towards Honduras and on to Mexico City or Miami or Houston or better still some field like this where there were no officials with curious eyes.

My hundred thousand dollars had bought this flight.

Well, not mine but the money I'd carried for Debilly.

I just hoped I never had to explain the difference to some hot major. Such as Major Portillo. Wasn't that the thug Beatriz mentioned?

# 8

I returned to a ghost village. Guazatan's population was wiped out by the plague.

When I'd first arrived it had been empty. So I had thought. The shacks had been as quiet as gravestones, until the figures rose from the dead. Now I walked the circuit and found no one. The young men had been conscripted into the army or pressed to join the Brigada. The old people feared to stay because the guerrillas would demand to be housed and fed. And when they'd gone the army would return, rape the prettier girls and shoot the old people for looking after the guerrillas.

That's the way it would be. The story never varies, only the location: Spain, Congo, Biafra, Afghanistan, this place. War is war but civil war is more bitter than any other.

The empty village made me uneasy. The vanished guerrillas too. Also the mystery plane and the man who wanted to shave the back of my neck. But more than all of these the prospect of the army.

*C'mon, move your ass, girl.* That Marines sergeant in Virginia, Moesser, that's what he used to scream at me. Used to come right up and yell it in my face and then he'd step back and watch with his greedy eyes and sadist's smile while I tried to outwit some brute on the mat. Okay sergeant, what would you do if the Salvadorian army was sending one of their *cazador* battalions over the hills? *Cazadores* are hunters, sarge, in case you didn't know. They could blast this place off the map. Tell you what I'd do: move my ass.

Slight problem with the car. Beatriz had told her fella to search it. I searched it myself in case he'd left a present. A little plastic explosive moulded round the exhaust pipe, for instance. That would move my ass. I drew blank. A pack of

Lifesavers purchased at Miami Airport had volunteered for the revolution. Nothing else seemed missing. They'd looked at the map. I could tell that because they'd refolded it all wrong. They'd decided against taking it. Ace of them. The map was generous with its awards of coffee beans, cattle, cotton bolls, beach umbrellas and other symbols. But roads were not meant to interest the traveller. The road to Chalatenango was marked. Likewise the one to the Honduras border. But the road to Guazatan was beneath notice. And the tracks the guerrillas used, the map denied their existence too.

I sat behind the wheel with the key in the ignition and my fingers gripping it. This was another danger point, something wired into the electrical circuit. In Europe or the East that would be a worry. But it was too sophisticated for Central America. Anyway, why should Beatriz want me dead? I had simply done my job, acted as go-between. I was no threat.

Don't crowd me, sergeant, I'm just taking a few deep breaths. One of them might be my last.

I started up and swung the car round and left Guazatan on the road I'd come in on. Sometimes life is just too full of stuff. By my watch I'd had less than three hours of army checks and guerrillas and ransom money and a knife in the back of the neck. Too much. All because I'd trusted an old movie star. I'd neglected to take a long cool look at his credentials because . . . Well, because a love affair had blown apart and my feelings were in chaos and I needed to *do* something to take my mind off it. Such as flying to El Salvador with a thick wad . . .

The engine stammered and picked up and stammered and died. The car dragged to a halt on the slope. I pulled on the handbrake and stared at the fuel gauge and thought: You bitch, Beatriz, may the rest of your hair turn white. She had syphoned the petrol out.

A whore's trick, Alonzo's whore, that's all she is. Put her in a cheap hotel room and she'd have flicked through some punter's wallet while the oaf slept off his frenzy. Why had she done this to me? Wanted me to fall into the army's hands? Or afraid I was their spy and would race back to tell tales? She'd taken out each-way insurance.

The army camp wasn't far away. Nothing is far in El Salvador. I hadn't been counting off the kilometres but the car must have run dry not far from the river. I could even hear the camp: not boots or shouts but the grinding of military vehicles.

So thanks, Bea, thanks a million. If she hadn't done it in person, she'd given the order. I knew she had because I'd have done the same if our positions were reversed. She was my left hand, my ugly sister.

Now calm down. She's only doing her job, furthering the revolution.

I got out to test the power of the sun. No good waiting here for a lift. I was going to have to walk. Out of the car the sound of the camp was louder, much louder, and I listened to it.

Not just louder, closer. And moving.

The army had picked up its toys and clambered into trucks and was coming to see what was going on in Guazatan, why a plane had suddenly sprung to life. If they met me along the road, why naturally they would pop me into the bag for questioning. What was your real purpose in going to Guazatan? What did you deliver to that plane? How did you make contact with the *terroristas*?

Anger against Beatriz flashed and was gone. The prospect of action cleared my mind wonderfully. Always has. A powerful drug is action. It can hook a person for life.

They weren't far now, no more than a couple of curves away. I had ten seconds, five seconds, while a choice was still open to me. After that the decision was no longer mine. The smart thing to do was to tear my shirt and go pelting up the road towards the trucks and scream in the nearest officer's face: Help, help, the terrorists have robbed me and beaten me and they're escaping over the hills thataway. Then admire the gleam in their eyes as they set off in hot pursuit.

One second, zero. I did the other thing, the smarter thing.

I scrambled back into the car to put the gear in neutral and release the handbrake. I jumped out again as the car began to roll. Like a snail it moved. I shuffled beside it, a shoulder to the doorframe, a hand through the window on the steering wheel. Faster, *faster*, I shouted in my head. Brute had a will of its own, picking up speed so that I trotted a dozen steps, then dawdling, then gaining strength again and I let it go and commended it to the gods and the law of gravity and at the corner it said goodbye to the road. There was a rending of metal which must have been the exhaust and the crack of a young tree and a snapping of twigs. Finally came a sound like a muffled gun report and I saw the car rear up the way an unbroken horse tries to throw its rider. It sank to earth, its nose against a rock formation, its tail big and blue and only half hidden by shrubs that shivered and went still. A little dust rose like campfire smoke.

The noise up the hill swelled. There was no time to drag branches across that big blue tail. There was no diversion I could work out in the second or two before I went over the edge of the road and rolled down the slope, jamming my body among loose stones, drawing the branch of a shrub down to break the outline of my shoulders. I blessed the yellow and grey stripes of my shirt. They were camouflage, better by far than a solid block of colour. The smell of dry earth was in my nose. Why so dry when there'd been a rainstorm? Why weren't the bushes and grass greener? Must have been a freak storm and the water had boiled away under the onslaught of the sun.

In front of me, leaves shook. Keep still, leaves. The leaves were scared, trembling with nerves, my nerves.

First came a jeep. It held a driver and two soldiers and an officer with a pulled-down beret. Automatic rifles threatened the countryside. Next came a truck with a heavy machine gun mounted on the rear platform. Sandbags protected the gun crew up to chest height. Next two trucks of soldiers, a couple of dozen in each. Last, another jeep with a very tall aerial that whipped back and forth like a trout rod.

Fifty or so of the brave. If they looked to the right, there was the tail of the car sticking stupidly out of the bushes. If they looked to the left, one Englishwoman sheltering just as stupidly with a branch held in front of her like the holy cross.

Fifty pairs of eyes stared forward. It was the corner that was my best friend. Those soldiers hated the corner and what lay in wait round it. They were conscript boys, fifty of the not-so-brave. They strained forward with the fervour of lads who've heard tales of horror, of booby traps and ambush round every bend.

I huddled and listened to the sound dwindle and die away. A powdering of dust drifted over me, along with the rank smell of diesel. I got to my feet with a muddle of thoughts and emotions. That I'd been careless and stupid. That I'd been lucky the car hadn't caught any soldier's attention – though when I checked the bushes there was only a small patch of blue visible, made huge by my distorting eyes. Also that I'd been excited. Admit it.

It took less than thirty minutes. I did it on the road. The corners I took with the caution of a little old lady in a Morris Minor. When the hill gave way to flat ground towards the river, I stood stock still to look and listen.

I'd been crazy even to contemplate driving the road. You can hear nothing in a car. If the army was going to check Guazatan, trucks were what they would use and a child would have known that. I'd been too long in Paris. I'd grown soft, lost the fine edge of self-preservation. In Paris the biggest threat is the traffic wardens. *Bluets* the Parisians call them. The guerrillas weren't cornflowers and neither were the army.

I was half a kilometre from the bridge. A rough track wandered off between black basalt boulders to the river bank. Cattle had been driven down this way to drink. Hoof-prints were like fossils in the dried mud. As I went I caught glimpses of barbed wire, sentries, sunflashes off the metal of the bridge. In the river the rocks were still my protection. If Beatriz ever wanted to raid across the river, this is the place her group would use. The army faced a daunting task. They couldn't patrol the whole length of the river and keep the roads open and go hunting in the hills as well.

I waded barefoot through mud and water, ducking from rock to rock, startling birds, startling myself. Once I'd climbed the bank on the far side I felt safer. A little safer. It was only that morning I'd come across a body by the roadside here. The corpse looked as if men had quarrelled over it, invaded it, dug for information in it, used it for war games.

Salvador is not the Cotswolds. Remember that. It's not Paris either. The people are not gentlemen.

Shape up and stay alive.

There was a truck carrying timber. The driver kept taking his eyes off the road to gape at me. He couldn't make me out: *gringa*, alone, torn and dirty clothes, rising from a ditch with an imperious wave of the hand. He may even have had some primitive fear of me, that I was going to steal his soul. He took me as far as the highway and sped away.

A bus picked me up, *confort y seguridad* all the way to San Salvador. A boy sat beside me holding a string of freshwater crabs. The crabs wanted to shake hands. I sat sideways on the seat to give the crabs more legroom. The boy thought this hugely funny. When he grinned all his front teeth were edged with steel.

'Señorita, why do you worry?' the boy asked. 'They pinch only a little. And they're good to eat, very good.'

'That's what the crabs say about me.'

This joke lasted the whole way into the capital.

A full length mirror hung on the wall. I caught sight of somebody's reflection and stopped for a closer look. No one else was in the room. I was the somebody.

The shoes were still all right. Ridged composite soles, leather uppers that had begun the day dark maroon and ended it beige. The rest of my clothes looked as if I'd stormed the Bastille. Stains and rips were everywhere. They'd never

90

let me past the front desk of the George V in Paris, but the Camino Real in San Salvador is used to the humours of reporters and I just looked as if I'd been having my own personal war. Buttons were missing from the shirt and it hung open at the side as well from a close encounter with the agave. My roll away from the road had left streaks of dirt on the slacks. River mud fringed them.

I took the clothes off and slung them in the bin and stood naked in front of the mirror. There was a tide mark where dust and sweat had mingled. It ran round my neck and plunged like an arrow down the valley between my breasts. Pointing the way in case anyone got lost. A knee was grazed. And something under one breast. It looked like a love-bite and I peered closer at the bruise. I must have knocked my ribs hard. I'd felt nothing, had no idea when I'd done it. I'd had other things clamouring for my attention.

I stood the way I always do, leaning forward, shoulders slightly hunched. You see tennis players standing like that as they wait for a serve. Or fighters wary of an attack.

And the face that stared back at me: it belonged to a fighter who'd gone ten rounds. Dark hair lay in rat-tails. Eyes seemed further apart. A day in brilliant sun does that. They had the staring quality of the slightly mad.

I was a mess.

I wanted a long bath with something by Guerlain to take the smell of dust out of my nose. I wanted a scandalous dress and dinner with someone who smiled as his hand reached across the table. I wanted moonlight and strong arms and hot blood to erase the memory of Philippe. But more than anything I wanted the Taca flight to Miami first thing in the morning.

So what did I get?

The rush of water nearly drowned the words. I half heard what he was saying and stepped out of the shower very fast, slipping on the tiles, pulling down the shower curtain, racing into the bedroom. I was blinded with shampoo and rubbing my eyes made it worse.

A foreign spy, the newsreader had said, had been captured by the army at Guazatan.

I peered at a television screen blurred by shampoo. The newsreader was a young man in a sincere suit and tie who was going to be president when he grew up. The picture changed to show a truck packed with soldiers. It was a meaningless bit of stock footage to go with the voice-over. Units of the Quezacatl Battalion had made a powerful sweep through territory infested with communists. It was when they reached Guazatan that they discovered the foreigner in incriminating circumstances. The terrorists had indulged in an orgy of murder and destruction at an important ranch and then had withdrawn. Major Portillo, the officer commanding the camp at Puente de los Negritos, said he believed the *terroristas* had received warning of the army's approach from another spy, not yet captured.

I dripped on the carpet and stared at the stupid pictures on the screen. Very slowly the army truck passed in front of the camera. A couple of soldiers raised rifles in the air. The rest simply stared. The faces were those of peasant boys. Yesterday, kill a pig. Today, kill a terrorist. It was all the same. Orders were to be obeyed. Nothing was explained.

Abruptly we were bounced from the crawling army truck into an interview with Major Portillo. From the squawky sound, the major was at the other end of a telephone. I listened, not just to the words but to the sound of the voice itself. His voice was vigorous, forceful. He spoke fast and without hesitations. Portillo was sure of himself. He told the story all over again.

'The task force from the Quezacatl went with all speed to Guazatan. There was evidence everywhere of terrorist activity. Many buildings were destroyed. The local people had been murdered or driven away. At an abandoned *finca* the spy was discovered. My lieutenant reported to me that he had been aiding the enemy.'

'You were not there in person?'

'I was directing operations from Puente de los Negritos. You understand that I command the camp there. At the

92

same time I have to be in communication with the authorities in San Salvador and Ilopango. It is to this camp that the spy was brought on my orders. Here he will undergo close interrogation into his links with the terrorists.'

They showed a photo of Portillo. It was a blow-up from some entirely different occasion. It might have been a political visit to inspect the Quezacatl because over Portillo's shoulder there was a pompous civilian and in the background a fuzzy pattern such as an out of focus line of soldiers might make. Major Portillo had his mouth open, speaking to someone who had been cropped out of the photo. I got down on my knees close to the TV set. His face was in two halves. You would almost have said it belonged to two different people. He wore a beret pulled down over one ear with a disconcerting kiss-curl peeping from under it. A pair of metal-rimmed glasses perched on his nose, giving him the look of a soldier-scholar. But then his face changed character. Below the high cheekbones were sucked-in cheeks and thin lips. His mouth opened wide as if he shouted a lot. It didn't make a perfect O because the lip on one side reared up. It was a sneer, despising others.

'Major, what nationality is this spy?'

'Most likely he is Cuban, though naturally he denies this.'

'What explanations –'

'I pay no heed to what he says now. By tomorrow morning we shall have the truth out of him. He has an accomplice – a foreign woman – and he must tell us about her. She travelled to Guazatan earlier today. I believe she took vital information to the terrorists. We are still hunting for her.'

'Thank you, Major Portillo.'

'This is another success for the Quezacatl Battalion in the war against communist terrorists.'

'Thank you, Major.'

'They are lower than cockroaches and will be crushed under our boots.'

'Thank you.'

'By Independence Day they will be utterly destroyed.'

93

'Thank you, Major Portillo. And now football. There is a fever —'

I pressed the button and the set went dead. From the bathroom came the rush of the shower. Let it run. Let it empty the whole reservoir. The sound of it comforted me. It was as if someone was in there and at any moment would appear and smile and tell me not to worry.

What did he look like, the man who'd pricked my neck with a knife? I'd never seen his face, seen only a snatch of his body through bushes. He'd spoken English first because that's the international language of money and flying, spies and terrorists. He'd spoken French next, hardly enough to guess at the accent. But he wasn't a Cuban, I would swear that. Why did Portillo say he was? Cubans had African blood where Salvadorians had Indian blood. But most likely Portillo saw through prejudiced eyes. What did he look like before the Quezacatl got him? I'd seen what a man looked like when they'd finished with him.

I shivered.

I was wet and the air conditioning was fierce. I switched it off and opened the window. The night sky had the velvet promise of espresso. Trees hid the lights of the city centre.

Portillo would be a tough one to meet. He was a rising star. It's unusual to get a major strutting in the limelight like that. It is the colonels and the generals who grab the glory without risking their necks.

Close interrogation.

I was still cold though the air through the window held the heat of the day. Down below was Boulevard los Heroes. I could see a couple of heroes. Their helmets bobbed like Chinese lanterns under the street lighting. They carried machine pistols and in daylight their helmets were canary yellow. They stood like Alsatians, turning with each passing car.

No one had given a name to this spy they'd caught. No papers on him or they weren't saying. Who was he? I had a burning curiosity about that. He'd put a knife against my skin, an action as intimate as love-making. What was he doing there? Had he seen me hand the money over to Beatriz?

I walked back across the room to the closet, choosing what I should wear. Something sexy no longer suited the evening. No frills, no black satin, no come-hither. I chose a safari jacket and matching slacks in blue. It was almost the same blue as the car I'd been driving. When the army found that they would check with Avis and then I would also be closely interrogated by the major with metal-rimmed spectacles and a sneer to his mouth. But for this one night I was safe because darkness hid the car and the army wouldn't venture out into ambush territory until daylight.

I dressed without hurrying and took care with my hair. Lipstick, I decided. Perfume, no.

# 9

---

Businessmen move out. Reporters move in. That's the sign of a country on the critical list.

I came down the stairs and made a circuit round the second floor which the media had made their home. A communal noticeboard was crowded with anguished cries: *Lost – Pisces pendant – sentimental value; Peter Downing – Hablo Roxana – Importante; Is anyone going to New Orleans this weekend?* A typed sheet gave Advice to Reporters on Dangerous Assignments. Don't be a hero, it advised, no story is worth a reporter's life. Beds had been thrown out of the rooms and typewriters, telexes and coffee machines moved in. Doors carried initials instead of numbers: ABC, NBC, AP. There was a door marked: *UPI – One up on the world.* It stood open like a welcome. I paused and listened to a weary American on the telephone. Had there been, ah, no combat at all? Couldn't they find the Brigada 24 de marzo? Were they perhaps not looking with, ah, great zeal? The man asked his questions in slow English and repeated them in slower Spanish. Only the swear words came easily. Is Major Portillo saving himself for more heroic deeds in the field? How about the other spy, this woman? The mad major would like to, mmm, get his hands on her, right? You bet he would.

I slipped back out of the door without putting any questions of my own.

In the front lobby two photographers waited by the ornamental pond. Round their necks hung voyeur's cameras, long lenses to tease out every screaming mouth and twisted limb. They sneered at me. Photographers don't think much of the rest of humanity.

And so I reached the bar. I was ravenous. My body needed fuel. But my soul needed drink.

This was the heart of the Camino Real. It was a big room, long, boutiques on one side, plate glass on the other with a view of palm trees round a pool, tables and chairs half-occupied, a deep counter with tall square stools and a crowd of war groupies from the world's media. Deep Throat I'd call this bar. There were American, British, German and French voices. Not much Spanish being spoken. The Salvadorian stringers kept to the fringe and answered questions and thought their own thoughts. Various reporters checked me over and lost interest. I pushed my way to an empty stool and waited for one of the barmen.

'*Ron con Canada Dry*,' I ordered, '*un doble.*'

'Make that two,' the voice at my shoulder said.

I'd seen him already, of course, seated at a table by the wall. I knew he'd get up and that's why I'd made it a double. No point in running for the exit. He's like an eel through a crowd.

'I'm not mistaken, am I?' he said. 'It is Anne-Marie, isn't it? We met last year.'

I paused a long time before answering. In my mind was the foolish thought that he might get discouraged and go away. You might as well ignore a shark when it's smelt blood. It was Crevecoeur and he would always appear at the difficult moments of my life. Indeed we had met last year, and the year before, and the year before.

'In Marienbad,' I said.

'You *do* remember.' His delight sounded genuine. I'd never heard him so pleased before. I didn't think he had so much joy in him. He'd switched to French but even so paused while the barman put down our drinks and a saucer with a couple of cocktail sausages. 'Old times, good times. We've got so much to talk about. Why don't we sit somewhere quieter. Here, I'll handle the bill.'

I put a toothpick through both sausages and popped them in my mouth.

'You haven't eaten yet?'

'I had breakfast.'

97

'After a drink or two we might have dinner. Provided, of course, a lovely lady like you isn't already invited.'

He led the way back to his table by the wall. He didn't even bother to see if I was following. I'd have to, he knew that. This wasn't a Paris café and the tables were well spaced. Nobody would overhear. But he still leant close to speak.

'Cody, I could spit in your bloody face.'

It was only when I looked into his eyes that I saw how angry Crevecoeur was. He'd been holding himself in while he went through the social niceties. All the time anger had been building inside him. He has narrow shoulders and a thin chest and a face like an accordion squeezed tight and you wouldn't think he'd be able to contain so much rage.

'I should take you outside and shoot you straightaway. Nobody would pay much attention. Just some Death Squad throwing another party. It's what you deserve. Better than you deserve. Bitch.'

I should have hit him. I should have pushed the drinks in his face and stormed out. I made the mistake of treating him as a rational being. 'Crevecoeur, I have no idea what you're talking about. So if it's . . .'

'You stay put.' His hand clamped over my wrist. He had an amazing grip. 'You're not running away. I haven't decided what to do about you yet.'

'Let me go or I'll break your arm.'

'You do that,' and his eyes were exploding, 'and I'll shoot you dead right here in the bar, with all these newshounds as witnesses. Know what, I wouldn't even stand trial. They'd give me a medal instead. I'd be a hero. You've broken more laws in two countries than I can begin to think of. You've destroyed an operation of mine that stretches from South America to the United States and ends in France. You're about to send one of my men to a screaming death. You have given a whole lot more muscle to the Marxist guerrillas. Is that enough to be going on with?'

I stared and stared at his eyes. It was like the children's game of staring out. His anger was real. It wasn't an act. But I simply had no idea what caused it. He's a Chief Inspector in the Sûreté Nationale and his job is the security of France, so what was he doing here? He is long overdue for his step up, so if he's still Chief Inspector that's because he has made enemies in his service, which is to his credit. It means he's honest according to his own complex code. In all honesty he will trick you, cheat you, use you, drop you, throw you to the dogs, provided the security of France dictates it. He's a Gaullist who despises de Gaulle for his inflated ego, a Stalinist who thinks Stalin failed in the end, a Jesuit without the beliefs, a Calvinist who likes his pleasures. He's his own man, his own law, his own judge, his own executioner. And I'd last seen him going into my apartment block in Paris forty-eight hours ago. Or forty-eight years ago.

There's a line where anger and abuse reach their limit. Cross it and there's no more human contact. Crevecoeur had reached that line, had even stepped across it with one foot. Now he drew back. In the silence between us he reached for his glass and drained the double rum.

'I don't know what you're talking about,' I said. 'Do you believe that?'

Perhaps he did, perhaps he didn't. He lifted his glass and drained it a second time, though there was only ice and a slice of lime in it.

'You never were a great thinker,' Crevecoeur said. There was no put-down in his voice. It was just a fact he was stating. It probably came out of my file. 'Not an intellectual giant. But you were smart. You could look after yourself, even if you couldn't unravel all the world's complications. You had a brain that could add two plus two, eyes that saw in the dark, and a nose for trouble. What's happened to you?'

'What are you on about? What laws have I broken? How have I helped the guerrillas? You're lying, Crevecoeur. You always twist and trick and cheat.'

'*Ne fais pas le con,*' he whispered.

Why did he speak so softly? And his face had changed. He'd lost that look of self-confidence. Events had slipped through his fingers and he could no longer control them. Even the cold grey eyes had changed. They were red as if he hadn't had time to sleep since I'd glimpsed him in Paris. He'd seen his world go mad and it showed in his eyes.

He beckoned a waiter and ordered more drinks and searched in his pockets for cigarettes. Gitanes he always smoked and he lit one with his little Cricket lighter. The drinks came.

'And sandwiches,' Crevecoeur said. 'Can you bring us sandwiches?'

The waiter thought he could when he saw a five dollar bill. We waited in silence for the food to come. Crevecoeur was working out in his mind what to tell me. Or he was giving me a chance to worry. Or he was just spending time with me to establish links again. I had had dealings with him before. The first time we met he accused me of being an accessory to the murder of a CIA agent in Paris. The last time I had flown with him into the Sahara to track down hijacked weapons. In between times I could amuse myself, earn an honest franc or dollar or pound. But when Crevecoeur stole back into my life, business was always serious. Like now. He was letting me brood on that. The sandwiches arrived and the waiter departed, looking happy. He didn't have to deal with Crevecoeur often.

'Eat,' he said. 'You need food.'

In Strasbourg they lock up the geese and force food down their throats and when they are bloated and their bodies degenerated, the geese are slaughtered. I was Crevecoeur's goose.

'You were hired by a certain Jules Debilly,' he said. 'Who gave him your name?'

'Maybe you did.'

I said it on impulse, to annoy the man. But he just sniffed in disgust.

'You didn't even ask him that? A depraved former film actor with criminal connections asks you to do a risky job and you never checked up on him?'

Crevecoeur waited for my defence against the charge of professional incompetence. What could I say? That I'd found Philippe was cheating on me and I was angry and hurt and

100

full of doubt. Yes, the greatest sin, doubting myself. Couldn't I hold Philippe's interest? Had my body begun to sag? Or my spirit turned dull? And here was Debilly suddenly wanting my skills and I swallowed his story because it gave me the chance to prove myself.

How could I tell Crevecoeur that? It was painful enough admitting it to myself.

'He hired you to bring a sum of money to El Salvador. Not a fortune, but large enough.'

'One hundred thousand US.'

'I know. I've talked to Monsieur Debilly. Talked quite hard to him. He told you the money was to help a medical mission in the back country. And you believed this fiction, even after a gangster shot him in the street. You found the money in his apartment and flew here and went through fire and flood to deliver it to Guazatan. Only there was no medical mission. There were guerrillas who were grateful and let you go. And provided the security forces don't catch up with you, it's your intention to fly out tomorrow. Right?'

'Stop the cat and mouse game.'

The sandwiches were chicken and lettuce and mayonnaise. He ate a neat quarter in two bites. A dribble of mayonnaise crept from the corner of his mouth.

'You know, Cody, the smart drug in California and New York these days isn't marijuana, it's cocaine. After dinner parties the host offers brandy or coke. And he doesn't mean Coca-Cola. Rich people are buying the stuff so there's a lot of cash to be made. Since it's illegal, it means the mob is involved. They bring it in, distribute it, and grow fat. With the mob on the scene, you naturally get violence. Sometimes a body with bullet holes because he got in the way. Or of course a body that died of an overdose. This cocaine trade is what your friend Debilly was involved in.'

'Not my friend.'

'Your employer. You involved yourself in the drug trade.'

'Shut up.'

'Oh, you're in very good company. You see, Debilly was nicely placed to peddle to certain elements in society. Come to a Snow Ball – smart invitations to smart people. You know the sort: actors, actresses, big names on television, the people who ski in St Moritz and yacht among the Antilles, currency brokers, politicians. A minister's son, for instance. We knew about that, we were quite concerned. But no, hands off I was advised, because of the importance of the father. You understand all this?'

'It's not my life.'

'No, but you understand it? Not too difficult for you to follow? Because the complications start now.'

A light went out and I looked away from Crevecoeur and saw a woman shutting up the magazine shop. Over at the bar they'd stopped drinking beer and started on tequila. At the other end of the room a pianist was playing to himself. I came back to Crevecoeur.

'Troubles crowded in on Debilly and his pals, far more than they could handle. Misfortunes come in threes, isn't that what the English say?'

I began counting my misfortunes and when I reached seven I gave up. The biggest of them was sitting with me. I picked up my glass and found it was empty. I'd drained it, like Crevecoeur, and never noticed.

'The guerrillas had captured the plane carrying the cocaine and were demanding a ransom. Another gang was set to muscle in. And I began taking an urgent interest. Are you listening? Do you need another drink?'

'I'm listening.'

'Okay. The cocaine originates in Colombia. Once a month a plane flies down to collect it. All right, it's not a 747 but the cargo it carries has a high street value. The plane flies north again. It has to stop somewhere in Central America to refuel and that used to be in Nicaragua. All the smugglers used to use Nicaragua. The Sandanistas were happy to facilitate the collapse of bourgeois civilization through drug abuse until Washington warned them they'd blast the airfield out of existence unless they stopped it. The drug runners all made other arrangements. Air Today took to refuelling at Guazatan.'

'The army would know about it, Crevecoeur. They'd see this plane coming in.'

'Don't be naïve. Who do you think was supplying the aviation fuel? The army was. More particularly a gentleman by the name of Major Portillo was growing rich. You know the Salvadorian army ranks? Captain, Major, Colonel, Millionaire. Portillo is a shooting star. Blum made the arrangements, looked after the money side. Then the aircraft flew on to LA, Blum's home town. Here it was transferred and carried by certain cabin crew on AF004 to Paris. Now, there are a lot of important people involved, Cody. A general and a police chief in Colombia, a major and an air force colonel here, a deputy police commissioner and customs chiefs and various state politicians in LA, police and customs protection in France too, a minister's son, plus all the middling to little fish. How am I going to crack that open? Is it even worth doing when only a few jet-setters are scrambling their brains? No, was the answer. Observe and take note but leave well alone.

'So I busied myself elsewhere until last month. One of the people I pay to listen reported to me that a new and more ruthless gang were about to break in on the drug scene in Paris. They called it the Snowline, the route from Colombia to Paris. They weren't going to the trouble of setting up their own Snowline, they were going to take this one off the shelf: the generals, the middlemen, the Guazatan refuelling, the LA staging post, the delivery to Paris. Warnings were given that Debilly and the rest should go on a long vacation. The shot in Debilly's leg was the latest reminder. Next time the bullet would be higher up. One of Debilly's associates got angry and was removed. They killed him slowly. You could tell from the body.'

The ice in Crevecoeur's glass was melting and he drank the water. I had never known him talk so much before. It made him thirsty.

'I have been involved in wrapping up the entire operation before the new gang takes over. The whole of the Snowline has to be destroyed, not just the distribution network in

Paris. You can always buy yourself some more pushers. The drug business is like a lizard: you cut off the tail and it grows a new one. You have to kill it. Have you any idea how tough that is? Three foreign countries are involved. I have to mount operations in them without anyone knowing because maybe their security people are getting a rake-off too. I need names and dates and photos and tapes and licence numbers and routes and bank accounts and passport numbers. I must have all this in a tearing hurry without any hint getting back to Paris.'

I could hardly keep up with him. It was a flood of words. He was doing it deliberately. I realized that too late. He was overwhelming me until I nearly drowned and would grab at any arm for help. Which would happen to be his arm.

'So the snow, the coke, the moondust, whatever friendly name you call it is flown up north and on the way the plane refuels at Guazatan. That's a place the world has never heard of, which suits the smugglers well. I need evidence from Guazatan that cannot be ignored. It's part of the package and the authorities in Colombia, in El Salvador and the United States will be forced to act because of the weight of the whole package. You're listening well? You're taking all this in? Because this is where you stumble in, make your entrance on stage and kick the scenery over.'

My attention was rivetted on Crevecoeur as if he was the judge who had delivered the lecture on how wicked I was and how society had to be protected from the likes of me and was making a pause before pronouncing sentence. Crevecoeur darted a look round the room and checked that no one at the nearest table was listening. He lit another cigarette and inhaled the smoke and it seemed not to come out again. His body absorbed it. His eyes returned to me and fixed on my face.

'Paul Darcy is one of my top men. He's worked for me in Cuba, in Algeria, all over. I entrusted him with the job of getting the evidence in Guazatan. Photos, tapes, whatever it needed. Gave him a radio for emergency use, told him to live rough. But he must get the evidence that Portillo was

appropriating aviation fuel for his own gain. I was told w
the plane flew down to Colombia so I knew when it wo
be coming back. Paul went over the border from Hondur;
It wouldn't take him long. He carried food and drink for .
couple of days plus emergency cover. Only of course the
plane arrived in a storm and the guerrillas held it up and a
ransom demand was sent to Blum. Blum wasn't interested.
He's just a fixer. He wasn't going to be a hero. So the demand
got relayed to Paris and you were hired to deliver the money.
How much has Debilly paid you?'

'Nothing yet.'

Crevecoeur shook his head at my gullibility.

'He got shot before he could pay me.'

'This might be a job you never get paid for. Teach you a
lesson.'

'Get to the point, Crevecoeur.'

'The point is very sharp,' he said. 'The mob who are taking
the Snowline over have a rather different deal in mind for
the Guazatan refuelling. Their idea is to treat with both the
army and the guerrillas. Double insurance. Portillo they will
offer money in his Florida bank account against the day he
will abandon the patriotic fight against the insurgents – and
never mind his bloodthirsty public statements. The guerrillas
they will offer – for guaranteed safe passage – certain
weapons. They will fly the weapons into Guazatan on the
southward journey when the plane is otherwise empty. They
need this guarantee because the Snowline is about to grow
very big. They plan at least a plane every week. That's a lot
of cocaine, a lot of pushers in Paris, a lot of addicts, a lot of
gang trouble and underworld fighting. The opportunities for
blackmail and corruption are immense. The profits are so
huge they will buy politicians, not just their sons. Next thing
you know, they'll be selling the politicians. *That* is what my
concern is. Meanwhile you . . .'

I knew what was coming and shook my head. 'No, Crevecoeur, no.'

'You have wrecked things by taking money to the guerrillas
and releasing the plane.'

'Stop it. That's not what I was doing.'

'The next time that plane comes south, it will have weapons on board. The Snowline will be established.'

'Stop it. It's none of my doing.' Why didn't he listen? Even if I shouted, he went on relentlessly.

'And my agent Darcy who was there for the evidence –'

'Enough.'

'– you have had him captured by the officer he was to expose. You have ruined the operation and cost Darcy his life.'

'Shut up,' I screamed at him. I'd had enough of his lies and heaping the blame on me. 'Stop it, stop it, stop it.'

He reached over and gripped my thigh. Did he think I was about to run away? His fingers dug deep. They were a dog's teeth sinking into my flesh.

'Stop it,' I yelled and smacked his hand away. How dare he touch me? I wasn't his to handle. I wasn't his woman or his prisoner or his agent. 'Take your hand away.'

Crevecoeur had a new mannerism I hadn't noticed before. He was grinning to conceal his anger. His lips were drawn back and his teeth gleamed, all the better to bite me with. But he was no longer looking at me. Following his gaze I saw that people at the bar had turned to stare. His hand had been on my thigh and I'd yelled to stop it, so a sexual advance was being repulsed. Happens every day. Though not often in the Camino Real.

'Your man's name was Darcy, right?'

'Yes.'

'Good man?'

'This is no country to send a probationer to. Yes, very good.'

'Then why did he let the army catch him?'

'How should I know?' said Crevecoeur through thin hard lips. 'I wasn't there.'

'Can't the French ambassador –'

'Have you seen the French embassy? A dog and two fleas. The ambassador creeps round with diplomatic bags under his eyes. By tomorrow morning, when he's put on his striped suit and trimmed his moustache and requested an interview with the President, Darcy will have been chopped into small pieces and fed to the dogs. What Frenchman? Major Portillo will demand, the man confessed to being Cuban just as I predicted.'

'Can't you get in touch with Portillo direct?'

Crevecoeur simply stared at me. He was right: I'd lost my brains somewhere along the way. He couldn't ask for his man to be released and please make sure he's got all the evidence with him.

'Let's get out of here,' Crevecoeur said. 'Let's breathe some air that isn't conditioned.'

One or two faces turned as we left. So, a lovers' quarrel, a tropical rainstorm, thunder and lightning and death and destruction, soon over, blown itself out. And the two lovers were hastening to bed because they'd worked out this amazing new way to do it and the urge was overwhelming.

'Have you bought one yet?' Crevecoeur jerked his head at the boutique. Among the kaftans and sandals and soft toys and wood carvings were tee shirts. Comic strip heroes struck bold poses. *Death to the Commies* shouted one. *Don't shoot – I'm a journalist* urged another. 'Do people wear these things? I mean, really put one on in the morning and go out and report on the war? They have to be damn certain which side of the field they're working that day.'

'Crevecoeur, I've met your man.'

He stopped and swung to face me.

'Darcy? Where? In Guazatan?'

'Yes.'

'Why didn't you tell me before?'

'I didn't know he was yours.'

'Did he say anything to you?'

' "Who are you? Why are you here?" '

'I mean, did he have some message for you to pass on?' The eyes were on fire again. 'Come on, what are you hiding?'

'I never saw him. He had a knife at the back of my neck.'

'What were you doing?'

'Watching the pilot refuel the plane.'

'Then you'd already handed over the ransom to the guerrillas. Darcy must have seen you do it. He assumed you were one of the gang.'

'Could be. I just don't like people pricking my neck with knives. The Mafia, the Sûreté, the KGB, the thug with a skinful of booze – I don't like anyone putting a knife on me.'

'What happened?'

'I got away.'

So much for his 'very good' man. I left Crevecoeur standing by the boutique window.


He caught up with me in the lobby. The photographers with necklaces of cameras had vanished.

'Where are you off to in such a hurry?'

I pushed out through the swing doors. I'd had enough of Crevecoeur. He's a con man, a trickster, a promoter of shady deals. He makes me sick. He always has. His anger and accusations this time were more than I could stomach.

'Where are you going?'

'Out.'

'Where to?'

'Anywhere. Just to get away from you.'

Taxis were lined up and a driver opened a door but I wanted movement, exercise, and I turned aside.

'Ashamed to hear the facts?'

'Go to hell.'

I was walking fast and took half a dozen skipping steps which brought me out on the boulevard. But I couldn't lose him.

'Leave me alone, will you.'

No, Crevecoeur wouldn't. I waited at the corner for the lights to go green and lost patience and dodged through the traffic. Crevecoeur was wrong-footed and a car's horn blared and then he was by my side again.

'What do you want with me?'

'Running away, are you? Can't take it anymore?'

Street lamps threw an ugly glow over trees and shrubs.

108

The traffic came in bursts, bunched by traffic lights. The boulevard was broad, divided by low concrete blocks that would blow the tyres of any car making a getaway U-turn. The air was warm and I was sweating again.

'The American embassy is this way. Is that where you're heading?'

I wouldn't answer. Treat him like any other man. Ignore him and he'd get bored and give up.

'At least your brain's working again. After all, this country is Uncle Sam's backyard and they don't let the Salvadorians step too far out of line. I've thought of the embassy. Unfortunately the ambassador has flown to Washington for the weekend. He's the only one with real clout.'

There was an amusement park on my left. Not much of a place, not many on the roundabouts or buying ice creams. Perhaps if I hopped on a dodgem, I could make a getaway.

'But I tried the embassy anyway. Got to speak with the chief spook. He wasn't any help. To tell the truth he was angry. How dare the French set up an operation without clearance. You'd think the CIA owned the country. Come to think of it, maybe they do. They bought it after a good lunch one day with all the funds Congress keeps voting. The spook wanted to know if I'd contacted the Treasury Police. The Treasury Police! It sounds medieval. Thumbscrews and the rack. What do you suppose Portillo uses? I talked to one of the Agence France Presse men in the hotel about Portillo and they call him *Commandant Casse-Couilles*.'

Just shut up, will you. There was a McDonald's on the other side of the boulevard and I crossed towards it. It was like a customs post at some Cold War border complete with floodlights, barbed wire and armed guards. The security men checked inside every car before letting it into the car park. How could anyone live here? You're going out for a Big Mac and someone puts a rifle on you.

'I guess that would translate as Major Ballbreaker,' Crevecoeur usually talked French to me. Switching to English was a big favour. Knew the language perfectly well. He'd been at the French embassy in Washington. Rich pickings round there. CIA, IMF, World Bank, other embassies.

'He likes to use cigars and matches, I'm told. Also keeps a blowtorch on the table so –'

'Will you shut up.'

We stopped dead, facing each other. The street lighting made him look sick. He was, in his mind.

'Well?'

'Well what, Crevecoeur?'

'Are you just going to forget about Darcy?'

'He's your man. I didn't employ him. I didn't betray him.'

'You brought the money that freed the pilot. The army remembered you coming, you can be sure of that. So when they saw this plane suddenly taking off they came to investigate. You were the match that lit the fire. Maybe you think you weren't strictly to blame. But the army doesn't work by logic. And Darcy under the blowtorch has no time for logic at all.'

'Don't try and involve me.'

'You carried money to the guerrillas. The army saw you going. They caught my man because they saw the plane taking off. You are involved. They'll be asking again and again who you are and where you've gone and they won't believe Darcy's screams that he doesn't know.'

I closed my eyes and tried silence again.

His voice was soft. 'You never believed in laws. Laws were for ordinary folk who couldn't think things out for themselves. You believed in something bigger: your own sense of morality. It didn't concern you whether a thing was illegal or dangerous but whether it was right. You believed in natural justice. You were a pioneer. You used to walk tall and my, how you've shrunk.'

'Crevecoeur . . .' I searched for the right words. 'You are a used-car dealer trying to teach Sunday school. It's unbelievable.'

He didn't answer. When I opened my eyes he was already on his way. He walked without hurry, as if there was no

110

particular place to go. A black and white police car cruised past, rifles bristling from every window. He didn't give it a glance. He never turned back to look at me.

'Tell me more about the weapons,' I said.

'Maybe it'll be rifles,' Crevecoeur said. 'Maybe grenades. They're easy enough to pick up.'

'You don't know? In other words, you're bullshitting me.'

'Weapons will come in. I know that. I just don't know what will be offered. There's a rumour that Gadafy has been approached about surface-to-air missiles. Even a couple would keep the Salvadorian air force out of the sky. They wouldn't dare go up. The whole course of the war would change.'

'In your view it's okay for the Salvadorian air force to bomb the guerrillas but not for the guerrillas to shoot down the planes.'

He walked a bit in silence. We were almost back to the Camino Real. I could even make out my own bedroom: it was the only one with the window open.

'Terrible things have happened here,' he said. 'In the thirties the army used to make the peasants dig their own graves and stand in them to be shot. And the Death Squads – just the army and the police out of uniform. But for the first time they've had a fair presidential election – well, fairish. The guerrillas refused to take part on the quite reasonable ground that their candidate would be assassinated. Instead they issue shopping lists of demands and try to destroy the country's economy. If the CIA did that, it would be called destabilization. If the guerrillas do that, three cheers, it's the revolution. In my view things are a little better here, democracy is creeping in and the Death Squads are reined back. And by and large I am not in favour of French drug dealers financing foreign wars.'

'But the army is interrogating your man . . .'

'Portillo is. And I want the evidence to blow that man wide open. I want to smash the Snowline.'

We walked some more. He'd said everything he was going

to say. He wasn't going to say 'please'. He had his pride and it was bruised enough even trying to get my commitment. He wouldn't go down on his knees.

'Okay,' I told him. 'Okay.' It was all I could think of to say. But everything was summed up in that word and he understood.

We had reached the hotel car park. He stopped while he patted his pockets and found his pack of Gitanes. He tapped a cigarette on his thumbnail. He wouldn't say 'thank you' either. Didn't even offer me another drink. He sighed and said minutes were important now. He seemed subdued. We'd spent all the emotion in us.

'I'm going to see a man called Serpollet,' Crevecoeur said, 'though he doesn't know it yet. He used to be a pilot in the French air force during the Algerian war. Like many disillusioned military men he went a little wild after de Gaulle gave Algeria independence. You know the sort of thing, joined the OAS, planted a few bombs. Well, he settled here in the end, runs an air taxi company.' He drew breath. 'I imagine it will come as a bit of a shock for Serpollet seeing me. He believes he killed me. I was only a kid then of course. So I think, for his peace of mind, he'll agree to fly me to Guazatan tomorrow. Darcy is smart so he'll have hidden his tapes and films. If the army isn't there and the guerrillas leave me in peace, I might be able to find the hiding place. I can't risk being in Guazatan long. But I'll stay until noon. You know what I mean, Cody?'

One quick look at me and he was gone. He walked up to the swing doors. I thought he was going to turn and wish me luck. But he'd only paused to light the cigarette. He carried on into the hotel.

For a moment I stood still in the car park. The street lamps played hide-and-seek among the trees and made shadows on the windscreens of parked cars so that I blinked and looked again. No one was watching. It was a trick of the light. I turned to face the city. Not far from the hotel was a *barranca*, a ravine with shacks and slum litter and cocks that crowed hours before their time. On the far side of the city was a dead volcano, black against the black sky. And beyond that, a whole world of darkness.

He'd tricked me, hadn't he? Crevecoeur had wormed his way down to some buried sense of guilt. He could have flattered me. He could have said: Go on, Co, there's nobody else who can do it, only you, your skills and your courage and your grit. Spat in his face if he'd tried that. Detest the man. Instead he'd talked and talked until the feeling simply grew that what had happened was my fault. It wasn't. But still I was about to go out into that darkness.

For a moment I felt peace and calm inside myself.

# 10

He was standing where he could look down and inspect me. The door behind him was open and the light coming out made the bulk of him even bigger. He was leaning against the wooden banister at the top of the stairs and one day it would kill him, the wood cracking and sending him tumbling to the floor below.

'So you've come, sweets.'

Blum hadn't been at home. 'He is working, maybe,' a manservant had said with a sneer in his voice. 'For you he stop working, maybe.'

La Linea Tropicana had an office in a side street off Calle Arce. This was the city centre, though you wouldn't know it. There was no blaze of neon, no elegant shops, no happy crowds. At street corners were stalls of plastic goods and food. The sour smell of cooking *pupusas* battled with the rankness of the drains. People stood and ate. These were the true poor with nothing left to lose, the victims of the war. Radios played *salsa* and rock and toothpaste commercials. The side street was lit in patches as if someone had forgotten to pay the electricity bill. Trees made it darker. A church had a roof of corrugated iron that rattled in the breeze. It looked like the kind of temporary repair that becomes permanent.

I'd rung the Tropicana bell and told Blum on the intercom who I was and he'd pressed the buzzer that unlocked the door. The building was of greyish plaster and looked old. It had looked like that from the day it was put up. Inside there were cracks in the skirting board where cockroaches had their homes.

'What the hell are you waiting for?' Blum called down. 'The butler?'

114

There was a wide stairwell and I climbed two sides of it to reach the floor where Blum waited. A lawyer and a carpet importer had offices here and the fanlights above their doors were dark. Blum watched me all the way up the stairs.

'Okay,' he said, as if I'd passed some kind of test. 'Hey, you look good, you know? Blue suits you, sets off the colour of your hair.'

An aesthete was Ernesto Blum tonight. When the hours of darkness came he obviously appreciated the finer things in life: a fine cigar, a rare cognac, a pretty lady, a Vivaldi concerto. Or he was just a drunk. As I passed him I caught a knock-out wave of booze. A quick drink wouldn't do that; it took hours with a bottle. He'd splashed on aftershave too. He hadn't used a razor, just the aftershave in honour of my visit. It certainly wasn't to impress the two murderers who waited in his office.

Blum followed in and stood with an arm out in a wide gesture, an opera singer's embrace. 'This little lady is blessed with the name Cody. Don't ask me what her other names are. Carmen Miranda. Queen Elizabeth. Brigitte Cody Bardot. Oh yeah, she's come from Paris. That's Paris, France, not to be confused with Paris, Texas. Different kind of *pueblo* altogether is Paris, France. A colleague of our faggy French friend. She's a lady of mystery. As women should be. Secrets and mystery. A magic lady then, foxy. And these fine citizens are called Luis. Both of them. Confusing. I call them Luis I and Luis II, like kings. Ha!'

He was smashed. He missed his mouth first time with the glass. The two citizens Luis looked at him, looked at me and looked back at him. There was no telling how much of this speech they understood.

'Luis and Luis are associates of mine,' Blum explained. 'Very fine people. Very go-ahead. Very tough.'

'Very tough employees of the Linea Tropicana?' I asked.

'Uh-huh,' Blum said through a cloud of smoke. He inspected the burning end of his cigar and found inspiration there. 'I am a man of many talents, sweets. The shipping line, I tell you honestly, is not so good as it used to be. But fortunately with associates such as these I develop other interests. Okay now boys, this lady and I have got some private business to go into. So if you'll leave us for an hour. Go and have a beer someplace. *Vamos*,' he ended, in case his thumb hadn't been understood.

What had they been doing before I came? Just dropped in for a drink and a chat? Planning a bank robbery? Deciding which horse should win the big race? Both Luises were standing but not because I was the lady that Blum insisted. In their world you got to your feet when you heard the doorbell. Just in case. I was entering their world and should learn that lesson.

'We see you later,' one Luis said to Blum.

'Have a nice day,' the other Luis said to me. Out of Blum's sight, he smirked.

'A couple of my boys,' Blum said. 'Fine boys.'

'Very go-ahead,' I agreed. 'Very tough. Very well armed.'

'Listen, in this city you're nothing without a gun. In this city, without a gun you're already dead. Jeez, I could tell you some things would make your eyelashes turn green.'

He peered at me to make certain I didn't have Martian eyelashes. His face had half a smile on it. You could tell he was pleased with himself. Alcohol made him more extreme. He was bigger, louder, more brutish, more smug.

'It's been a big day,' he said. 'Luis I – he's the smooth one – is getting himself married next week. So I tell him we got to celebrate now because he'll have nothing to celebrate after. Ha! We went down to La Libertad, drank some beers, ate some oysters. You got to eat plenty oysters, I tell him, they're an apho . . . aph . . . they make a man strong, right? Four dozen oysters he eats and he's feeling so strong we have to go right out and find some girls. He says – his English is not so good – he says: "One dozen oysters make one girl." Ha!'

He came over and chucked me under the chin and I didn't hit the slob then but only because he continued on to a side table with a bottle of Johnnie Walker Black Label, soda bottles and an ice tray.

'Scotch do you okay, sweets? Don't have a lot of choice. You can have scotch with or without rocks. I would bet you're a girl who goes for rocks.'

'Coke,' I said. As I had said this morning.

'That is a problem. I tell you frankly. Coke I cannot manage. You're right out of luck there.'

He had put his cigar down and was pouring whisky. Then he stopped and turned and looked at me. Slowly he nodded his head. His eyes no longer looked drunk. They looked hard and dangerous. He stared and seemed to take me in for the first time. I wasn't hot pants and a pretty face. I wasn't a little woman hungry for a superior male. But nor was I quite Wells Fargo who had delivered the gold to Cheyenne. He couldn't figure out what I was.

'Well now,' he said, 'look what the French fairy sent us. Not just carrying the money but doing a little private-eyeing while you're about it. You got there and got back, which is not a trick everyone can pull. And while you were there you asked a few questions and poked your pert little nose in places it shouldn't go. So what is it, sweets? A shake-down? You think maybe Debilly didn't pay you enough and I might be persuaded to contribute something to your personal fighting fund?'

'Nobody told me it was drug-running,' I said. 'Nobody told me I was delivering a ransom to guerrillas.'

'Would it have made any difference? You feel bad, so go to confession on Sunday. We don't hire people to take their conscience for a walk. We hire people to perform. You got paid and you performed. End of story.'

'I haven't been paid. I wouldn't have done it if I'd known.'

I wouldn't have got involved in the whole mess. I would have stayed in my apartment, warring with Madame Boyer and being sweet to Monsieur Roussy on the floor below, smiling no to Guy and no to Erica, smiling yes to no one, waiting for winter to end, waiting to see what the rising sap would bring in spring. That was my everyday life, my sensible self. I would have kept clear.

And yet.

117

This was the salt that gave life flavour. The danger, the adrenalin, the physical effort, the will to live and win, the need to discover the secrets of the world – they were my drug. They made colours brighter and sounds sharper and smells more haunting. They were what I lived for.

'Sit down,' Blum said. 'Make yourself at home while we have our talk.'

I stayed standing. With someone like Blum, you always keep on your feet. He went to the front door of the office and shot a bolt home. I could see keyholes to two locks but bolting the door on the inside was what Blum liked. Nobody could come in without that bolt being pulled back.

'You don't want a drink. You don't want a screw. You don't even want money. Or do you? Just tiptoeing round before you get to the point? Dollars, is it?' He was working himself up to a fury, his face reddening, spit on his chin. 'A great pile of green ones? Or do you want a fancy bank account in Curaçao? Or maybe you're into gold? Why don't you answer? Where's your manners?'

It was Mr Manners himself who began moving in on me. I took quick steps and put the width of a desk between us. It wasn't Blum's desk, it belonged to a secretary. There was a typewriter and an appointments diary and a telephone through to the holy of holies itself. We were in the outer office. To my left was a window, uncurtained, looking over the street. At my back was the door to Blum's private office.

'Who are you? I mean, where did Debilly find you?'

'I never asked.'

'Holy mackerel. You never asked. He hired himself an amateur. Well, I'm going to ask him where the hell he heard your name – went to the priest or what?'

'I'm going to ask him the same.' Who disliked me enough to involve me in this mess?

'So what is it you want?' Blum asked. 'You haven't said yet.'

He began to circle round the desk and I moved to keep it between us. He went the other way and I moved back. Ridiculous. He was too out of condition and too full of booze

118

to clamber over the top. It was futile chasing me round the desk and he knew it and stopped.

Something outside caught my eye, a movement through the window. The breeze blew leaves across a street light and I caught a flash of metal.

'One of yours?' I asked.

He glanced out of the window.

'Nice night for a ride. Is that what you want? Go down to the coast and skinny-dip? Eat some oysters maybe?'

A Cadillac stood at the kerb. It was leopard-spotted by the pattern of leaves.

'I don't mean the car. The man standing in the doorway beyond.'

He looked again and shook his head. 'A cop. A soldier. My boys are at Choy Tan's having a beer and imagining me enjoying a piece of tail up here. Ha!'

I couldn't have hoped for more. Blum didn't realize it but he'd told me everything I needed. He was a tough who thought with muscles and steel and didn't dream there was any other way. You meet them all over – New York, Paris, London, San Salvador. Wasn't that what the poster for Doberman jeans had boasted? Blum had the killer instincts of a Doberman; he didn't have the speed.

His lips moved back from his teeth. It was a smile.

'They picture us together. Maybe they prefer a woman to have longer hair. And of course you should be blonde. That has class here. They don't realize that every hooker in the States is a bottle blonde. But you've got the figure. I could see their eyes light up when you came in. Too bad you didn't come for a screw.'

'I'll tell you all I want,' I said. 'I want you to make a phone call.'

Blum's attention sharpened. No more thoughts of the two Luises or driving down to the Pacific. I wanted a favour, so he could expect a favour in return. Or I was going to bargain for something and he needed to know what.

'I'm listening.'

'I want you to telephone Major Portillo and tell him to stop

119

interrogating the foreigner they picked up this afternoon. Let him go free.'

It was worth trying. It was a thousand to one against his making that phone call but I wanted to try him first. The alternative was much harder. The alternative was getting Darcy out myself.

'Well now, Major Portillo. What makes you think I know him?'

'Just an idea I have. He's a big man out in those parts and with your business interests I think you'd keep on the right side of him.'

'So,' Blum said, which wasn't much of a response. 'And what foreigner is this? You fix yourself up with a boyfriend?'

'You haven't heard?' Was he serious? He was the kind of fixer who picked up every whisper.

'I told you. We've been celebrating. I've been out all day.'

'Major Portillo's men made a sortie to Guazatan and took a prisoner. A foreigner. Portillo says he's Cuban. By the time Portillo's finished with him, he'll admit to being Fidel Castro. He's not Cuban, he's French. A colleague of mine.'

And may God forgive me for saying one of Crevecoeur's men could be my colleague.

Blum took a sip of the drink I hadn't wanted. Then he took a serious pull at it. He'd been drunk when I arrived. Now he was sober. Eyes sunk in the flesh of his cheeks peered at me. He was a rhino, uncertain whether to charge. 'You came to Salvador alone,' he said.

It wasn't really a question. He was stating a fact. He could have checked at the hotel.

'Yes,' I said, 'I came here alone. But I wanted some protection so I had a colleague come over from Honduras. It's only ten or twelve kilometres to the border. Paul Darcy is his name. I wanted someone who could handle a gun in case . . .'

I stopped. It had been worth a try but the odds had always been discouraging. There was no sense in continuing because Blum had slipped a hand inside his jacket and pulled out an automatic. He held it loosely in front of him.

'You're a liar,' he said, 'and not even a clever one. Jeez, Debilly picked himself a dog. You had no colleague. You made no arrangement to meet him in Guazatan today. You couldn't have. You didn't even know where the dump was until I told you. Tell me what your game is. Come on, sweets, talk. It would be a shame to have to hurt you, a crying shame.'

He began walking round the desk. The gun was still not pointing at me. There was no need. He could jerk it up in a second. It made him feel good. It made him strong and powerful. With a gun in his hand, the rest of the world became pygmies. He was a thug, that's all. He was a male chauvinist. Beatriz would say he was a capitalist pig and she would be right. B is for Blum. Blum is bad. Blum is a drug-smuggler. Blum is a mobster. Blum is a rapist and a murderer. What shall we do with Blum? We shall annihilate Blum. I'm with you, Bea. I'm on your side, sister. It's just that Blum is the guy with the gun and he's walking round the desk and if I'm to get out of here in one piece it's now. I've got to move, *now*.

I disappeared backwards.

One moment I was there. The next I had gone. I'd had my fingers on the handle and as Blum reached the corner of the desk, I twisted the handle and rolled back through the door to Blum's inner office. It was a backwards somersault, dropping below the level of the desk so he couldn't shoot, ending up inside his office and jumping to my feet and looking round in one sweep, searching for a handy weapon and finding none, but seeing the room in every detail though the only light was what came through the door. There was a desk with a telephone and pens and paper and a swivel chair and three more chairs and a window out on the back of the building and an air conditioning unit sitting on the sill and a metal filing cabinet and a table with a tape recorder and a casting couch where Blum had planned a wedding night with me and a ceiling light and a map of Central America on one wall and gaudy tropical butterflies pinned to a board on another wall and an old-fashioned safe let into a third wall but no hunting rifle and no vase and no heavy-based ashtray stand and no potted plant and not even a whisky bottle or water carafe. I could smother him with the rug but that would only slow him for seconds and if I couldn't lay him out cold he'd be on me again.

'Ha!'

It was his all-purpose shout. It saved him having to think whether he was pleased or angry or triumphant. But I could hear victory in his voice. I'd gone through into the inner office and there was no way out. He was wrong, of course. There was a way out. It's just that, from the darkening of the light in the room, I could tell he was blocking it.

He was twice my weight and his temper was roused and he had a gun. My weapon was speed. It wins every time. And if it doesn't win, that means you were too slow. So speed it up. If you're fast enough, the other person's brain cannot cope.

He came a couple of steps into the room and stopped with his gun jabbing forward. I was to one side and the light was dim and for half a second he didn't see me and by then it was too late. I dived to the floor in front of him and got on all fours and was scampering and squirming between his legs before he could drop the gun on me. In the Foreign Legion they call it *le petit chat* and it's the last resort trick. You push through the enemy's legs and for a crucial moment his brain is blocked by three possibilities: that he will be attacked from in front, from underneath and from behind. Be quick enough and the enemy is too bewildered to counter. By the time he does turn, you have surprise on your side.

Blum blundered round and I hit him once, a rising chop with the blade-edge of my hand directly up into his nostrils.

Strike hard enough and you shatter the bone at the bridge of the nose and splinters of it can even penetrate the eyeball. You can blind a man that way. Even with the power I used the pain was overwhelming.

'Ha!'

It was a shout of agony this time. He let go of the automatic and clapped both hands over his eyes. He wouldn't have been able to see to shoot in any case. Tears would turn me into an underwater smear. And in the morning when he looked in the mirror he'd find purple bruising from the bridge of his nose right across the top of his cheeks – classic black eyes.

I scooped up his gun and prodded Blum with it so he lurched to the wall. He leaned against it, glad of the support. And while his whole attention was on the lightning striking through his nose and eyes, I felt first one trouser pocket and then the other until I found a big bunch of keys. Even the key-ring was typical of the man: a woman's body moulded in plastic. Not the head or the limbs, just this relief map of the promised land.

As I locked the door to his inner office I heard him begin to threaten me. He threatened violence against my sex, of course. I ripped out the telephone wire that ran through to his office, stubbed out his cigar, switched off the light and locked the outer door.

I stood a moment with the sense that something wasn't right. It was his gun. It was in my hand still. I don't like guns. I don't like them pointing at me and I don't like one in my hand.

So I unlocked the door, dropped his gun in the wastepaper basket and left again.

The thing about guns is that you grow to believe in them. If you have your finger on the trigger, sooner or later you end up squeezing. They laughed at me in the CIA when I told them that.

# 11

<hr>

Close your eyes. It was a tropical night. Soft heat on your skin, insistent beat of dance music, smells sweet and rotten. Open your eyes and you saw the soldier watching you, every move you made.

Go on, I told myself, it's just a man looking at a woman.

But why was he positioned directly opposite the building where Blum had his office? Blum would be on good terms with some colonel in the military command and could ask for a guard. Though what could the soldier do if one evening Beatriz and the comrades came to strike a blow for the revolution? One soldier was useless. Loose off a few shots and be cut down in the return fire. Or Beatriz might push the young children ahead; the soldier would hesitate to shoot at seven and eight year olds; they'd lift the rifle out of his hands.

I pulled the front door closed behind me and heard the lock click. Glancing up I could see the window of Blum's outer office. It was dark. His inner office was at the back. Even if Blum switched the light on and off, on and off, it wouldn't be visible to the soldier.

A bunch of traffic went past at the end of the street: buses, old cars, taxis, a truck with the army out on patrol. The night belongs to guerrillas. The army knew that. They were watchful. They would be extra suspicious at checkpoints. At the corner an illuminated sign jutted out over the pavement. *Choy Tan*, it said, *Chop Suey Restaurante y Bar*. Sounded terrible. Sounded the kind of place where all the stray cats ended their lives.

Okay, soldier, are you watching closely? Pay attention to what I do. Observe this big ring of keys I'm holding up to the streetlight? Well, I'm holding it up on purpose so you

124

can see I'm all above board and a great pal of Blum and it's really very sweet of him to lend me his shiny Cadillac. Well, naturally I had to do him a teeny favour in return but that was no problem. I mean, where's the harm in a little screw these days? It's how a girl makes out in a man's world, if you know what I mean.

The car was dark grey. From upstairs it had appeared leopard-spotted. Close-to, the leaf shadows looked like some disease. I unlocked the door and got behind the wheel and started the engine and checked over my shoulder for traffic and yes, the soldier was still watching. You'd swear he was a cardboard cut-out except that he'd moved his rifle so he held it at his side for a change. I hoped things wouldn't go badly for him when it was discovered that a *terrorista*, as I would be called, had gone up and brutally assaulted a prominent American business executive and stolen his car.

I didn't go far. Just to the corner, easing up in front of the Choy Tan. Ancient election posters cheered the wall. *¡Vota Verde!* one commanded and showed a green fish. *Vota Arena – Vota asi* was in blue, white and red. Or maybe you'd prefer to put your trust in *Tic Tack – El Licor Nacional de los Salvadoreños*. Dust as thick as net curtains blurred the windows. The door stood open and I could see a blue painted wall with a calendar for tyres. Men sat at tables in twos and threes. A waitress walked past carrying a tray with beer bottles.

I blared my horn. I wasn't getting out. I was a *gringa*. Also I was a close friend of the boss.

I blared again. Nothing like sitting in a Cadillac and ringing for room service. A young boy appeared in the door and looked at me. In Guazatan he'd have been in revolutionary school. C is for Cadillac. A Cadillac is bad. A Cadillac is a symbol of capitalist repression and American exploitation of the masses. What shall we do with the Cadillac? The boy vanished. I waited. Let's blow up the Caddie. I was right – this was known as Blum's car and the two Luises were known as Blum's men. One Luis came to the door and frowned as he saw it was me in the car and on my own.

'Come here,' I called out.

He held a beer bottle with a paper napkin round the bottom to stop his hand getting wet from condensation. He took a swallow of the beer, frowning all the time.

'Move it,' I said and hurried him up with a hand.

He spoke over his shoulder and then both Luises came out of the door and crossed the pavement to the car.

'What you doing in Mr Blum's car? Mr Blum say you to drive it?'

'No,' I said, getting out and bringing the keys with me. I put them into the hand of the Luis without the beer bottle. Make him accept the keys and he'll accept the idea of driving. 'He said you were to drive me.'

'Me drive you? Where he say me drive you? You go your hotel, you take taxi. Cost six colones, maybe eight colones, is nothing for you.'

So then I had to lay it on the line. I wasn't returning to my hotel, I told them. I was going nowhere in the city. I was going to a village up north of the capital. I had some business to do there and Mr Blum said I was to have the car and both Luises because it wasn't safe for a woman to drive alone in the country at night. Ernesto had said they were very fine and very tough boys. But if they were scared, then I'd go to Pulapeque without them. When Ernesto heard about it, I didn't think he'd be pleased, but that wasn't my worry. And if something unfortunate happened to his car, well my guess was Mr Blum could have quite a temper.

I made a point of speaking English. I was an arrogant *gringa*. They didn't like me. I didn't like myself. Beatriz, you should blow me up too.

'Do you believe her?'

'Foreigners always lie.'

'So you think she is lying?'

They were speaking Spanish.

'All women are liars. It is their nature. They are weak therefore they lie to make up. Even Aurea, though I love her, is a liar.'

'So we should check with the boss, you think?'

126

'I think . . .' He helped his brain with a swig from the bottle. 'I think the boss might not be pleased if we go back to check. Why are we doubting his orders? Anyway, she is only a woman. What could she do?'

'That is the truth.'

I breathed more easily.


'What did he say her name was?'

'I forget. It is not important. She is nothing.'

'She is called Maria, maybe. All whores are called Maria.'

'Is Maria a *Yanqui* name? Wait, I remember now, he said she was called Bardot. Do you want me to stop the car under those trees so we can take her? We must drive all this way so she should pay. You can have her first.'

'I don't think the whore is any good. She was only fifteen minutes with him. She knows nothing.'

'In America the women know nothing. And the men only know about baseball and hamburgers.'

'They know about rockets into space. They went to the moon.'

'I don't believe they truly went to the moon.'

'I saw it on television.'

'I saw Superman on television. Do you believe a man can fly? It is all tricks.'

There was a pause as we went past a bus, *confort y seguridad*, a waving boy, the conductor leaning far out of the rear door to shout at us.

'They know about whisky too, the *Yanquis*. They invented whisky.'

They ignored me. I couldn't understand. I was a *gringa* and a *puta*.


There was a restaurant at the side of the road but it was closed. It had been closed for years. We parked among rusting cans and old newspaper.

Luis the passenger said: 'We take off clothes now.'

They struggled out of lightweight jackets and folded them

127

neatly and laid them on the back seat beside me. The guns under their armpits showed dark, like stab wounds.

'You no frightened of this?'

Luis the passenger removed his shoulder holster and showed it to me.

'As long as it doesn't point at me.'

He laughed. 'In the city we must carry guns because there are plenty of bad boys. Is protection. Boys know Luis has gun and leave us alone. Then we are peaceful people, yes?'

'I'll take your word for it.'

'In the country there are plenty of bad people too but we no carry guns. You know why? Because the army. The army find us with guns, they go little crazy, they shoot us dead maybe, they say *we* are bad people. So we take off guns.'

The holsters were stored behind the sun-visors above the windscreen. They did it without discussion. They must know the places the army searched: round the radiator, under the spare wheel, in the glove compartment.

'Is no true we are bad people,' he insisted. 'Bad people are all out there. The soldiers, the *terroristas*, they are bad people sometime. I think they all *loco*.'

A car went past the restaurant's parking area. It was a taxi with its interior light on. A whole family crowded it out, grandmother, parents, children. The taxi was weighed down and drove slowly. We swung out on the road and overtook it. Faces crammed the windows on our side.

'They frightened, you see?' Luis the passenger said. 'They keep the light on so everybody see they is ordinary people, kids, no bad guys. But they is frightened because our car. Big car, big trouble maybe.'

I refused a cigarette. Luis used the lighter from the dashboard, his face glowing orange as he lit cigarettes for both of them.

'I tell you story, you see we no bad people. Many years ago, before we meet Mr Blum, we do many small jobs. We young, you understand, we know nothing, just boys, but we work hard. Is district by market with many cafés, cheap hotels, girls, you understand. You no go there, is no good place for you. One night in bar three men come and drink one beer with us. Their leader say: We hear about you, you tough boys, you have guns, you do one thing for us, you kill Archbishop Romero, we give you plenty dollars. He speak very quiet. His friends watch door all time. They worried men. Who is you? we ask. Never you mind, says leader, kill archbishop, one thousand dollars. We is poor boys, that is lot of money. We tell no, we no kill archbishop. Archbishop is good man, speak for poor people, speak no more killing. Okay, you see what I say? We no bad boys.'

He flicked his cigarette out of the window, half smoked, as if it didn't taste right.

'Listen what I say now. Somebody else kill archbishop. They shoot him absolutely dead in cathedral. He speaking peace in cathedral, then he dead. Everybody say it is army shoot archbishop, police maybe, because he speak for poor people. Is not true. You listening? I tell you men who ask us to kill archbishop not police, not army. Is true.'

'You mean they were guerrillas?'

'Maybe, I think. They want make *martir*. I don't know how you say *martir*.'

'The same.'

'So maybe army kill archbishop, maybe terrorists. Arch-bishop is *martir* anyway. You understand?'

No, I didn't understand. Who could understand? Truth didn't exist here. Only madness existed.

'Anyway, he dead many years.'

'One thousand nine hundred and eighty,' said Luis the driver, the silent one. '24th March he killed.'

In other countries they called streets after important dates. Here they named guerrilla armies after them.

Speedbumps in the United States, sleeping policemen in Britain, *tumulos* in El Salvador. The warning signs shone bright and we slowed right down to walking pace as we went over three bumps and approached the soldiers. Sand-filled barrels striped black and white narrowed the road to a single lane and provided protection in a shoot-out. Eight or nine soldiers were grouped among the barrels. They were a herd of deer caught in our headlights, rifle barrels pointing above their heads like antlers. They were turning their faces aside, eyes screwed up.

'Switch off the lights, idiot. You want them to shoot out the headlights?'

Luis the driver dipped the headlights and then switched them off. We cruised the last few metres on sidelights and the army's lamps.

We stopped and at once there were soldiers on both sides of the car. They were leaning very close, gun barrels pointing through the windows. They had been blinded by the headlights and now they peered with hard suspicion. They were looking at the two men in front and then they were looking at me. They were staring at me, all of them were.

What had Blum said when we first met at his house? When taxi-drivers flash their lights at army patrols, the soldiers haul the passenger away for questioning. Luis had dipped the headlights before switching them off. What a damn fool thing to do. I might only be a foreign whore but I was the personal friend of his boss. If they didn't like you, the army would order you out of the car, keeping their rifles on you in case you made a run for it, glance at your papers and then march you away to a cell where no one would come in answer to a scream.

'Switch off the engine,' a soldier said, 'and get out.'

Luis the passenger half-turned in his seat and translated this to me. To the soldier he said: 'She is a foreigner, a French-American I think. We were giving her a lift.'

They were going to drop me right in it. Those very fine and very tough boys had as much brains between them as a parrot and they were going to disown me until the army's curiosity was roused and I was taken away for more rigorous research. And the Luises would go to Blum and say: *Sorry boss, the army was suspicious and they've taken her away to see if she's hiding anything under her fingernails.* And Blum would say: *Boys, you've done a great job. Ha!*

The soldiers took a pace or two back, giving us room to

get out of the car. Luis the driver got out on one side. Luis the passenger and I got out the other. We moved in the stiff way you do when rifles are pointed at your stomach.

'The men to stand with their hands on the roof of the car.'

Two soldiers searched them, patting chests, backs, under arms, crotch, legs. Others put flashlights over the obvious hiding places in the car.

'Raise your arms.'

It was a sergeant who said this to me. Luis the passenger repeated it in English. In the morning I had refused to be body-searched because I had a moneybelt round my waist. I didn't have that reason now. Also this roadblock had a different feel to it. At night everyone's nerves are a little more exposed and I didn't like the edgy eyes of the soldiers or the fingers inside the trigger guards or the jeep with the whiplash aerial. I raised my arms to shoulder height and the sergeant patted my breasts and stomach and thighs and legs. He gestured for me to turn round and he felt my shoulders and back. I was facing across the roof of the Cadillac and I found myself staring into the eyes of someone in authority. A lieutenant, I supposed. I mean, they don't send generals out to man roadblocks, do they?

'What is your name?'

I replied nothing.

Luis the passenger said: 'She doesn't have the language.'

'Then you ask her.'

'What is your name?'

'Cody.'

'Where are you from?'

The questions came twice. They came first in the angry voice of the lieutenant, who didn't like my being here on the road at midnight. They came a second time from Luis; his voice repeated the anger because he didn't like being here either.

'From England.'

'Show me your papers.'

I moved without hurry. My passport was in a pocket of the safari jacket and the lieutenant walked round the car to take it. Luis and Luis had their identity cards out and lesser soldiers inspected these.

'What is her profession?'

Luis looked at the entry in the passport. 'Teacher.'

'You are a teacher?'

Luis translated this to me.

'I'm a teacher, yes.'

'And where are you going?'

'Pulapeque,' Luis answered for me.

'I'm not asking you,' the Lieutenant swung round on him. 'Ask her.' He looked back at me. He had examined my passport with care. My face got the same scrutiny as he watched the effect of his questions.

'I am going to Pulapeque. Is that in a prohibited zone?'

He wasn't going to answer questions. That wasn't in the rules. But it was important to establish from the start that I was an independent kind of person, doubtless because of coming from one of those northern countries that was accustomed to ruling large chunks of the globe. Luis translated and I got the next question.

'Why is a teacher from England going to Pulapeque in the middle of the night?'

The temptation was to answer before the translation came.

'To visit the father of one of my pupils, the boy Francisco.'

I found myself speaking English as if it was Spanish. I doubt Luis noticed anything strange.

'You come all the way from England? A teacher from England here?'

'Yes.'

'Pulapeque is a poor place. It is a very poor place. There are no rich people there. There never have been. It is not like other places where there were many poor people and a handful of very rich people. Nobody in Pulapeque could even afford to send a boy to school in San Salvador. To send one to England is impossible.'

I waited while Luis gave me his version: 'This army officer is very angry with you. He say Pulapeque is very poor village and the rich people have all been killed. He say there is nobody who sends a boy to school in England. Why you lie to this officer? He get plenty mad. He kill you a little maybe.'

'Tell him,' I said, 'it is the priest's son.'

One of the soldiers began a laugh and killed it. Suddenly it was deeply quiet and still. With the army's lamps casting a glow, they could have been faces round a camp fire. It was as if there had been the cough of a leopard out in the darkness and everyone had frozen. I could feel the tension tighten.

'Señorita Cody, it is perhaps different in England, I do not know. All I know is what is true in El Salvador. In my country a priest cannot marry. A priest does not have a family. He does not send a son to England. Why are you lying?'

I was glad the lieutenant's remarks had to be translated. If you are to build up tension, you need to let time pass. You must make them wait for you. It is only in that way, when you answer the accusation, that you relieve the tension and gain acceptance. I looked only at the lieutenant. But I was aware of all the other faces surrounding me, aware that the guns were no longer on the two Luises but had moved to cover me.

'Lieutenant, you are right,' I said. 'A priest of the Catholic Church does not marry and have children. Not in my country, not in your country, not anywhere. It is for that reason that the authorities of the church decided that the priest's bastard son must be sent away. It was to England he was sent. I do not know what happened to the woman.'

They had the windows closed because of the dust and the air conditioning was full on. The sweat was drying on me and I felt chilled. We hit a pothole and my spine jarred and I wished the driver would keep his eyes on the road and stop trying to watch me in the mirror. Once we pulled off the road altogether and stopped as a truck came towards us and his eyes were on me the whole time. I was exotic and he was overwhelmed with curiosity.

We took a bend in the road and his eyes flicked up to the mirror again. Dark eyes, very round, the way men's eyes go in the heat of passion. Philippe, your eyes were perfect circles. Do you remember our first time? Of course you do. The first time is always burnt into the memory. That Friday afternoon in May, driving to Normandy '*pour passer le dirty weekend*', you said. And your lovely smile. 'At the hotel we shall be monsieur and madame.' And I laughed because of the way you put it, half prim, half lecherous.

But you couldn't wait for the hotel, remember? We'd crossed over the Risle and were heading for Cormeilles when you pulled into the side of the road. We walked through an orchard with apple blossom drifting down. Hand in hand, like kids we were. Your hand was hot and when you pulled me round your mouth was hot on my mouth and your breath was hot. That was the first time, in the apple orchard, behind a haystack, with a brown and white cow watching through a gap in the hedge. 'I love you,' you said, 'I love you,' louder, 'I love you,' you shouted. And I believed you. And when I looked up your eyes were huge and round, like full moons in the sky. It was beautiful, Philippe, and what went wrong? Why did you drift away? Why *her*? How did you meet? Did she trap you? Were you pretending it was her when you were in bed with me? God damn her. Did you take her to the Auberge les Rosiers? Did you stop on the way in our orchard? Did the hay tickle her skin? Did you shout out your love for her? Were your eyes round and enormous for her?

I hate her, hate her. I hope she . . .

Had the driver spoken to me? Concentrate, you stupid woman, stop picking at the wound.

'*Señorita?*'

'What is it?'

'We are nearly in Pulapeque,' he said. 'Do you know where this priest lives? It is late. Pulapeque is a small place and it is dead at this time of night. There will be no one to ask.'

I said: 'There is no priest any more. He has no illegitimate son at school in England. But do you think those soldiers would doubt a story like that? It was the best way to pass the roadblock.'

134

The driver turned to look over his shoulder and the other Luis grabbed the wheel.

'Look where you are driving.'

'There is no priest and no boy?'

'None. Drive until we get in sight of the village.'

Very tough boys, were they? They drank beer straight from the bottle with a napkin to stop their fingers getting wet. Just boys. In some of the places I've been they wouldn't last five minutes. Toughness isn't in your muscles or your gun. Toughness is in your brain and your willpower.

'What do you think she really is?' the driver asked.

'Why don't you ask her?'

They were speaking Spanish again.

'Maybe she's not the boss's woman.'

'She should be the boss's woman. She has *cojones*, that whore.'

And how goes the night with you, Monsieur Paul Darcy? How are your *cojones*? I hoped, I prayed, I was not going to be too late. Men shouldn't get into this sort of game. If ever I saw Crevecoeur again, I'd tell him that. Hire only women, I'd tell him. Men have got more to hurt. Hire women but not *me*, thank you very much.

The road curved round a hill and Pulapeque was a short way ahead of us. I could make out a huddle of shacks under the starlight, a single street lamp in the centre of the place, a lamp in a window. Otherwise, as Luis the driver had pointed out, it was dead.

'Where you want we take you?'

'Switch off your headlights. Go to where that big tree is and stop.'

With only sidelights to cast a glimmer on the road, Luis drove slowly. I was tired of the air conditioning and opened my window to let my body start acclimatizing. The moment I stepped outside I knew the sweat would come. There was a smell of hot dry earth and once, as we passed a darkened shack, the stink of a chicken shed.

'Here?' Luis asked as we passed under trees.

'Yes.'

He stopped the car. It was dark here with the starlight cut out. Suited my purpose.

'Okay,' I said. 'I'm leaving you here. When you see Mr Blum, thank him for the use of his car. He said not to go to his office before lunchtime tomorrow. You got that?'

'Sure,' Luis the passenger said.

'On the way back you'll have to pass through the army checkpoint again. That lieutenant is bound to ask you questions about me. Tell him the truth: that you dropped me outside the village. Tell him I said I didn't want to arrive by car outside the priest's house in the middle of the night. Tell him you think *I* am the mother of the priest's child.'

Teeth gleamed against their faces. They understood that. They thought it a good joke. I got out while they were still happy with me.

'Okay, get going.' I slapped the side of the Cadillac as if it was a horse.

The car did a three-point turn in the road and went on its way. Just before the curve on the hill, Luis switched on the main beams. I watched the car out of sight. When the red of its taillights disappeared, I listened and heard nothing. I was all on my own. The decision was made. It was too late to go back now. I could only go on.

I had started to walk towards the darkened village when I caught approaching headlights bouncing in the night sky. At once I got off the road and crouched among rocks, watching and listening. Lights appeared on the far side of Pulapeque. Someone was pushing the car hard in third gear. Or pushing the jeep. Yes, more the sound of a jeep. It drove into the village. I could see the wash of light between shacks.

Of course it might be a regular army patrol. But to my mind that lieutenant had got to worrying and had used his radio to check about the priest in Pulapeque and had been told there wasn't one any longer. He'd decided I wasn't simply mistaken but lying. And instead of giving chase, he'd ordered a reception committee out from the army camp to cut me off on the road.

But what choice was there? I had to go on. In Pulapeque

there was someone I had to see, the only person I knew who might help me find a way into the camp where Darcy was held.

As I watched the headlights faded and the engine noise cut out. Ahead it was dark and silent. So it wasn't a regular patrol. They were waiting for me.

# 12

I knew where the jeep would be.

The order would be given: You are to go to Pulapeque and wait for the woman who spies for the terrorists. Where do we wait? Where is the priest's house? Do we knock on doors and wake the whole village and frighten her off?

Pulapeque was not a big place. It had a square with cobbles round the edges, a big guanacaste tree in the middle and a slab of stone made for a statue glorifying the local bigshot, only the village had never had one. The square had all the important buildings: shops with a bit of everything, the café, an agricultural supplier, a place that repaired vehicles, the church. That's where the jeep was: parked in front of the church.

It was just another shanty. No rich citizen had got pious in his old age and rushed up a fine church as insurance. It was constructed of corrugated iron, painted red and white, with rust gnawing it into holes. You could tell it was the church by the cross on top. The jeep waited there because they were expecting me to arrive in a chauffeur-driven Cadillac. The village had perhaps a hundred houses and four or five mud tracks led off from the square. The priest's house wouldn't be far away. They would see me go to it.

That's how their minds work.

A dog barked as I worked my way round the buildings opposite the church and I froze. Dogs bark at strangers in the night and soldiers know that. I stood and waited and the dog growled low in its throat. It was tied by a piece of rope to a barrel which was its home. It couldn't bite me. But its bark was worse, if it brought the soldiers.

I moved a foot and the dog barked again and a man's voice from inside a shack told it to shut up. That's only guessing.

There were expressions he used I never learnt in Madrid. The dog hung its head and cowered in the barrel.

Good boy.

I passed the square and rejoined the road that led on to the army camp at Puente de los Negritos and across the river to Guazatan. On the outskirts of Pulapeque was the house I wanted, the home of the woman whose son had been tortured and murdered. Armando, wasn't that his name? It was Portillo who had gone to work on his body, I would bet on that.. And was working on Darcy's body now? There was no time to waste. I mustn't be too late.

I recognized the house. It was better than a shack because its roof had been tiled and the breeze block walls had been plastered but not painted.

'*Señora.*'

What was her name? Nobody had told me. It had been no time for formal introductions with her son's blood on the back seat of the car and her kneeling beside me as I drove. I called again, louder, and knocked on the door. She should be home. Perhaps she was too grief-stricken to come to the door. The night after her son is murdered is not the night a mother sleeps. She has carried him for months, given birth to him in pain, raised him with love, been proud of him as a man. And her hopes and dreams have been killed. I knocked again and there was the noise of a hinge needing oil and a voice from next door said:

'What do you want? Dinora's not there.'

I had a name for her. That's something. You feel a fool asking for someone when you don't even have a name. I looked at the neighbouring shack and the door was open but only a crack. You don't open the door wide at night in case the bogeymen sweep in. I couldn't make out much: an eye, a scrap of hair round the door. But it was an old woman's voice.

'I need to speak to Dinora. Can you tell me where to find her?'

'Her son is dead. She doesn't want to speak to strangers. She wants to be alone.'

'I know Armando is dead. I brought his body here in my car.'

The door opened another fraction as if she wanted a closer look at me. I still couldn't see much of her in the starlight: a high cheekbone, fingers gripping the door.

'Yes, well . . .' She was grudging with her trust as if she had to pay out good money. 'I don't know that she wants to speak to you . . .'

And when she came out with it, I didn't know I wanted to go back and speak to Dinora.

'She's keeping a vigil over the coffin.'

'Not here?'

'No. In the church.'

Oh hell.


I looked at my watch and it said 00.49. There's no romance in a digital watch. You get the naked truth.

Romance is a tropical starlit night, the village *plaza* with a spreading guanacaste tree, four soldiers in a jeep. They smoked and talked and were quiet and talked again. The talk was of football and Bo Derek.

I was so close to the jeep that when one flicked away a spent match I could have picked it up without stretching. They were settled, that was the main thing. They'd been told to come here and wait and they weren't about to go out on patrol for me.

I was at the corner of the church, in a crouch, with just my head breaking the line of the corrugated iron. If one of the soldiers turned, he wouldn't be looking down at ground level. Even if he did register the dark shape of my head, there was a chance he would dismiss it as a prowling cat.

And have you seen the film 'Indiana Cojones', one wit asked. That broke them up. Each of them practised the joke in turn. Hey, another said, I tell you what's happened to this foreign woman – she's in bed with Cojones. Their laughter echoed off the corrugated iron. There was no talk of Major Portillo interrogating a Frenchman.

140

The church had a side door and even that was of iron sheeting. I put a hand to the knob and turned and found the door locked. At waist height a piece of iron had rusted away. I knelt down and put an eye to the gap. A single candle gave the church the look of a cave. The walls had been whitewashed. Paintings of bible scenes were so garish they stood out even in the candle light; they were done by a kindergarten class or by a genius. A Salvadorian Christ with wide cheekbones stared fiercely from a cross. Wooden chairs were ranged against one wall. Dinora sat in one. The coffin was in front of her. It was open but I couldn't make out the corpse. She wore the same mauve dress as before. She wasn't praying. Her eyes were vacant and she waited for dawn, the burial, an end to the country's agony.

I put my mouth to the gap and whispered her name. When I looked again she hadn't moved. I tried a little louder and had no success. I couldn't hammer on the door because the church was like a drum and they'd hear the knocking in the jeep at the front. I found a small stone and flicked that inside and it rolled up against the coffin. Finally she looked up.

'Dinora, do you remember me?'

I couldn't talk and look at the same time. You feel a bloody fool whispering and then moving your eye down to see if your words have had any effect.

None.

'We carried Armando in the back of my car. Do you remember?'

All she remembered was that her son had died in agony and was laid out in a plywood box and she was spending a last night with him by the light of this one candle because candles cost money and the night was long.

'I would come to sit with you in the church except this door is locked. Is there a key in this lock? Can you see? I can't use the front door because there are soldiers there. The army is looking for me. They think I'm a spy because I went to Guazatan. That's where I was going when I met you.'

All you can do is keep talking and hope that the sound of

141

your voice and the things you mention will bring her back to present reality. I thought her face had sharpened.

'I'd like to come to the service in the morning but it's not going to be possible. What happened to the priest who used to be here? Did he run into trouble? It must be a problem when you want to get married or need to hold a funeral. I spoke to your next door neighbour. She told me where to find you. What's her name?'

She still wouldn't open her mouth. I looked again and saw she'd turned her head aside. The neighbour wasn't a subject that appealed. *She wants to be alone*, the neighbour had said. It looked more as if Dinora didn't want that neighbour with her.

'Dinora, when I was in Guazatan I saw your nephew Alonzo. He was in –'

'Go away, *go away*, GO AWAY!'

It was shocking, a rising scream, shattering the night. I couldn't budge from the door because the soldiers had jumped out of the jeep. Two had stumbled into the square. If they looked round the side of the church they'd see a solid black shrub that grew by the door. If the moon had been up, that would have been different, they'd have seen a person. But starlight didn't betray me. I believed that with all my heart. I had to.

'What's wrong? Who are you shouting at?'

I looked through the gap in the door. A soldier with sergeant's chevrons and a machine gun stood in front of Dinora. The waxy light made him a whole size larger.

'I'm talking to you, mother.'

She didn't hear him. She didn't see him.

The sergeant pivoted round where he stood. His machine gun threatened the coffin, the paintings, my eye, Christ on the cross. A draught fluttered the candle flame and his shadow swayed and he swung his gun back, startled.

'It was a ghost. A ghost, mother. Is that what you were shrieking at?'

'Is everything all right, Carlos?'

'It's just the old woman shouting at spirits.'

'Tell her to come and sit with us a spell.'

'She's an old woman. Her son is in the box. She's got to sit with him.'

He lashed out at the coffin with his boot. The plywood splintered. It made a soft noise like a fist in the mouth. The woman was on her feet, ready to tear the soldier to death with her nails, but he was already on his way out. The church door slammed. It gave a metallic clang, like a cracked bell. The whole flimsy structure shook. The candle flame was sucked towards the front door and shivered back upright. Soldiers' voices from the comfort of the jeep were on edge and angry.

'Dinora.'

She looked towards the side door. 'What do you want with me?'

'Come here where the soldiers can't hear.'

She knelt at the other side of the door. We whispered through the hole. We could have been in the confessional.

'He is dead,' Dinora said. 'Tomorrow a priest comes from Chalatenango to say prayers over his grave. There is a special place in the cemetery for the ones who are found dead at the roadside. Five from our village. There are others who have disappeared and we have no news of them. Others are with the guerrillas and we hear sometimes that one is dead. The whole of Pulapeque is dying.'

'Your nephew is alive.'

'I don't care. I hate him. He is alive and Armando is dead. He is a slave of that witch-woman and she will destroy him. She says to him: Do this, do that. And he does it. He lies in wait and blows up soldiers because she orders him to. He comes here to Pulapeque to get food. He comes to my house because his mother who died last year is my sister. Give me food, he says. What have I got? I give him a meal, *pupusas* and beans, but I have no food for him to take. Someone sees him, someone tells the army. Understand, it is a village and we have our secrets and our hates and our desires. There is always someone who betrays. The Lord Christ had twelve disciples and one of them was Judas.'

143

Boots halted the flood of words. I couldn't move. I was flattened behind the bush. My shelter, my trap. The soldier came to within a couple of paces of the side door. My hand scooped up dirt to throw in his eyes. My thigh and calf muscles were tensing for an explosive burst that would get me across open ground to the shelter of a grocer's shop before they started shooting. There'd been fighting here before. Bullet holes tattooed the wall of the grocer's. Seconds from now there would be more.

The soldier stopped. Between leaves I could see his hands moving. Then came the steady patter of rainfall as he pissed against the iron wall of the church.

'That's better.'

As if he knew I watched and listened. He returned to the jeep.

'There's something I want you –'

But she hadn't finished. 'I don't come from here. Is that any reason to betray my son? I come from the west, near Sonsonate. You are a foreigner, you don't know our country. My parents fled fifty years ago and came as far as Pulapeque because even this village was better. If offered hope. They had lived in a place too poor to have a name and one day soldiers came and took my grandparents away. That is the mother and father of my mother. The army took them out to a field where tomatoes and pumpkins were growing and told them to run. Run? Run where? Why run? My mother was hiding and heard them ask. Run, they were told. A soldier put bullets by their feet to encourage them. Run for your lives. So they ran and the soldiers shot them in the back and left them in the vegetable field. Perhaps that is what the army will do with me. I am too old for them to rape. So they will shoot me and leave me for the crows.'

A soldier was whistling. Sometimes it is terrifying being a soldier; mostly it is boring. He was bored with the waiting. He whistled 'Here comes the bride'. He repeated the opening bars over and over again. He couldn't remember any more. It was like a wild nightmare that defies reason. I kneel by a tin can of a church while an old woman tells how her

144

grandparents were hunted like big game. The army lies in wait for me. A soldier whistles a nonsense phrase of pop classic. It's dark and I'm exhausted and my nerves are jumping. I feel just about every bad emotion it is possible to feel. I feel anger and hate and shame. I feel them at myself, no logic in that. I feel desperate pity for this mother, overflowing with madness. I feel furious with the army, striking through the generations of her family. And despair for a country that even with elections and a democratic president can still have such blots of darkness. For Crevecoeur who manoeuvred me into this grotesque position, nausea. And for lesser characters – Blum, Debilly – lesser emotions.

'Do you imagine it will ever end?' she whispered.

She meant everything, I supposed, the whole tragedy of the country. 'Yes, everything comes to an end.' Even the Hundred Years War. Even if it lasted a hundred and sixteen years, it ended. Then men draw breath and give us women time to bear sons for the next war.

'They say that the Brigada 24 de marzo is on the run. They have said that before. They've said it about the army too. They say there will be peace. They say the Pope will command it. Will we still go hungry? The Brigada says we must join them and fight for victory or the landlords will return and give us orders again. And if the Brigada wins, won't there be Nicaraguans and Cubans and Germans giving us orders? I have heard in Germany they have a wall and fences and mines to keep their people in. Is this true? Will they put up a wall round our country?'

I looked at my watch. 01.16. I closed my eyes. Bone tired. There was a lot of the night still to come, a lot to do. This old woman could talk until dawn. The dam had broken and a torrent of words swept through. By morning the dam would be dry and she'd go to the cemetery, following the coffin, with her mouth shut.

'Dinora, I need your help.'

'I am an old woman. I have nothing to give.'

'Information. You can give me that. You're the only person I know who can.'

145

'Information? What do you mean?'

I heard her shift and when I put my eye to the hole she'd taken a step back. It was too dark to see her expression but her voice held suspicion.

'Come back. Nobody must hear.'

'There is nothing I can tell you.'

'Listen to what I say. There was a Frenchman at Guazatan. He should have come away with me but he stayed behind and now he is a prisoner in the army camp. Major Portillo has him.'

'Then he is dead.'

'I don't think so. Not yet.'

'Then he wishes he was dead.'

'That is why I can spend no more time with you. I have to get him away before Portillo finishes with him.'

'You? What can you do?'

'I can get him out of the army camp.'

'No. You can do nothing. You are one woman and they are six hundred soldiers. When they catch you they will torture you. Shall I tell you how Major Portillo kills a woman? Have you heard of the bayonet rape?'

Six hundred to one? I closed my thoughts to those odds. It was Major Portillo I was up against. One to one. Keep that in mind.

'I must get in, find the Frenchman, and get out. That is what I must do before dawn.'

'How can you?'

'It is my work, it is my skill. You can tell me how to get in.'

'Have you seen the camp? Barbed wire fences, floodlights, armed sentries.'

'There are girls in Pulapeque. Do they visit the soldiers?'

'Some go with the soldiers. The young men here are all gone,' she said, her voice dropping. Her mind was on the box behind her.

'And do they walk up to the main gates and ring the bell? Is it allowed for a girl to spend the night there?'

'Of course not. It is forbidden for civilians to go to the camp.'

'Then these girls, who feel such strong desires that they risk being caught in the camp, how do they get in?'

'You are right,' she said. 'There is a way to avoid the barbed wire. Estela told me after she found her daughter's dress so dirty.'

# 13

———◆———

I can move.

If a cop swings his club, I can move so fast it hits air.

If a thug throws his fist at my face, I can sidestep and turn and have his arm over my shoulder at the breakpoint of his elbow before he can use his second fist.

That's part of the training. They do it for real in Virginia. They warn you: Get fast or get hurt. Pain is a ruthless teacher.

Nothing much you can do about an ICBM coming down. The four minute warning would see me 1270 metres away, which is no help at all. But you don't get four minutes any more. Missile technology has advanced, human capability hasn't.

I ran and walked and ran. I would walk the final half kilometre. When I arrived at the army camp I didn't want eyes blinded with sweat and ears deafened by the pounding of blood. The dirt road was grey in the starlight. Stones tripped me as I ran. Memories tripped me when I slowed down. Here was the place where I had picked up Dinora and the body of her son. Major Portillo had done his worst, demanding connections with the guerrillas. But even the worst is useless if there's no information to be got. So before dawn he'd given the order and Armando had been killed. Dawn was the danger hour for Crevecoeur's man. But two nights in a row might tire a man even of Portillo's appetites. He might signal the execution earlier so I had a narrow margin of time left.

02.12. A little glow lit the numerals when I pressed the button and I turned the watch inward on my wrist.

Running again, stumbling over a stone the size of a grape-fruit. The road was bad for running. It was too rough to

148

supply an army camp of six hundred men. Another route to the main road must lie on the far side of the camp, a blacktop for all weather. That meant the main gate wasn't on this side. Not that I was going to ring the bell. I was going in the way the itchy village girls went.

'You can do nothing,' Dinora had said.

'I can get the man out. I have to. Portillo will kill him if I don't.'

'They will catch you and have their fun with you and you will die too.'

But I was cheered. If girls from the village could get into the camp, I could.

'They will see at once you are not from the village.'

'It is better they don't see me at all.'

'Why do you run the risk?'

I'd hesitated. Because it was my life. It was what I'd been trained to do. It made my blood race and my nerves tingle and my brain leap. It made my whole being sing. Nothing else compared. Nothing else used my body and my wits and my willpower to the utmost. I found out things about the world that nobody else knew, and things about myself that I didn't know. It was a secret drug and I had become an addict.

'Perhaps I'm doing it because of Armando,' I'd answered. 'So there won't be another Armando.'

The road was dropping now and at the curve I slowed to walking pace to let my pulse rate drop and get my breath back. I went through the huddle of shacks. They were long abandoned. There were no smells of fires or animals or cooking. Ahead the road aimed for the bridge. I supposed it was guarded at night. That was one posting where sentries wouldn't sleep on the job.

On the left was the army camp.

I set off on a path towards it with the thought that if there was a path there must be a back gate and therefore a guard hut. And that not only the back gate but the whole perimeter fence would have sentries on look-out. And that if this had been at the time of the full moon I would have been totally

149

conspicuous. Even so I was relying too much on the subdued colour of my safari suit. I left the path whenever rocks promised shelter. I was doing well, pat on the back, when floodlighting was switched on ahead of me. I was so close to the fence that I threw a shadow and I dropped to the ground and wriggled like a snake to the shelter of long dry grass.

More lights were coming on and voices were raised too far off for me to catch the words. When I looked up I could see the solid block of the old ranch house, with windows showing lights. And beyond was an area with tall clusters of lights like a railway yard or a football pitch. The voices seemed to be coming from there but the rise of the land meant I couldn't see what was interesting them. No lights shone along the perimeter fence or among the rows of tents. I could make out the silhouettes of three sentries. They were turned inwards. Now, while everyone's thoughts were inside the camp, now was the time to cover the last part.

'You will be exposed at the very end,' Dinora had said. 'They have cleared a firebreak round the fence. The sentries will see you.'

'What do the girls do?'

Dinora was ignorant on this point. She had had a long heart-to-heart with her friend about the waywardness of modern girls but that hadn't included what you did when a sentry saw you approaching. 'Estela's daughter has no shame. Most likely she waves.'

'Where do I go?'

'You aim for the corner of the fence near the bluff that looks over the river.'

I was half way there when the sound began. A machine gun, and I nearly threw myself to the ground. Executing Darcy, floodlights, too late. No, an engine starting. I sprinted the last part and huddled by a rock and waited. A light was moving now and then up into the air rose a helicopter. They've got Hueys now, big troop-lifters, a gift from the United States. But this was smaller. I could see the vague outline of heads through the Plexiglass. It doused its landing lights and tipped forward to move away, gaining height as it went. Navigation lights winked. The sound faded. The helicopter was gone and the floodlights were switched off.

Have they flown Darcy out? My mind was full of him; it was natural I should assume the helicopter was to do with him. Is he being rushed to hospital? Is his corpse going to be dropped in some remote area? Are they going to threaten to push him out unless he reveals the darkest secrets of his soul?

And am I going to wait like a wallflower at a dance? Come on, move.

The fence was two and a half metres high and had triple strands of barbed wire at the top to make hand-holds impossible. The trick was not to go over the top.

Raising my head I could see two sentries from here. One was staring at the night sky where the navigation lights had lost themselves among the stars. The other was staring at me. He wasn't moving his head, wasn't checking on the approaches to the fence on the river below or the road or the bridge, wasn't on the look-out for changing patterns of shadow. His gaze was locked on me. He couldn't see me. I swore he couldn't. I wasn't here. My body lay between rocks and my head was just another stone. But inside a little voice whined: He can see the whites of your eyes.

I closed my eyes. When I opened them again, he'd altered his position and was staring towards the river and beyond where the badlands began. He was humming a bit and then stopped. He shuffled his boots in the dirt and did a couple of knee-bends. He was tired, bored, stiff and perhaps a little scared. I almost made a move, and waited, and almost made a move again when he shifted his rifle from one shoulder to the next. I felt so big and clumsy and obvious and the night was so still.

'Juan, how much longer?'

The sentry nearest me shifted his rifle again and lifted his arm, angling the watch on his wrist for starlight and I moved. Juan, the sentry, answered something but his voice came muffled. There was a storm drain under the fence. It had its own bit of barbed wire but this had been cut through.

Guerrillas could crawl through and no doubt would one night. But the drain had been opened to let through visiting girls and now it let me through. It was a big drain, like a culvert under a road, but the storm waters must be heavy here.

The pipe was short but the important thing was it got me under the wire with nothing worse than dirty knees. I got to my feet in the lee of the terrace, hidden from the sentry, with the big house beyond. I stayed absolutely still while I used my senses one by one. No smell of tobacco or aftershave or sweat. No sound of foot grating or metal clinking or deep breathing. No sight to chill the blood, no shadow moving, no outline of a body. Infinite care was needed now. This was the forward camp of the Quezacatl Battalion and if I was discovered the reaction would be violent.

I hadn't wanted to question Dinora about where her son had been tortured to death. But she'd lowered her voice until it was barely audible. 'It's known where they interrogate prisoners because ordinary soldiers have to clean up afterwards. At the back of the big house is the old laundry. The floors are of stone so . . .' But she'd choked there. It was too much to think about.

Some of the windows showed lights and I could hear two men arguing in an upper room. I couldn't catch the words but you can always tell anger: voices at a higher pitch and neither letting the other finish a sentence. I was skirting a courtyard behind the house and I stopped because it could be Darcy they quarrelled over. It wasn't. Eventually I caught the phrase *junta de la culata* and moved on. Their disagreement was about cars and I wasn't interested.

'It's at the back,' Dinora had said. 'That's all I know.' It shouldn't be too difficult. All I had to do was follow my ears. The courtyard was stoned and sloped gently to a draining hole in the centre. On the far side of the courtyard from the house was the same clutter of buildings that I'd seen at Guazatan: stables, store rooms, tool sheds. One must be the laundry.

Follow my ears.

152

That's how you find a torture chamber.

And then? Cody, one-woman cavalry, creates diversion and escapes with victim. The thing is, I didn't even begin to have a plan until I knew the lay-out, the odds, the condition Darcy was in, the possibilities for disruption. The camp had electricity, for instance, either power lines or a generator. I hadn't been certain of this. Short-circuiting the supply was a useful trick. It sowed confusion but didn't always rouse suspicion. My supreme weapon was surprise. I mustn't squander it.

I halted. I listened hard. Now in an army camp you can't have the sounds of a prisoner's screams echoing through the night. On all available evidence Portillo was a sadist, the very worst kind. But he would recognize that screams would keep his men awake and induce unhappy thoughts of what might happen if the guerrillas captured them. Terrible for morale. So he would soundproof the old laundry. Timber cladding, plasterboard, thick rugs on the walls do a lot to damp down sounds.

But in extremity the human voice reaches a very high pitch. It's something a bastard like Portillo would thrill to. And high screams penetrate home-made soundproofing.

My ears were giving me no guidance.

Some thin screech, some imploring *No*, some bellow however faint should come on the night air. Nothing.

I walked on. The first outhouse I came to was no problem. I put my ear to the door panel and there was no sound, no vibration, no movement within. I took half a minute with the handle and cracked the door open and it was pitch black inside. A smell drifted out: paint and thinner and oil and sawdust. Store-shed for maintenance men.

Between this building and the next concrete had been laid. On it, very narrow, was a line of light from the join of two curtains. Even if the window was double-glazed, some sounds should have been audible at this distance.

I was puzzled. I kept against the wall while I ran through the facts and my theories.

Fact: Paul Darcy had been captured and brought to the

camp for questioning. Evidence: Major Portillo on television.

Fact: Portillo was an inhuman sadist who enjoyed torturing suspects. Evidence: the body I'd seen with my own eyes, Beatriz, the French journalists who called him Commandant Casse-couilles.

Fact: torture and beating up require movement and noise. Lack of evidence: nothing moved across the split in the curtain; there was no sound of instruments bruising flesh or cries of agony.

And various assumptions: that this wasn't the old laundry, or Darcy was elsewhere, or Portillo had extracted every scrap of information, or the helicopter had left with Darcy on board.

02.56 by my watch.

There was another possibility: I was too late and Darcy was dead.

I crossed the concrete on the balls of my feet, freezing once when some small stone scraped. The window was barred and one of the bars was awkwardly placed so that I couldn't move my eye across the crack in the curtains for the widest arc of vision. What I could see was a wall draped with sacking and covered by clear polythene sheets. There were twin sinks so large they must originally have had to do with the laundry and now would be useful for cleaning up blood. A naked bulb dangled on a flex. A blouson hung from a hook behind the door, as if it might belong to Darcy. Perhaps it did. He was in shirtsleeves, sitting on a military iron bed, slumped with his elbows on his knees, his chin resting on one hand. He hadn't the Salvadorian bone structure or skin colouring. He was dark-haired all right but his face looked Mediterranean, a man from Corsica or the Midi. He was smoking. I could just decipher the pack on the bed beside him: Windsor.

He wasn't tortured to death but he'd been badly roughed up. His lips were split and blood had dried in a trickle down to his chin. His face was lopsided, half of it swollen as if a tooth had been knocked out. Contusions showed red and raw on one cheek and the eye was partly closed. That was what I could see. His clothes hid what other punishment he'd

154

taken. But the way he smoked was a clue: he lifted the cigarette to his mouth slowly, pain flickering across his face as if his ribs were bruised, even cracked.

So, Monsieur Darcy, it has not been a pleasant night but it could have had a much worse ending.

Darcy had been smoking. The sentry outside the door was smoking too. I watched while he worked the whole way through the cigarette, went for a little walk to the courtyard and returned to his post. There was still only starlight and not even a crack between the curtains on this side of the laundry so I couldn't make out the details of his face. But I had the feeling that the dozen paces he made to the courtyard hadn't been through nerves or zeal but because he was bored.

He was on his own but there was no knowing how long that would last. The interrogation of Darcy might just have reached half time and the inquisitors might return at any moment refreshed and with a sharpened appetite. Or this had merely been an initial softening up and now the real party was going to begin when Portillo put in his appearance. I couldn't afford the time waiting for this sentry to go off round the corner for a pee.

So I wandered out from the end of the outbuilding and he saw me at once and I hissed:

'Hey, psst, Carlos.'

The rifle lifted at once.

'Who are you? What are you doing here?'

I began moving towards him, one step and pausing. There was still a lot of ground to cover. I hesitated because the rifle was on my chest.

'I thought you were Carlos.'

Another step.

'What?'

My voice was a stage whisper. It was entirely reasonable for a village girl to be leery of discovery by an officer. More important, the whisper masked my accent.

'I mistook you for Carlos.'

'Carlos? What Carlos?'

155

'He told me he was on duty tonight.'

I moved again.

'Carlos Tobar?'

'Yes.'

'Or Carlos Ganuza?'

Never hesitate. Never show doubt.

'I don't know him. Carlos Tobar is my Carlos.'

'He has been sent to the village.'

'You mean I've come for nothing?'

He didn't respond to that.

If the moon had been up he'd have had a clear view of my face and been suspicious. But also he'd have seen the top two buttons of my safari jacket were undone. I had made five steps and I dropped my voice lower. Now it was the whisper of conspiracy, of two people in the night.

'What is your name?'

'Miguel,' he said. 'And you?'

'Carmen. Has he spoken of me?'

'Carmen? I don't think so.'

'Has he spoken of others? I'll kill him.'

'I don't know. He's not really a close friend. How did you get into the camp?'

'Oh, the usual way.'

Let him work it out for himself that I was a frequent visitor at night and that I was friendly and that my regular boyfriend wasn't available and that the buttons of my jacket had a way of coming undone. So he appreciated that I rubbed myself just inside the jacket where the second button was. *Puta*. Those two Luis boys had known a thing or two.

I was close now and I said:

'Do you have a cigarette I could share with you?'

His teeth showed in the starlight as he smiled. He said: 'Certainly.'

He transferred the rifle to his left hand and got out the packet. He stepped forward to offer it to me and that's when I took him. He wasn't tall but he was a soldier and had trained on the parade ground and on military exercises and he was stronger than me. Also he was armed with a rifle but

156

this worked in my favour as one hand was useless in the initial phase. If he had been taller than me I could have used a simple *ogoshi* but with someone my height it was better to go for the *harai-goshi* which looks marvellous if you're a spectator but is disorienting if it's done to you when all you were anticipating was sharing a cigarette and maybe a bit more with your new friend.

The packet was held towards me and I reached out and grabbed his elbow and pulled him nearer and maybe he thought he was going to be treated to a bit of sudden passion as I stepped in close turning my right foot so it was touching his and arching my body into him. I kept pulling him closer and turning sideways and thrusting my right leg in front of him and still pulling him until I felt his balance break. By now he realized he was in for a tumble and he gave a grunt and loosed his grip on the rifle. The barrel had got tangled up under my arm and now it swung away and I never heard the gun hit the ground because I was too intent on getting him over. I was now twisted three-quarters round and I kicked my right leg back and swept his legs clear of the ground. I kept turning and slipping my arm round his waist and increasing the pressure until I drove him over my leg and he went in a flattened arc and hit the concrete.

A mat in a training gym provides a softer landing and also he had the weight of my body on top which smashed the breath out of his lungs. He was lucky he had fallen on his shoulder and the back of his skull hadn't struck the concrete or he'd have suffered permanent brain damage. He was winded and shaken but there was fight in him yet so I rolled on top and tried for a normal cross strangle. I didn't get my knees pressed high enough and he looped a hand over my wrist and was tugging me to one side and I had to break his grip first and then jam my knees higher into his armpits and go for a half-cross strangle because he was struggling so hard. I grasped the collar of his shirt right round at the back with the thumb-edge of my hand against his neck. My left hand I crossed under my right wrist, keeping the palm down with the little finger edge against his neck as I gripped at the back.

157

I pressed both blade edges against his neck and pulled back towards me, easing the protective muscle and exposing the carotid arteries. He was struggling, trying to reach my wrists with his fingers which was the worst thing he could do because the direction of force along his shoulders simply added to the pressure on the arteries.

One, two, three.

He heaved. He got a knee up into my back but my grip was locked on and all he succeeded in doing was tipping me further over his head and increasing the pressure.

Four, five.

'Stop it. What are you . . .'

He could speak. He could breathe. I wasn't choking the windpipe. I just seemed to be holding him. He may even have had a stubborn bit of hope that this was extreme sexual passion.

Six, seven, eight.

He convulsed. His heels kicked the concrete. The thing about the strangle if you're not tense yourself and apply it properly is that your opponent feels not so much pain as discomfort. The jerking of his heels wasn't agony but a sign that the blood supply to the brain was cut off and unconsciousness was nearing.

'Carmen,' he whispered in my ear. We were lovers in an embrace of death.

Nine, ten, eleven.

Limp.

Twelve, thirteen, fourteen, fifteen.

I released him. His head flopped to one side. His breathing was ragged. You can kill someone so easily with the strangle and they never know it, feel no panic or warning stabs through their nerves. Fifteen seconds was the maximum I would ever use. In training I stop at seven because if your opponent has the skill to escape he will do it by then and if he hasn't done it what is the point of going on to the inevitable?

I got up and dragged the soldier to the building and sat him upright against the wall. There was a slim chance, if

158

anyone saw him, they'd imagine he was dozing and a chance they'd let him dream a little longer. Whereas if he was spotted sprawling over the concrete with his rifle tossed aside there was no chance at all.

I stood a moment and filled my lungs and breathed out and filled them again and waited for control over my pulse and lung action. I listened and heard no sound to worry me, no rush of boots. I looked left and right and saw only ghost-shadows.

What did the soldier say his name was? Miguel. If the light was better the flush on his cheeks would show. He wouldn't be unconscious for long but I didn't want to do anything more to him. Miguel had done nothing to me. He'd just been standing between me and Darcy. There was no time to lose now. I had no more than two or three minutes at most.

'Darcy.'

I had a hand cupped to my mouth as I stood against the door.

'Darcy.' I tried a fraction louder. 'Can you hear me?'

'What?'

I'd spoken French and his reply was the same, muffled by the thickness of the wood and the sacks and the polythene sheet.

'I've come to get you out and we've got very little time indeed and once I open that door we'll only have seconds so –'

'Hold on, who are you?'

'I'm called Cody. You met me yesterday. You stuck a knife in the back of my neck.'

'Holy cow. I mean, who *are* you, Cody?'

'Leave the explanations. Crevecoeur told me –'

'Crevecoeur?'

'He's gone to collect your photos –'

'That old *pète-sec* here?'

In spite of everything, I smiled. I had to. So that was what his juniors called him. I wondered if he knew. You don't call someone a dry-farter to his face, not if you ever want promotion.

159

'We'll meet up with him –'

'What for?'

'The bloody army –' The hell with him. 'Get back against the wall.'

'Are you crazy?'

'Once the door is open –'

'What are you doing?'

The hell with explanations too.

'Ready?'

'Two seconds. My blouson. Okay.'

We'd spent twenty golden seconds on introductions. No more time to waste. I picked up the soldier's rifle and put it to single shot. I laid its muzzle against the doorframe by the lock and listened one last time to the silence of the night.

# 14

The night was shattered.

It was something past three in the morning and a lot had happened since I'd got up twenty hours ago and some of the polish was coming off me. Not an excuse; an explanation. Until now I'd been on top of events: Blum, Beatriz, the Luis boys, Dinora, assorted soldiers. Not Crevecoeur. It's beyond anyone to control him. He's an eel and he's slippery and there's no useful way of handling him. One day someone's temper will snap and Crevecoeur is going to be too slow sidestepping the bullet. Will that stop him? Kill an eel and it still keeps wriggling.

There was the onset of exhaustion. Adrenalin had pumped while I chatted up the soldier Miguel and threw him with the *harai-goshi*. My effort had been explosive and the adrenalin was used up and my brain slowed. From the moment that I pulled the trigger I lost the first-strike capability. I was reacting, recovering, trying to keep one jump ahead, even half a jump ahead to stay alive. This was a camp on the edge of the badlands with a revolution across the river and the noise of a rifle within the camp in the middle of the night alarmed the sentries, stopped the officers bickering and smashed into the dreams of every sleeping soldier. Six hundred men had a single fear: guerrillas had penetrated the camp.

I had been in a tearing hurry to leave the camp and a bullet in the lock had seemed the quick answer. Why didn't I pause to think? Better to pick the lock or try the soldier's pockets for the key. As it was I was engulfed in chaos. And Darcy, well his mind seemed to work in a different way from mine.

'Jesus Christ, why didn't you warn me?'

161

Did Darcy imagine I was going to knock on the door and ask permission to enter? I checked the soldier on the concrete but he hadn't been jolted out of unconsciousness. A million things were happening at once and my brain couldn't cope with all the information streaming in: shouts, cries echoing from the tents about *terroristas*, someone shooting out into the darkness, always some fool doing that, door slamming, dog, ringing bell. It was a speeded up film and you needed to slow down the projector and analyse every detail to sort out where the most immediate danger was coming from.

'Darcy, are you all right?'

'What?'

'They haven't broken anything?'

'I'm bruised.'

'Can you run?'

All this before I even put the heel of my shoe against the panel and slammed the door open and got inside. I found him with his arms still flattened against the wall and his head angled round to stare at me with wide cat's eyes. He was in his mid-thirties. He had black hair rather longer than the current fashion but a neat man all the same. He looked taller than he was because he stood on tiptoe, pressing against the wall. He had the stance of a matador about to challenge the bull. There was only me. But in thirty seconds we'd have half the Quezacatl with rifles at our throats.

'Run?'

'They're going to shoot first and identify the corpses later. Come on.'

What was he hanging back for? A bloody limo service?

'Are you . . .' he began and changed his mind. 'Do you work for Crevecoeur?'

'Have you ever seen me before?'

'No.'

A sudden rush of boots in the courtyard of the big house decided me and to hell with Darcy. Could be he was a male chauvinist. I'd grated against several *types* in the DST and they were all macho cowboys and maybe Crevecoeur's colleagues in the Sûreté were the same. If he didn't fancy a woman leading him out of the camp, he was welcome to stay and have his body used as an ashtray. Not me.

'Get moving,' I said.

I checked outside the door and there were figures moving in shadows by the tents. No one was visible in the courtyard though more windows were blazing in the big house. The soldier on the ground was stirring but he was no danger yet. Darcy was moving now but whether he followed or not I was going. I dropped the rifle and turned away. I got as far as the end of the laundry building on the side away from the blazing windows of the house. My plan was to make an immediate break for the fence until I saw a detail of half a dozen soldiers with a sergeant in the lead come at the double from the tents. I kept in shadow and waited until they cleared a shrub. They changed tack. The sergeant was aiming for the laundry. I turned to find Darcy picking up the rifle.

'Other way,' I said. 'Army's coming.'

He swung the barrel up and didn't they teach them any-thing in training? You never point a rifle at someone unless you intend business – never as a joke, never as a trick, never through carelessness. People get shot by accident. Also it makes the nerves jump all over the place and mine were bad enough already with the sound of boots hitting the dirt growing louder.

'Come on,' I said. I was so close to him I slapped the rifle barrel away. 'Move it. You can't shoot it out with six hundred soldiers.'

I got to the courtyard and was in time to see an officer disappear in the direction of the tents. He went down the path by the next hut. That close. There was a pistol in his hand and he shouted an order and then he'd vanished. He saved our necks – I'm sure of it – because the boots behind us faded as the soldiers changed direction.

He was at my back, Darcy was. I heard a slight clink of metal as the rifle scraped across a button or a zip. Jesus, I hoped he was keeping the muzzle pointing down.

'Listen, Darcy, we've got to get round to the other side of the house, the side facing the river. There's a mousehole through the wire there. I came in that way. There are sentries but –'

'You don't work for Crevecoeur but he sent you. What are you?'

'For Christ's sake,' I hissed. Someone comes to save your life. Do you ask for a character reference?

'So what do we do when we get out?' he asked.

'If we get out.'

I didn't like anything about the situation now. I'd let exhaustion dull my thoughts. The result was this ants' nest I'd kicked. A door slammed in the house and a man came out buckling his belt. Taken his time. I mean, it was a couple of minutes since I'd squeezed the trigger.

'You got a car or anything?'

'We walk.'

'Steal a car,' he said.

There wasn't the time to argue because at that moment the floodlighting went on at the helicopter pad. There wasn't much light thrown where we stood but the danger was that the floodlights eliminated a large area of the camp where the army had to search for intruders. I believe in myself. I believe I can always win through. But a nasty voice had begun to whisper inside me that I'd run into a dead end and it was suicide to go on. That's all very well if you're a junked-up Shi'ite who believes in a *jihad* and going straight to paradise. But I was trying to get out with a whole skin and bring Darcy with me. He looked handsome and he had tough instincts but he didn't seem trained for this sort of situation. I was. I spent several seconds reviewing possibilities such as concealment, hostage taking, crashing the main gate, disguise, and decided they were useless, all of them.

'Give me your matches,' I said.

He looked at me as if I was simple-minded. What a time to be smoking. That sort of look.

'Matches, hurry.'

He had a lighter. A Cricket, same as Crevecoeur. I hate lighters. You never know when they're going to sulk and refuse to work.

'Watch our backs. Don't shoot at anything, just warn me.'

He walked beside me, twisted round to look over his shoulder and we passed from the laundry to the store shed I'd tried first. The door opened with a protest from the hinges and he groped for the light switch and I hit his hand away. I knew there were lights going on all over the camp. I just didn't want my woman's body to show at any window.

'They're going to search everywhere,' he said, 'can't hide out here.'

I flicked his lighter and shadows leapt all over the place. 'Correct,' I said. I didn't look at him. My eyes were already searching. 'We need to give them something else to work on.' It was a jumble room without military order and I stumbled over a saw and kicked aside electric flex and considered a blowlamp and wondered if the major knew of it and at last found among cans of white and orange paint a bottle labelled *Trementina*. It was a large bottle, the army size, but it was half empty. I would have liked more. No time to spare looking.

'Hold the lighter a moment.'

There were rags that had been used to wipe oily hands. I tied one round the neck of the bottle of turpentine, having first unscrewed the cap. I took the lighter back from Darcy and he followed me out to the courtyard.

'Once I've thrown this,' I said, 'we run like hell that way.' I pointed at the corner of the house. The tiniest strip of fence was visible. The drain was past the end of the terrace, out of sight.

'Suppose –'

Great one for objections. He didn't trust me. It didn't matter what this objection was. Boots were running towards the laundry and stopping and voices were raised. At last they'd checked their prisoner and found him gone and his guard still coming out of unconsciousness. I turned the bottle upside down and waited until I felt dampness through the rag and righted the bottle and flicked the lighter. It was at this point that the lighter should go temperamental. It sparked at once and I touched the flame to the rag and abruptly the end of my arm was a flaming torch.

They used to call them Molotov cocktails when they made them in Budapest and chucked them at tanks to protest at the Soviet army crushing their freedom. If you've got an old Soviet model tank with a hot engine, just sluicing petrol into the works can make a most impressive funeral pyre. Doing what I was doing was the suicide's way because you only have a couple of seconds before the glass heats up enough to crack the bottle and you end up in flames yourself.

I took a couple of steps back to get a better angle and hurled the bottle over the shed, away from the big house, in the direction of the tents. There was a smashing of glass and a satisfying crump and a great sea of flames lighting up the night sky.

'Fantastic,' he said.

I was already back at the door of the hut. 'Come on, do some work. Get a blaze started here.'

He was a little boy playing with fire. It was something he was enthusiastic about, driving all thoughts of bruised ribs from his mind. He banged down the light switch and fell on the bottles like a drunk and kicked open cans while I found some paint stripper and fixed another fire bomb. Outside was the sound of a riot with a lot of yelling and a few wild shots and boots pounding. Our luck had held and held and suddenly it ran out with a bang as the door was flung wide and a rifle poked in. There was a few seconds' hesitation as if the owner of the gun hadn't been expecting a light on in this store shed and was reluctant to find out why. The barrel wavered and then the soldier stepped into the room and halted. He was appalled. He didn't expect to find us here. I've never seen anyone so frightened. He was only a kid. Beatriz would have sent him back to school to catch up on his alphabet.

Q is for Quezacatl. The Quezacatl Battalion is bad. The Quezacatl takes me from my home and my parents and my mates. The Quezacatl forces me into a uniform and sticks a gun in my hands and orders me to hunt *terroristas* in the black hours of the night. What shall we do with the Quezacatl?

The rifle was on automatic and a short burst hammered in my ears. It was Darcy, behind me. The boy took the shots in his chest. He was thrown back against the wall. The look on his face changed to amazement. His rifle clattered by his feet and he touched a hand to his shirt and looked at the red on his fingers and brought his hand closer to his face as if his sight was fading. He began to slide down the wall and then he convulsed and tripped forward into the room and toppled over on his side. He jerked his knees and was still. He was curled like an unborn baby.

I twisted round and Darcy's face was white and glistening with sweat. His mouth twitched open in a kind of smile.

'It was him or us,' he said.

He was a kid but he'd also been a soldier and he had a rifle and he could have shot us in the next second. I knew that. And we were in an army camp and shouts were very close. I knew that. We had no more than a couple of seconds to get out of this deathtrap of a shed and make for the fence and try to get clear and that kid with a rifle had stood in the way. I knew all of that. But Darcy smiled. He shouldn't have done that. Nobody should kill and smile.

I hated him.

'Come on,' I said. 'Let's go.'

I still held his lighter and I fired his heap of wood and paint and whatever else he'd poured over and flames leapt to the ceiling. Darcy was first out of the door while I knelt to lift the dead soldier under the arms and drag him outside.

'They're onto us,' Darcy shouted.

I had to leave the boy. I joined Darcy at the door and two more soldiers were coming towards us and I felt the whole of our situation shrivelling and our chances closing down until our lives flickered out in the impossibility of escape. I'd prepared another Molotov cocktail but that was useless now we were known and the noose was tightening by the second. Darcy was shaping up to shoot and I punched his shoulder and got him facing away from the soldiers.

'Save your ammunition.'

There were shots behind us but it's difficult to hit running targets, particularly at night. I believed that. All of me believed. I believed as if our lives depended on it as we raced to the courtyard and slammed into each other like a sequence out of the Keystone Cops. Good for a giggle.

'You said the way out's down there.'

'Bloody follow me.'

I struck out across the width of the courtyard. Darcy swung round with the rifle aiming back down the path we'd taken. Fed up with him. One last try.

'Run.'

He got moving at last. True I'd said the hole in the fence was to the right. But if we went straight there the soldiers would follow and there was nowhere else to go and they'd finish us off before we could wriggle into the drain. No damn good at all. I was working by instinct now because there was no time for rational thought. But if I'd had to spell it out I'd have said: if we're very quick across the courtyard, the soldiers will follow and at the far side we'll be out of sight for critical seconds and when they come out by the prefab hut ahead they won't be able to tell for certain which direction we've taken.

Concentrate on the prefab. It's fifty metres away. I'm there already. My mind is waiting by that corner and my body is flying to join it. And it takes no time to cover forty metres. Don't think about feet and legs. Don't heed the fire in the muscles as they burn up oxygen. Muscles won't get me across thirty metres. Willpower does it. I float ahead of my body, urge the body on, flesh and bones are useless, dragging me back. There's a pinpoint of intensity twenty metres away and it is me, and my gravity-bound muscle-slowed body is not going to accept separation another nanosecond. I can feel nothing any longer. The two halves of me are going to rejoin and I shall be whole. I am floating the last ten metres and this cylindrical metal object that floats past me so close I can feel the angry wind of it is not going to stop me. My body and my mind will be divorced no longer.

168

I hit the corner and swung round it, my fingers straining to break my speed. I seemed to hear the explosion of the shot that had been fired. My brain had refused to accept it, holding it back. Now it came like an echo followed by a louder crack and a cry from Darcy and then he lurched round the corner.

'Bastards.'

'Where are you hit?'

'It's not that,' he mumbled. 'I tripped when they shot.'

He about-turned and was going to avenge his wounded ego and it was hopeless because that would still leave 598 of them. He loosed off a short burst and there was a scream from the courtyard. I jabbed an elbow into his bruised ribs because that would get his attention.

'Let me go, bitch.'

'You escaping or committing suicide?'

I didn't wait for an answer. To hell with him. Maybe he'd slowed down the two who were closest but I could hear the whole camp after us. I sprinted straight down the side of the big house to the terrace that ran the whole length of it like the promenade deck of a cruise liner. Flick of my eyes over my shoulder and Darcy was after me. He was coming fast now, seeing the point of getting round the side of the terrace. He made it before anyone called out or shot at him. We now had the luxury of no one snapping at our heels. When the first soldiers reached the prefab hut they'd lose precious seconds while they tried to work out which direction we'd taken. Straight ahead into the old banana plantation? It was dark and full of shadows. Or down the side of the house? If they followed us they would be confronted by the fence five metres beyond the terrace and another choice: gone left or right? We might even have cut the wire and that was another thing to check.

'Keep tight against the terrace,' I whispered in his ear.

I could see the sentries. Two of them. They stood on the terrace itself, straining their eyes into the night.

169

The ranch house had been built in this position because of the view. The ground fell steeply down from the bluff to the river valley. The terrace itself jutted from the level ground so that we crept along in the lee of its wall. No moon. Couldn't have hoped to get away with it in moonlight. Stars were enough for us to see our way.

A voice, somewhere above in the house. It was muffled. An officer leaning out of the window and throwing his authority around.

'No, nothing.'

It was the first sentry. He was directly on top of us. Darcy and I froze together. There was noise all over now. It was like a crowd coming out of a football ground. The sentry would never pick up our creeping footsteps. Never hear the thump of our hearts or the breath through our nostrils. Never. My nerves weren't convinced.

The officer, calling out another order.

I could hear movement above my head. It was so close. It was that kind of closeness to danger which drives you to panic. I could have reached up and grabbed an ankle and pulled him over. Or I could have lost control and bolted like a rabbit. I looked at Darcy. *Don't panic*, I yelled at him. My voice was a scream in my head. My eyes blazed with the message. He stared back at me. The sentry had only to peep over the low wall of the terrace to see these two ashen faces. *Terroristas* he'd call out. The only terror round here was in our hearts.

A flashlamp flicked on above us and a beam of light went out through the fence, probing down the steep hill, searching among rocks. I took hold of Darcy's wrist. There was sweat on it. Maybe on my fingers. He raised his eyebrows. I nodded. We moved again while the sentry's concentration was elsewhere.

There came shouts from the fence at the corner of the house where we'd been a lifetime ago. I didn't think they could see us because of the darkness that grew in the shelter of the terrace. I still had hold of Darcy's wrist and I could feel the tension in him. He ached to whip round and blast

170

the pursuit off the face of the earth. *One of my top men*, Crevecoeur had called him. Worked in Cuba and Algeria. What had he done in those places? Made work for the undertakers?

Soldiers were checking the wire behind us.

'Nobody,' I heard one shout. 'Nothing moving.'

'Keep looking. A whole gang has broken in.'

Me and Darcy.

We'd passed the second sentry. We had to leave the shelter of the terrace. We were in open ground, half a dozen steps from the mouth of the drain, when some officer somewhere used his brain and pulled a switch. Big white lights blazed to life along the fence and we were exposed like a couple of lovers holding hands.

'*Terroristas*,' a sentry shouted from along the fence.

'*Terroristas* here,' a sentry on the terrace echoed.

'Two of them,' someone shouted behind us.

Darcy broke my grip and lunged round. He stood with his legs apart and his knees bent and he looked like a man making his last stand. He was a marvellous shot. He hit the sentry nearest us and he toppled off the edge of the terrace and before he'd hit the ground Darcy swung the rifle and got the floodlight on the cornerpost of the fence and then one about forty metres away which went with a noise like a stungrenade and shorted the whole circuit and he turned to give a blast back along the fence at the pursuers and got a click from the rifle and he hurled it up on the terrace where it clattered among chair legs.

'It's finished,' he said. The rifle, us, everything. It was a simple fact to him.

I was more than frightened. For a moment I knew pure terror. I was the hare frozen in the headlights. I was Butch and Sundance waiting for the hail of bullets.

Luckily someone took a potshot and it broke the spell. The shot went wild because in the seconds after the lights go out your vision is no good. Already a flashlamp was dancing along the fence and a jeep was turning round on a piece of empty ground to train its headlights on this corner. This wasn't my idea of a perfectly planned escape. They knew where we were. They'd be on our tails in seconds. What choice was there?

Boots were a growing thunder.

'This way,' I said.

We got out like rats through the sewer.

# 15

***

'It ain't going to be easy,' the sergeant said.

'I'm not a powder puff.'

'So long as you don't kid yourself it's a Sunday hike.'

'If I thought it was going to be easy,' I told him, 'I wouldn't want to do it.'

He put his head on one side to look at me and gave a slow nod. We've got a right one here – that's what that slow nod means. Only a madman would *want* to climb up this part of the Grand Canyon. Or, in my case, a madwoman. It didn't add to the fun that it was raining. It's always raining on some bit of the canyon. That's my theory. You get cloud and mist and hot sun and purple shadow and lightning but always somewhere there's a patch of rain. I wasn't going to have any sun though. I was doing the climb at night. Awareness Under Stress this phase of the training was called. What they meant was they work you until the sweat blinds your eyes and your heart is breaking loose from your ribs and there is a white pain inside your forehead from tension and then they throw the man-eating tiger at you.

That's overstating.

No, it isn't. In the CIA there's an expert for every situation. If you need to know how to outwit a tiger, the computer at Langley will print out name, qualifications and availability before you can take one sip of their incredibly tasteless coffee.

'It ain't much of a track in places either,' the sergeant said. I nodded. Well, I wasn't going on the Bright Angel trail but up to the north rim. 'Remember not to look directly *at* the track but slightly to one side. Just slightly. In night vision you have a blind spot at the centre.'

'**Why?**'

'How do you mean?'

'Why is there a blind spot where your eyes focus at night?'

'Do you need to know that now?'

Some day it could be important to know the reason. I never have found out.

'Remember,' in the sergeant's parting words, 'you'll have three challenges from unseen men.'

The rain was the last of that afternoon's thunderstorm and it cleared and there was a half-moon for the climb and that helped me spot the first man who wasn't much hidden. The second I caught because of the smell of cigarette smoke. With the third guy it was something I can't explain, some instinct left over from the wild that said danger was waiting in the shadows above that boulder. I picked up a tremor in the ground or an electro-magnetic current or some body radiation. There are times to use the brain and times to have faith in instinct and this hadn't been one for rational thought. I doubled round and took the man from behind while his mind was one hundred per cent on the path below.

Three men Sergeant Kellerman had warned of. I'd taken all three and a certain amount of euphoria set in. I should have analysed his words because before I reached the top it wasn't a man I blundered into but a black widow trapped between double nylon webbing. I struck it away and got a bite on my forearm. If it had been on the inside of my wrist and got to a vein the poison would have pumped through my system. I ducked under the torn netting and ran in the dark, stumbling and picking myself up and getting to the top in fifteen minutes and was so angry I wanted to lay out the medic who had been waiting with the serum, just in case. *I am the bloody case.* I screamed that at him, something like that. In the morning I saw Sergeant Kellerman. He smiled and gave his slow nod and said one word to me: 'Smartass.'

I've hated spiders ever since.

I didn't think there were any black widows here. But I assumed a danger behind every rock as we climbed. This was no Sunday hike either. The sweat was stinging my eyes and kept stinging even when I wiped it.

Darcy stubbed his toe and stumbled again. He said, '*Merde*.' That made four times. He didn't seem to notice stones and roots. I waited until he caught me up.

'The thing to do,' I told him, 'is not to look directly at the spot where you're going to put your foot but slightly to one side. There's a central blind spot in night vision. Do you know why?'

'I don't want to know why.'

That was the difference between us. I would think my way out of danger. He would shoot his way out. One night he would run up against someone who shot quicker.

'Let's catch our breath here,' he said.

Or against someone who thought quicker.

'Let's just make it to the top,' I countered.

It wasn't far. Psychologically it was important: to have climbed right out of the valley. We chose a rock each to sit on. Darcy slumped over. I rubbed my feet, feeling the wetness of the river. No, not possible after that climb. There were cuts all over my feet. Darcy's feet must be bleeding too.

I'd insisted on shoes off to ford the river. There's nothing that slows you and absorbs so much attention as sodden footwear.

The first soldiers had been coming out through a side gate. Five seconds wrenching off the shoes. Figures began running along the fence. Torches bobbed.

'And socks.'

I'd stopped Darcy at the water's edge. Another five seconds for the socks. Fingers awkward with the socks, too hasty. Into the river. Gravel underfoot, weeds trailing, stepping into slime, Worthing beach when I was a girl and the tide was out and the stink of it as I slithered and shrieked at the fun. This wasn't play. This was real. They were coming down from the bluff at the same place we had, a gully eroded by storms, and so close. Faint illumination from flashlamps sent our shadows dancing as we dodged between boulders.

A sniper would have got us. These were ordinary infantry and above fifty metres it's luck whether they hit a target or miss. They were closer than fifty metres.

Miss, miss, miss again.

It was night and they were overexcited and they weren't aiming. They caught glimpses of us and blazed away. Ricochets whined into the darkness.

Were they going to cross the river? Person with gun run slower than person without gun. Confucius he say. Person without gun run very fast indeed when person with gun is behind. Cody she . . .

Concentrate. It's not a joke.

Don't slip. You'll be a sitting target. So be careful.

But be quick, quicker than that.

Never mind the contradiction. Be extra careful, extra quick.

Darcy made his own way across the river. It wasn't deep, nowhere above knee high. He reached the bank ten metres away and we were on dry land.

'You okay?'

He cared. I'd never have guessed it.

'Yes. We run to that hill.'

'My shoes . . .'

'No time.'

'*Merde.*'

That was the first time.

Soldiers were following across the river. I didn't look back but above the pounding of our own feet I could hear splashes. Someone slipped and brought down the man at his heels. That's what the shouting sounded like. Had they taken off their boots? They'd be trying to run with buckets of water on their feet.

Up in the camp someone had brought a jeep with a searchlight to the fence. Its beam stabbed out and hit the hill and moved back, making a series of sweeps until it picked us up. We were caught, both of us.

'Go to the right,' I shouted.

I veered left and now the beam couldn't hold us both. It

was on me and then skipped over to chase Darcy. Back on me. I liked it on me. It lit up the ground ahead. I went like a hurdler over a fallen tree trunk, skirted a hole in the ground, picked up speed between tufts of dried grass. I hated it on me. It made me a target. But you can't hit a running target at night. Believe it. It's all you can do. Believe and put in distance from the men with rifles. I could still hear shots. I could hear bullets striking, sharp cracks against rocks, thumps into earth, smacking through branches.

The searchlight swung away and I was heading into pitch black and running blind. Pain in my feet was slowing me down.

I took my mind off my feet and put it on the hill. It had been half a kilometre from the river and now it was close.

The searchlight caught me again. I had a stupid thought: when they aim for me they hit the rocks, so why don't they aim for the rocks and hit me? The beam swung away again and searched among boulders and trees away to the left and then ahead of us up the hill.

As we reached the hill I glanced back over my shoulder: the soldiers weren't following. We were safe from everything except fluke shots, safer than crossing the quai des Grands-Augustin where the taxi-drivers grin as they aim at you. I took a longer look back. The flashlights were grouping together and there'd be an officer at the centre. What orders was he giving? What was normal procedure after a guerrilla strike? Tracker scouts? Dogs? Helicopters? Pincer movement? Of course the Americans had done a lot of the training of the Salvadorian army and had told horror stories about getting lured into the Vietnam jungle and so these soldiers could be holding back because they suspected an ambush.

That explained the new pattern of the searchlight, darting among the rocks, trying to catch movements or reflections off weapons. Its beam was growing weaker as we climbed. When it flicked across us, our shadows were ghosts.

Would they follow when they were satisfied we had no comrades in hiding? Wait until first light? That occupied my thoughts as we climbed, that and the memories of the haul up the Grand Canyon and the feel of the web on my face and the bite on my arm.

So we reached the top and sat a little apart, putting on our socks and shoes while the searchlight played hide-and-seek below us.

The attack came without warning.

I was tying the knot in a shoelace when suddenly my fingers twitched and my hands jerked and I straightened up, my whole body shaking. You can put the lid on worry and tension and fear because there are things that must be done and you impose your will and do them. When the pressure eases and you relax, the nerves take their revenge.

We did our best to warn you, my nerves said. Men were shooting and you should have got your head down and hidden. We warned you that death was in the air and you didn't heed the alarm signals. So now you're going to suffer and next time you'll listen.

'What's the matter?'

'I'll be all right.'

I'm just letting the devils out.

In Turkey I'd been shot at. In Tunisia when I was trying to get the Skyvan into the air and Antoine was giving me my first ever flying lesson, there'd been shots from the car that had raced beside the airstrip. But nothing on this scale. This had been war and I didn't like it, my body could have been smashed and my life ended. My nerves were right to protest.

'Were you scared?'

'I told you, I'll be all right.'

I wasn't scared. Maybe my nerves were scared but not *me*. Cody is never scared. It's just these stupid shakes and the choke in my breath . . .

'We're safe now,' Darcy said. 'They can't see us on top here.'

And he came and put his arms round me. It wasn't comfort he offered. He wasn't reassuring me with his strength. His face angled into mine and his mouth pressed on my lips and I could feel the heat in him, the excitement in his breathing.

178

'Get the hell off me.'

'Do you good. Straighten the shakes out of you.'

He had one hand in my hair and the other moving over my buttocks. He was pressing hard against me. I turned my face aside and his mouth kissed my ear and cheek and throat, his tongue licking, his teeth biting my skin.

'I need you,' he said.

He'd killed back in the camp. It had been a thrill for him. And now he needed me, any woman, but I was the only one available. Killing horrifies most men. A few are caught up in a blood lust. I hate those few.

I twisted my head so my mouth was against his ear and I could breathe into it. 'Don't make a sudden move, Darcy. Don't panic them.'

He slipped a hand inside the waistband of my slacks and inside my pants and his fingers dug into my flesh. Then he went still. He stiffened. 'What? What do you mean?'

'Softly. There are two of them. They must have crept along the other side of the ridge.'

'Where?'

'Directly behind you.'

The eagerness drained out of him. He'd been tight against me, trying to fuse our two bodies into one. The pressure slackened and his hands began to fall away.

'Soldiers?' he whispered. 'Terrorists?'

'I can't tell.'

The hand that had gripped my hair passed across my breasts. He didn't fondle. His attention was all behind him. He was straining his ears, listening for a click of metal. Slowly he turned, looking for menacing figures, pointing rifles, faces, even shadows.

'Where?' he asked. He stood off a couple of paces to look from a different angle.

'There's nobody,' I said. 'It's just I make my own choices, Darcy. I won't be imposed on.'

He swung back. The lust in him was dead and was replaced by a furious twist to his face.

'Bitch,' he said.

You're entitled to your opinion, Monsieur Darcy. But it was better than a knee in the groin, wasn't it?

From this distance they had the innocence of Christmas tree baubles. They were arranged in four clusters. They shone brilliant white with a tinge of pink reflected off the paint of the stanchions.

04.32 by my watch and I got to my feet and felt stabs of pain and had to will my attention away. Forget your feet. Forget the bruises and abrasions. Think about the floodlights in the camp. Not their pretty blushing colour. Think what it means that they have been switched on at something past four-thirty in the morning.

Three or four figures were visible. Impossible to tell if they were doing anything. They moved about, tiny movements, like insignificant insects.

Come on. They are very significant. They are planning to kill you or capture you. You have taken a hundred thousand dollars to the guerrillas and broken into camp and rescued a prisoner and if they do catch you Major Portillo's eyes will twinkle behind his intellectual glasses because you are the foreign woman spy he wants to get his hands on. So wake up and stay alive.

No sleep. But I had rested. My brain was wandering off on its own which is natural after twenty-two hours of action and now it had to snap fully alert. I stared at the army camp across the valley and all my brain could deliver was the idea that they were initiating some kind of security check in case more guerrillas had come in and were lying low. That didn't seem too clever. The trouble was that my brain was humming and it made coherent thoughts difficult. The hum was increasing until I realized it came from the sky. I caught sight of red and green lights moving across the stars. Louder, closer. Then it was like watching a Polaroid photo develop. First a shadow, then a shape, finally details firming as a helicopter flew into the glow of the lights. The helicopter hovered and sank to earth. The same one that had taken off a couple of hours ago? Major Portillo returning to take charge? I doubted he had been at the camp when I got in. Portillo was a vigorous forceful man. He was a sadist but intelligence stared out from his eyes. From what I'd seen on television, he would be a formidable opponent. He would have organized swift and deadly pursuit of two escaping guerrillas. But I had no proof Portillo had gone in the helicopter. Why hadn't I asked Darcy what had happened at the interrogation? No time. And when the opportunity came, Darcy had made his take-over bid for my body.

We had stayed on the crown of the hill after the struggle. Our feet were bloody and our bodies needed to rest. Also we were in a natural look-out position and could monitor the first signs of pursuit. Correction: I could. Darcy had taken himself off. He wasn't far. I knew that. He'd come back once and asked for his lighter.

'You had it last,' he said.

'Maybe. I haven't got it any more.'

'I want it.' His voice rose. He was a baby throwing a tantrum.

'It's gone. It's in the river. It's in the drainpipe. I don't know.'

'I want a cigarette.'

Then chew one. At least there's no risk that smoke will give us away.

He had limped away muttering. From the sound of it I was an *espèce de con*. I thought that was what he'd wanted. I was a woman and he was a man and while I was dealing with a crisis the sexual difference meant nothing to me. But Darcy's sex drive was all-powerful even in the middle of danger, maybe because of the danger, and I would have to watch him all the time. If he couldn't have me by consent, he would try to take me by force. If the frustration turned to rage, he might destroy me. It didn't matter a damn that he was a 'very good' executive in the Sûreté. This side of Darcy would never be revealed to Crèvecoeur.

There was this single patch of illumination to watch. Toy soldiers strutted round the helicopter. Impossible to tell who had got off. I assumed someone had got down, not just that the helicopter had returned empty after ferrying Portillo. The floodlights on the landing pad were cut and they faded to nothing, leaving an after-image on my retina, pinpricks of light that danced as I blinked.

I waited. If someone had come, if orders were given, if action was taken, it would happen soon and this was the place to observe from. Once the nature of any operation was obvious, then we knew how to react.

05.00. Nothing more than a distant shout once, a flashlight moving somewhere by the river, darkness again. They must be waiting for first light. They wouldn't shrug their shoulders and let us get away. I made one final sweep of the valley and the camp, circling my hands to form them into crude binoculars to concentrate my vision. Blank. It was time to leave. I turned and made my way through the rocks.

'Darcy.'

He'd gone to my left and I couldn't find him there. I was working my way back through the rocks when I caught the rasp of a shoe on dirt and I dropped to a crouch and span round. Darcy had been moving from the shelter of a bush. He stood there with the starlight making a fool of him. He held his fist forward with two fingers poking towards me like a pistol. I suppose the idea was to creep up behind and jab me in the back. Kids do it.

'Bang, bang, I'm dead. Is that it?'

'You should be more careful.'

'Of you?'

'It could have been anybody.'

'No. I knew you were here. Do I have to watch out for you? I saved your life, didn't I?'

I didn't expect gratitude. It's just that he shouldn't get it fixed among his emotions that I was an enemy. He stared at me a bit before putting his stupid hand down.

'Okay.'

'Let's forget about that tussle we had. Let's just pretend it never happened. We've got to move.'

'Okay,' he said again. His voice was dulled.

We set off. We were like a chain gang where they used to

couple together two convicts who hated each other's guts. They used to do it just for the hell of it.

Looking to the east there was a segment of sky that was paling along the horizon. Stars were going to bed for the day.

I said to Darcy: 'Do you know this terrain?'

'Not at all.'

'You were here for ten or twelve days.'

'I didn't go for country walks.'

The problem was that we could veer wide of Guazatan and miss our plane-ride out. Trying to map out from memory the route I'd done yesterday, I put the village as north-north-east from the shattered bridge over the river. But the angry little hills and valleys twisted so that it was impossible to hold a steady course. The alternative was to cut to the right until we hit the road and follow that all the way. The danger was that the army would use the road to come after us. This time I wasn't isolated inside a car. I would listen very hard for the sounds of vehicles.

'Let's make for the road,' I said.

I've thought about it since.

I don't see what else we could have done. We risked getting lost going across country.

But it was as if the night's darkness never ended.

# 16

The talk came bunched together. We'd had no opportunity until now to discover the most basic things. Why had I come to Guazatan in the first place. How had Debilly got hold of me? Did Crevecoeur pay me?

'You mean pay me to get you out of that camp?'

'Well, that seems to be the line of work you're in.'

'I wouldn't take money from him.'

'You took it from a drug pusher.'

'I didn't know Debilly was anything but a faded film star.'

'You wouldn't have brought the money if you'd known?'

'Never. Drug pushers are murderers. They kill slowly and never see their victims.'

That seemed to satisfy Darcy. He was silent.

I thought about my answer. It wasn't quite true. A pusher like Debilly with an entrée into smart society would mix with his clients. Of course they considered themselves too clever to get hooked. Only dumb kids and derelicts and human dregs were torn apart. And a pusher who sold to junkies on the street also saw his victims every day. Pushers were sadists. Like Portillo, they took pleasure in shivering bodies and pleading eyes.

Light was coming into the land and it was easier to find our footing. We still moved slowly because of our feet. We came to a shack. The doorway was a black hole and half the iron roof had been blown away. A patch of ground had been cleared of scrub and vegetables would have grown there. It was covered in weeds, a couple of years' growth. What had the family done for water? I was thirsty. I could see no well. Couldn't have drunk from it even if there had been a well. The risk was too great. In a civil war one side or the other always gets the idea of poisoning the water sources.

We went through the abandoned farm in silence. Darcy had no more questions for me. I asked one of my own.

'Why did Major Portillo stop interrogating you?'

'What?'

'It was Portillo interrogating you, wasn't it?'

He didn't want to answer. I got a foul glance from him. The place with the easy-wipe plastic sheeting and the sound-proofing had been a torture chamber and I was forcing him to go back to it.

'Yes. There were two others but Portillo was the boss.'

'I was afraid I'd be too late. Crevecoeur couldn't come.' Maybe *wouldn't* was more to the point but I wasn't going to sour the office atmosphere with that. 'Portillo has a terrible reputation. He began work on you and then gave up. What made him stop? That's what I don't understand.'

We were coming through long grass and we reached a cutting. The road lay directly below us. We'd made as much noise as a rogue elephant blundering through the bush and I was uneasy. It was after sunrise but the sun hadn't cleared the hills. Colours were steely. The danger was that the army could have posted look-outs in the bushes along the road. I hesitated.

No sound, no movement, no life. The light made it unreal. It was a world that had suffered some disaster and this was the aftermath. The bank wasn't high but we went down with caution. You'd think it was the marathon we'd run in bare feet. Nobody shouted a challenge and we began walking. Guazatan was at the end of this road, Crevecoeur, a plane out of the country. I liked that thought.

'So why did Portillo stop?'

Darcy shrugged. 'Someone called him away.'

'In the middle of an interrogation?'

'An NCO knocked and said: "Headquarters on the radio for you, sir." '

'And he simply left?'

'Yes.'

'When was this?'

'Half an hour before you shot your way in? I don't know. I wasn't keeping a bloody diary.'

'But Portillo was called away and later the helicopter took off?'

'Brilliant,' he said, and gave me a smile that wasn't.

What had prompted Portillo's helicopter trip? What had he been told? Perhaps Crevecoeur had succeeded in getting the defence minister to stir himself and Portillo had been called in. Or it was something entirely unrelated. Perhaps. But when you're running for your life, you never make easy assumptions.

'And he left you bruised but not crippled, with your hands not cuffed, even with a pack of cigarettes.'

Had I touched on a sore point? He swung round in front of me, his face grey in that flat light. His mouth was puckered as if he'd sucked a lemon. I was the lemon.

'Unlike when you kindly set me free and my feet got so battered I can hardly walk, my lighter is lost so I can't smoke, and half the ammunition in El Salvador chased me up a hill.'

This vote of thanks was delivered with great force. He gave a sneer and set off again. I put it down to the sexual thing. He was a man rejected by a woman. Happens a million times a day. And the man will walk away or go for a drink or find a different woman. But we were chained together and he hated it.

'Anyway,' he broke the silence, 'what's so special about going to Guazatan? You said Crevecoeur's there, right?'

'He will be. Looking for the evidence you collected. He's flying in by air taxi. We can hitch a lift out.'

'Fantastic,' he said, a hint of sarcasm in his voice.

More silence, except for our shoes grating on the road. My mind wouldn't leave the interrogation.

'Did you tell Portillo you were French?'

'Well, it's obvious I'm not Salvadorian.'

'But did you say you were from the French Sûreté?'

Again he halted and swung round.

'Cody is your name, right? You're not French, are you. You've got the language. If I heard you on the telephone I wouldn't suspect. But when I see you in daylight, you don't move like a Frenchwoman. Your face doesn't change – you could be playing poker. Your hands don't speak. Your shoulders are too still. What are you? American? English? Dutch?'

'Hasn't Crevecoeur told you?'

He took a deep breath. 'Amazing, aren't you? Want all our secrets.'

'What secrets? I'm on file at the Sûreté.'

He laughed. It was the first time I'd heard anyone laugh in this country.

'Have you any idea what it's like? Do you imagine we sit on our bums drinking coffee and passing round the files. "Here's a good one – what's the name? Cody. Juicy fruit this one." ' He gave a sneer. 'Come on, let's keep moving. Just stop interrogating me, okay? I had a wife once and she nagged like you.'

Really all I hoped for was gossip about Crevecoeur. I wanted to hear malicious tongues wagging – like calling him *pète-sec*. Give me a bit of dirt I could squirrel away to spit in his face later.

The road was climbing a hill. I caught Darcy up at the top where it curved round to the left and began to descend and I put a hand out to stop him.

'What is it now?'

I nodded ahead. There was a patch of blue.

'Someone's gone off the road,' he said.

It was a shallow gradient and I'd had trouble getting the car to roll back. I'd been trying to steer and put some pressure behind the doorframe at the same time. The patch of blue was at most a hundred metres away at the next curve, part way down the bank, in among rocks.

'Did you see the car when you came this way yesterday afternoon?' I asked.

'Oh sure. Listen, I was lying face down in the back of a truck, my arms tied, with a rifle between my shoulder blades. You imagine I was admiring the scenery?'

'Don't shout. It was a perfectly simple question.'

'You're full of questions.'

We were standing quite close, staring at each other. Yes, frustrated male was in his eyes. Something more. Confusion, worry, even fear. Well, that was natural. Wouldn't he see much the same in my eyes? Except I had a poker player's face. Got his word for it.

'There's a point to my questions. Did the soldiers notice the car?'

'I didn't hear anyone remark on it. The convoy didn't stop.'

'The thing is this, Darcy. I pushed that car off the road when it ran out of fuel. It wasn't hidden but there were branches breaking up the outline. The army convoy went past twice yesterday and no one spotted it. Now it's the first thing you see as you come round the corner. You can't miss it. Someone has taken all the covering branches away.'

'Who?'

But he didn't need an answer from me. The idea sparked in his own brain. At first just his eyes moved. Then his head, very slowly. The sun was on his face now. But it wasn't hot enough to account for all the sweat. I looked away towards the car. I inspected each rock round it. Next I tried the hillside opposite. It wasn't high. Rocks had tumbled down, some right to the bottom, others lodging half way. Then I moved on to the trees. A lot of leaves had fallen during the dry season but the trunks were sturdy. I tried the bushes. In a flat piece of ground was a stand of bamboos. I could see nobody. But they could see me. It made my flesh crawl. They were watching, perhaps through rifle sights. They had baited the trap, knowing the army would pull up to investigate, and they were waiting.

'Mary, Mother of Jesus, protect me,' Darcy mumbled.

What I wanted to do more than anything was back away round the corner. I fought down the urge. They wouldn't accept the idea of losing sight of us. We might go back and warn the army.

The most unnerving thing was the silence. They were watching but doing nothing, not issuing a challenge, not shouting a question. They were sitting in judgement: play it right and earn a medal; put a foot wrong and get a bullet. They were hidden in places I couldn't see, perhaps only the nose of a rifle poking forward, with their bodies and faces in shadow. We could be alone in this stillness but I knew we weren't. Gooseflesh was rising on my arms and I felt a prickle at the back of my neck. I wanted to jerk round and check no one was creeping up on me.

The other danger was Darcy. He was unpredictable. He might make a desperate dash for the corner and it would be an unthinking reflex that squeezed the triggers and brought us both down. The silence was appalling and I broke it.

'Beatriz.'

I shouted. It came out as a whisper and I tried again.

'Beatriz, where are you?'

There was movement at my side and I put a hand out to Darcy. The shots would ring out if he made a break for it.

'Beatriz, can you hear me?'

There was tension in Darcy and when it became insupportable he would take to his heels. I had wormed my way into the camp and brought Darcy out and nursed him this far but I had no faith in him. He was a worry because his nerves lay too close to the surface. He lacked Crevecoeur's cool. I would love to stroll away and face the situation without him. I work best on my own, without another person's mistakes to make me stumble. Give me odds of a hundred to one, provided I am the one.

'Beatriz, where –'

'Who is the man?' her voice called out. She was on the hillside, part way up. Three or four rocks could be her hiding place for the ambush.

'A friend. From Paris.'

'Is he the famous film star?'

'No, he –'

I'd had time to work on the story I'd tell and it depended on the self-assurance I showed whether or not she believed it. But she wasn't giving me a chance. She was too full of suspicion. It sounded in her voice.

'What's his name?'

'Paul. He –'

'Is he your lover?'

'Yes.'

'Why have you returned?'

'Paul has come to fix the car. It broke down on the road yesterday.'

Why wouldn't she show herself? Why didn't she trust me?

'How can he fix the car? You've seen where it is, crashed into those rocks.'

'I left it on the road.'

'I think she's lying.' It was a man's voice from among the bamboos. Most likely it was Alonzo. I'd heard him too little yesterday to be certain.

'I agree,' said Beatriz. 'She's lying. The car didn't break down, it ran out of fuel. Alonzo drained the tank. Didn't you check?'

I couldn't relax but I felt a fraction more comfortable. That was the first question that even hinted at a softening in her.

'The tank was full when I left San Salvador in the morning. Why should I check? I wasn't expecting anyone to syphon the tank dry. It simply went dead on me down there. An electrical fault is what Paul thinks.' I lifted a hand. It was time they accepted the idea I could move. 'Perhaps the handbrake went. It's not much of a gradient but it's either a weak handbrake or some of your people tipped it over.'

That brought her to her feet. She carried a rifle. Grenades dragged her belt down to one side.

'It wasn't us.'

'Then the army got it out of the way,' Darcy said. 'They were in a hurry and they just shoved it off the road.' It was the first time he had spoken. His Spanish was fluent but with cadences that were strange to me.

'I still say they are lying. What shall we do with them?'

'Don't rush things, Alonzo. You, Paul, where have you come from today? Why are you on foot?'

190

'The army is out on the road in force. There is some kind of panic.'

'How did you come?'

'In another car.'

'Where is it?'

'In the last village before the army camp.' Darcy turned to me. 'I'll go up and speak to her. I'll say if it's true the car is out of petrol, then we'll go to Guazatan to get some.' He turned to face the hill. 'Listen, rather than shouting at each –'

'Stay where you are.' Beatriz's sharp features and shock of white hair gave her the look of some giant bird of prey. She moved her rifle up, just a fraction, to emphasize her point. 'If you rented another car, show me the keys.'

'Listen, let me explain,' Darcy began. He took another step and halted. 'There are things that –'

'You don't have the keys,' said Beatriz, 'because there is no other car.'

'They are lying,' Alonzo said. 'They have been sent to spy.'

Darcy took another step. He was still smiling but it was costing him a lot.

'That is absolutely –'

From somewhere above and out of sight came a whistle, three distinct notes. Heads turned. Darcy and I were no longer the focus of attention. The signal was repeated. It could have been made by some gaudy tropical bird.

'They're almost –' Alonzo began.

'Ssh,' Beatriz went.

For another second or so we remained frozen. The whistle came a third time and now there was movement.

'A helicopter!'

'Are you prepared?'

'Beatriz, what shall we do about these two?'

There were figures, a dozen or more, who had come out of their hiding places while we were being questioned. I hadn't registered them until now as they vanished again.

191

What I did take in was the rifle that Beatriz levelled at Darcy, who had walked closer.

'Get down,' Beatriz shouted. 'The army will kill you.'

Urgency was given to her words by the growing noise of an engine. Abruptly there was nobody visible, not Beatriz, nor any of the other guerrillas. They were wild animals that had gone to earth. I never saw where Darcy hid. I found a rock just in time as the helicopter clattered into view. It was low, definitely following the road. It swung wide round the corner and snapped back. It hesitated, hanging in the air. I could see the pilot talking to someone. If I could see the pilot, he could see me. There – more than twenty-four hours on the go and my brain could give Einstein a good run.

The helicopter came nosing in. You could swear it was a shark smelling blood.

I fancied animals everywhere today. Exhaustion had turned my world into the jungle.

A hand was pointing. It was the car that drew their attention. The helicopter dipped down and edged sideways. It was about the size of a Cobra, able to lift a dozen soldiers into the combat zone. I could see them, their faces pressed against the windows. They were commuters going to war.

I didn't like it at all. I was in the worst possible position. I was sprawling in no-man's-land between two violent armies and I didn't fancy my chances when the shooting started. I should get away. It wasn't possible. It *had* to be possible. Nothing is beyond you provided your brain works hard enough.

Suddenly my brain wasn't there at all. *She died because her brain went out for a stroll.* Put it on my headstone. Would anyone come to read the inscription? Did anyone care enough to leave a bunch of flowers? I would have a grave in a field in Central America and nobody would mourn.

*Think.*

Don't maunder. *Think* how you can stay alive.

It wasn't far to the corner. It was a bit of a slope up through withered grass and on the road the dirt would be loose underfoot and I'd have to be careful not to slip. Fifteen metres. No distance. The guerrillas – with the possible exception of Alonzo – would hold their fire because it gave away their positions. The danger was the army. I could see a rifle poking through an open door. If I made the corner, the helicopter would be after me. There had to be some trick, if I could work it out.

My thinking was a waste of time because at that moment the road got up.

There's no telling with explosions. Like people, each one has a different character. No one knows them all. You come across loud ones and soft ones but that's not the end of it. There are braggarts, nothing substantial behind the noise. And assassins, silent killers. They can be flashy types that make you recoil. There are practical jokers that bring the house down, leaving granny's chamberpot on her head. And snobs, very picky about who they know, ignoring the people in the front row in favour of the folk in the royal box.

This was a street bully.

It only made sense if a culvert ran under the road. The Brigada had selected this place because they knew the army would stop to check the car that had ended up among the rocks. The Brigada wouldn't have had time to dig a trench and lay a roof back on top and make good so that it aroused no one's suspicions. But the car had left the road on a curve and it made it a natural place for a culvert to drain off storm water. It was a quick job to pack with explosives and lay a wire to somewhere safe so it could be detonated for maximum impact. They would expect a truck. A helicopter was a much richer prize.

The noise wasn't great. Not where I lay it wasn't. Or perhaps my brain was overloaded with visual impressions and couldn't take in sound. The road broke up in pieces, stones, gravel, earth. Large pieces flew up and split into smaller bits, into a million fragments of destruction. A flash lit the underbelly of the helicopter before the shock wave. The blast and the debris struck together with a noise like a car smash. Half a rotorblade went spiralling downhill and metal sheeting aged and imploded and a face at the open portal turned red and vanished and wind with the power of a tornado picked the helicopter up and hurled it sideways fifty metres and slammed it tail first on the road. It came to rest with the power dying and men screaming. An officer shouted orders and figures jumped out on the far side and ran and dropped in cover, safe from the fuel tanks going up, safe from bullets.

The guerrillas were shooting. It was a rapidly escalating war and if the soldiers had radio contact with the army base, reinforcements would be rushed here and that would be the end.

Something like that must have been in Beatriz's mind for she shouted an order and the Brigada pulled out. There must have been fifteen or so, in jeans and tee shirts, cast-off army blousons, vests and ragged trousers. A boy lost a baseball cap and turned back to pick it up. I was running from rock to rock, clambering up the hill, dodging behind trees, using bushes as cover. The bullets were flying the other way now.

Not again.

I was having to climb Everest twice in a day. I couldn't. Muscles were burnt out. Willpower was in hiding. I'd used up my ration of luck and couldn't hold out my bowl for a second helping.

But nobody else is going to get you up that slope, Cody.

I was exposed by brilliant sunshine. Every time I darted between cover I was a big tempting target. But I was only one of many. It's always the other guy who gets it. Scratch round for comfort.

It was a gutbust of a retreat, zigzagging, crouching, scrambling. It was fast because the essence of guerrilla fighting is to get far enough away so the army doesn't see where you melt into the bushes. From the brow of the hill the land dipped and rose again. I caught up with Alonzo who turned and fired a couple of rounds. There was no target. Squeezing the trigger made him stronger and braver. We clawed through scrub and raced across a large field that skirted the slope of a hill. There was no cover. Maize had been harvested and

194

then grazed to the ground. Crows blundered into the air in alarm.

'Stop! Stop!'

It was a yell from behind us. Alonzo did stop long enough to shoot back his reply. At the edge of the field Beatriz stood as steady as an oak. The shock of white in her hair made her distinctive. She was showing herself to the soldiers, a deliberate challenge: hit me if you can, chase after me if you dare.

'Did you bring them?'

'Don't be absurd.'

She turned angry eyes on me. 'They came close behind you.'

'The helicopter stopped because of the car. I made no signal.'

'Maybe.'

'Not maybe. It's true. You know it's true.'

'Maybe I know it's true then. This is the middle of a revolution. Do you expect me to trust strangers?'

We stared, puzzled, trying to make sense of each other. The crack of a rifle came thinly on the air, and another. Soldiers across the field had sunk on one knee and their rifles were pointed towards us. I moved into the trees. Beatriz didn't. She flung her arms wide, a scarecrow, a Christ on the cross, an embracer of death.

'Take me. I offer you my body.'

The soldiers were too far to hear. It was a piece of theatre for my benefit.

That three note whistle came again. It was a long way off to the right.

'Beatriz,' Alonzo said, 'they won't cross the field. We can pin them down.'

This is the end, I thought. I'm going to be killed in a dirty little war that's nothing to do with me.

Beatriz stared across the field, listening. When that whistle had come three times before, it had signified a helicopter. The whistle came a second time. She waited and then she spoke. 'It's always the same. If their numbers are too few, they follow at a distance. If they outnumber us, they attack. Now there's a truckload coming.'

'What do we do?' I asked. The knot was tied and my fate was bound up with hers.

'Burrow in the earth like animals.'

'We can pin them down,' Alonzo insisted.

'Until they outflank us. Come on.'

'Where?'

'The *tatu*.'

There was the briefest of pauses before he nodded. Sometimes he argued with her because he was a man, a peasant, and couldn't swallow taking orders from a woman. This wasn't one of those times. We went fast again, up a narrow ravine, through a plantation of coffee shrubs that had been left to grow wild, across a barren field, until we reached a shack. The first you saw of it was smoke curling up to the sky. A woman squatted by a wood fire boiling something in a pot. A baby was at her breast. She stood up and put the breast back inside her shapeless dress.

'They're coming,' Beatriz shouted. 'Hide.'

Alonzo kicked at the smouldering logs, scattering them. Using a rag as a glove he picked up the pot and dashed water on the flames. He used a palm frond to sweep dirt over the mess. He followed us, walking backwards, using the frond as a broom to obliterate our footprints.

At the back of the shack a hill climbed up. Here among the rocks was a black hole and into it we crawled: the guerrilla fighters, Darcy, me, the woman with the baby, Beatriz, and lastly Alonzo.

'Give me some light. Lazaro, lend me a hand.'

Someone flicked on a torch and by its light Alonzo and another man rolled a rock across the entrance. We were cut off from the world, buried in the hill.

'This is our *tatu*,' Beatriz said. 'Welcome.'

I'm part of the family now, I thought, as the light went out and blackness swallowed us.

# 17

Darkness clung to my face. I could feel the darkness. It was thick, a blanket smothering me.

I was crouching. Safe to stand upright? I straightened until rock bumped my head. Putting a hand up I felt a jagged ceiling that sloped away from the entrance. I moved until I brushed against another body.

'Who is it?' It was an unbroken voice, one of the boys who was considered old enough to carry a rifle. But young enough to squeak with fright.

'Cody. I was walking down the road.'

'You,' he whispered. 'I watched you in my rifle sights all the time. Just in case.'

Thanks a lot, *niño*, you've made my day. Twelve years old and covering me like a pro. I'd been within five millimetres of death. That's how far his trigger-finger had to travel. My safari jacket was clinging to my back and not just because of running.

Sounds of breathing were all round. It's the worst part, Commander Elton had told me long ago when I had pigtails and wide open eyes. Commander Elton RN (Ret'd) was on his calling card. I loved running my fingers over the engraving. He'd been a friend of my father, an old submariner, with breath that smelled of gin and false teeth. Never mind battle, my girl, picture yourself sitting mum on the seabed, not moving an eyelash, not talking, waiting for the unseen enemy to track you down. Nothing you can do. Nowhere you can run. Nowhere to hide. Battle was terrifying and stimulating at the same time. It was waiting that got to the nerves. Nasty, my girl, damned sticky.

My own nerves were screwed tight. I wanted all the forbidden things: I wanted to jump up and down, shout, run.

I became aware of smells. It was a triumph of training, using the senses one by one. Isolate, evaluate, initiate action. The smell of sweat was pervasive. Not the fresh odour of a man's body which puts all sorts of ideas in my mind. These were people who never washed and bacteria were rotting the stale sweat on their skin and clothes. In the cramped *tatu* the stink was overpowering. Other smells: mould, urine, vomit. This was their burrow and there had been other vigils in the past. How long was this one going to last?

07.46.

Time had slipped away. Where had the night gone? Two seconds ago I had been blundering round the army camp and now I was trapped in this tomb and the countdown to Crevecoeur's noon deadline at Guazatan had begun.

A current of air stirred and Beatriz whispered: 'Who's nearest the table?' She was close to me.

There was no immediate answer. We were all listening. There had been a shout in the outside world. You could feel ears straining to work out how close it was. The acoustics were odd and the rock over the entrance muffled the noise. The shout could have been anywhere.

There was an instant's light, not much more than a camera's flash. It illuminated the *tatu* and was doused. The darkness was thicker than before. The flash had taken me unaware. I'd seen a confusion of images and had to reconstruct them from memory. The *tatu* was a cave. An extinct volcano was always somewhere in the landscape of El Salvador and a few million years ago some seismic upheaval had split the earth's crust and made this cave. Humans had improved on nature. There were gouges where tools had hacked at the rock. At the back wooden props marked a rockfall. From the low entrance the cave opened up and the flash of light hadn't penetrated to the top. This is our *tatu*. Welcome.

'Mauricio.' Beatriz hissed the name.

Human figures had been straight from an opium den. Yellow skin, black spikes of hair, slanted eyes, mouths twisted with the pain of fear. Clothes were turned to grey.

Next to me, the boy who'd watched me through his rifle sights now aimed at my hip. Other rifles pointed towards the *tatu*'s entrance. The first soldier to come in would be flung twenty metres back by the force of the gunfire. Even the woman with the baby in the crook of her left arm held a gun in her right hand, a toy pistol, the kind that makes a snappy noise and with a following wind could drill a hole all the way through a soldier's uniform. Darcy had a hand to his face, covering his mouth and nose. He was blocking out the stench or craving a cigarette.

'Mauricio, get up on José's shoulders. Use the spyhole.'

A rough table made of packing case boards was jammed against the wall next to Darcy. On it like a row of carcasses were ammunition boxes, rifles, handguns, a water flask. Was it full? My mouth was parched. My throat hurt when I swallowed. Fear gave me the thirst. I was a trapped animal. Also on the wooden table, material like a bandage. Its whiteness had jumped out in the burst of light.

'Careful when you move the stone. Don't send any pebbles rolling. I don't have to tell you . . .'

Concentrate. Bring the image forward in the memory. Inspect it. It hadn't been a bandage on the table. It had been the moneybelt made from Erica's pillowcase. That had been in another lifetime, in another country where the luxuries of pillowcases and beds and sleep existed.

As the minutes passed my eyes were accustoming to the *tatu*. Shadowy silhouettes grew, charcoal grey on coal black. Bits of light leaked round the rock that had been rolled across the entrance. If the light could creep in, sounds could steal out. I understood that. My stomach and my pulse knew it. We all accepted the logic and that was why only Beatriz spoke.

A sound came from outside again. It was a sound with the life taken out of it as if there'd been a snowfall. Tropical snow, that's what had got me here, the Snowline from Colombia to Paris.

Think. What had the sound been? A bell with the clapper muffled? Beatriz had the answer.

'You should have put it in the hut.'

The cooking pot, a boot kicking it.

Alonzo bridled. 'Hell, I was doing all –'

'Ssh.'

Men's voices, like you hear outside a window when the curtains are drawn on a winter evening. Saying what? Arguing what the wet patches meant, why the fire had been scattered, why an ember smoked through dirt?

'Ask Mauricio what they're doing,' Beatriz breathed to someone.

On my right was the outline of a giant, Mauricio on José's shoulders. The face was too small for someone so tall. His cheeks were the brightest thing in the *tatu*, catching the light that came in through the spyhole.

Whispers came back. 'He says he can see seven men.'

'Is that all?'

'He says seven men. One of them is a sergeant.'

'Have we killed the officer?'

No one answered.

'More than seven soldiers got out of the helicopter. Then the truck brought more. The others are searching the hills.'

'We can kill seven men.'

'And then? The shooting will bring the others.'

The baby stirred in its mother's arms. It was protesting at being held so tight, moaning through its nose.

On one side of me Beatriz whispered: 'For God's sake tell Rosa to suckle it.'

The message was passed to the boy next to me and to a man on the other side and I heard him urge the mother: 'Rosa, give the baby your tit.' The sound of wet lips on skin came.

The soldiers will hear.

Careful. In the dark my sense of proportion was being corrupted. I was in a deep shelter waiting for the bomb to drop. I was in a coffin waiting for the rattle of earth on the lid.

A hand was on me. It patted my shoulder, moved up my

neck, felt the shape of my face and the commas of hair slicked to my forehead.

'It's you,' Beatriz breathed. 'Now you know what it is to be hunted. Do you begin to understand why we hate them?'

I understood this was the most vicious kind of war, citizen against citizen. These were family hatreds burning red hot. Half an hour ago the Brigada had done their best to kill those men outside. The bomb blast most likely had killed some. Deaths cried out to be avenged.

There were voices again and the whisper was passed from our spy at the rathole in the side of the hill: 'A lieutenant has arrived.'

'Do you know which lieutenant?'

'He wears dark glasses.'

This intelligence didn't seem significant to Beatriz. Or perhaps she concentrated on other things. The voices were louder. I could hear boots. Boots meant they had drawn close.

*Mary, Mother of Jesus, protect me.* That had been Darcy's mutter. So far it had worked. How much longer would we be safe? We were in a trap and the only way out was into the army's guns. I should go on my knees and try a prayer. Let me live and I'll build a chapel on this spot. Europe is littered with chapels people promised if a miracle was granted: a shipwrecked sailor coming back from the sea, a battle turned, a condemned man's life spared.

'You have no rifle,' Beatriz mouthed in my ear. 'You must have a gun.'

There are no chapels where the miracle was denied, where the prayer was considered but not granted. Those unbuilt chapels would swamp the whole of Europe.

I wouldn't take a rifle. How could I tell her? She would never be persuaded for herself but might accept I had my own reasons. If you shoot, someone shoots back. If you kill, eventually you will be killed. I might die anyhow. I was in the worst conceivable position, surrounded by armed people driven desperate. It's why I always work alone. A lone unarmed woman would pose no threat to the army and I wouldn't be shot on sight. As part of a gang of guerrillas, I would be cut down in a hail of bullets. That was the practical side of it. The moral side: I would never knowingly set out to kill. In self-defence, in the last resort, yes. The human animal fights to protect its own life. Yet . . . Let me think my way out of a tight corner, not shoot my way out.

Was this the corner that was ultimately too tight?

No, don't doubt. Don't give in to exhaustion.

I was staring at her, at the solidness in front of my face. There would be a frown dividing her forehead. I heard it in her whisper. I could make out nothing of her face but the shock of white hair was visible. And she was staring at me. I could feel the intensity of her eyes. They were a force even in the dark. I hadn't responded to her offer of a rifle and now she was testing the silence. Her brain and her willpower and her imagination were eager to enter me, try me out. Was I a traitor? A coward?

Suppose I found the words to say why I wouldn't take a rifle and shoot the men outside, would she understand? Cody, your morals are a luxury. In a revolution a taste for luxuries is weakness.

It didn't matter. Events took over.

'Beatriz.'

'Ssh.'

There was whispering from Mauricio. His face vanished from the spyhole while he bent down. In the leakage of light I saw his hand gripping the wall to steady himself. The whisper reached us. It was Alonzo, who always had a louder voice, who told Beatriz and I heard too.

'They've found Hector.'

'Have they captured him?'

'He's running on the far side of the ravine.'

'How can Mauricio be sure it's Hector?'

'He has the binoculars.'

Which made him the look-out, I supposed, the forward scout with the three-note whistle who warned of the helicopter and the truck. There seemed to be no other information. Mauricio had his eye to the spyhole again. He bent to give the urgent news to José and it was passed to us.

'He's running this way. The soldiers are spread out behind him.'

'Heading *directly* here?' Beatriz wanted to know.

'The shitkickers will run him till he drops,' Alonzo said.

'*Is Hector coming here?*'

The question was passed down the line. Mauricio ducked down and the answer came back. Ridiculous. First World War communications. Send three and fourpence we're going to a dance.

'He's vanished, turned up the ravine.'

The stink was growing. Nerves had goaded sweat glands into frenzied efforts. You'd think the stench would drift out and lead the army to us.

'Hector's reappeared.'

Three or four distant sounds like knuckles cracking in the next room.

'He's turned and shot at the bastards and now he's running again.'

'Which direction?'

A peppering of remote gunshots. Or not so remote. Remember the *tatu* deadens sounds.

'He's swerved and heading this way.'

I grasped the danger. My moral scruples were melting. A rifle might offer my only hope of survival, as once in Holland I had shot Yussif so that I might live. Hector knew of the *tatu*. He saw it as his final hope of escape. Like us, he wanted to burrow in the ground and be hidden. He would come to the hillside and struggle with the rock and the soldiers near the shack would see.

'Alonzo, Lazaro, be ready to move the rock.'

'You're not letting him in?'

'We go out shooting. Surprise will help us.'

But I heard another voice. It was the man who balanced Mauricio on his shoulders. The escalating danger made José reckless. 'Mauricio's counted more than twenty chasing him.'

Twenty soldiers. Plus the ones already here. Plus reinforcements brought by the sound of combat. Beatriz was planning a suicide run. Talk of 'surprise' was whistling in the dark. The first person out would have the benefit of surprise, but the entrance was low and the guerrillas could only get out one at a time. Each would crawl blinking into sunlight to face the firing squad.

Sounds of gunfire were drawing closer. Then one of the soldiers by the shack sighted Hector and loosed off the entire clip of his automatic rifle. A scream came thinly and was drowned by a scream that echoed inside the *tatu*. The baby, filled with alarm at the darkness and the noise, began to yell.

'Rosa,' Alonzo's voice was raised, 'shut the baby up.'

The head was clamped against the breast, the cries were muffled, the head turned and yelled louder.

'Give it to me,' Beatriz ordered. She pushed aside bodies while the yells redoubled.

'You're frightening her,' Rosa said.

'She's frightening us all,' Beatriz said.

Security was blown. The voices were at full pitch, the screams piercing, someone dropped a rifle.

There was an ache in my chest. I was holding my breath. What good would that do? Strangely there was no uproar outside. Mauricio reported no attack being mounted against the *tatu*. My ears had exaggerated. The sounds hadn't been loud. Or the soldiers were intent on Hector.

'He's been hit,' came the whisper. 'Badly.'

By a collective effort of will, silence was reimposed. Even the baby, comforted by Beatriz, stopped her yells and gave only a subdued moan.

'Hector's crawling on hands and knees.'

'Which way?'

But that wasn't the danger now. He couldn't reach us. The danger was he would be captured and a knife twisted in a wound as questions were shouted in his face: Where have the *terroristas* hidden? I know nothing, nothing. Where is their hiding place? Nothing, stop, know nothing, I can't stand the pain. Then say where you were running to. Don't torture me, I was running, just running away. Tell us and we'll take out the knife. Where? Nothing, can't you understand, nothing, no, stop, I beg you. Tell us before the knife is twisted again. Nothing nothing nothing, *yes*, in the hillside, behind that rock, just stop the pain.

A shot outside. There had been silence while the hunters stalked their prey. This single shot broke it.

'That was Hector.'

Mauricio didn't want to say more. In saying nothing he said everything.

Finally the confirmation: 'He turned the gun on himself.'

Beatriz urged: 'Remember always that Hector was a true hero of the revolution.'

Inside the *tatu* it was still and quiet.


09.08.

Less than three hours to Crevecoeur's deadline.

An hour and a half buried in here. How much longer? The stench grew worse. My nostrils could scarcely breathe it. I inhaled through an open mouth. The air tasted. To everything else was added a new stomach-turner. Fear had un-clenched someone's sphincter muscle and latrine smells spread like poison gas.

Of course, I didn't have to fly out of El Salvador. That was the millionaire's way home. The poor bloody infantry walked. It's just that I was bone tired, my feet were blistered and cut, my body was dehydrated, my reactions slowed through lack of food, the Honduran border was up in the hills a day's march away, the army was hunting me, and I would have to cross the *bolcon* where unknown guerrillas made the rules.

I wanted the Rolls-Royce and chauffeur treatment.

09.10.

'Why do you keep looking at your watch?'

It sparked like a firefly when I pressed the button.

'How much longer are we going to be shut in?'

'Once upon a time,' she began like some fairy tale, 'Alonzo and I and two other comrades were in another *tatu* for thirty-six hours. The fascist army knew we had gone to earth but didn't know the spot. *Tatus* differ. This one was a tunnel dug under the yard of a peasant's hut. It was a dirt yard and chickens pecked for grubs. The army never found us. The entrance was under the cooking fire, actually under it. The whole grate was mounted on a trapdoor that lifted up.'

Thirty-six hours. The air in this *tatu* would be solid with smells by then. And it would be a long hike to reach the border.

'Mauricio, what's new?'

'Nothing.'

Hector's body had been searched, the binoculars and gun taken, and then he'd been abandoned to the scavengers. The army had blundered around, stabbing sheath knives into the earth outside the hut, quartering the wooded slope of the ravine, combing the hill behind us. At nine o'clock, running to some rigid military timetable, a whistle had blown and they had withdrawn.

'Tell us when it's nine-thirty.'

Orders for me.

The time dragged. I saw 09.18 and 09.22. More than four minutes surely. Four hours, four centuries. You'd swear the mainspring was winding down if it wasn't a quartz model.

'It's time,' I said.

There was movement, a new sense of purpose.

'Alonzo, you know what to do?'

Alonzo knew. He grunted. Why was this stupid woman always teaching him his job? The rock was rolled aside, Alonzo crawled out, the rock was rolled back. He was lucky. If he ran into an ambush, at least he'd die with a lungful of fresh air. It had smelled so sweet for the few seconds the entrance was unblocked.

Alonzo had gone on a scouting mission. There was no sophistication to it. If nobody shot at him, it was safe for us all to come out. Perhaps this would be the day the army hid out of sight until he reported all was well and we gave away our secret sanctuary.

'Nothing,' Mauricio reported. 'He's waving from the edge of the ravine.'

206

At 09.40 the rock was rolled aside and we all came out. The world was new made. I stood in the garden of Eden on the sixth day of creation. I breathed scents of earth and trees. I warmed to tropical sun. I gazed at rocks and grass and blue heavens and banana leaves like tattered green umbrellas. One by one the Brigada filed out, the kid with the rifle, Lazaro, Mauricio, José, all of them.

A scream pierced my ears. Rifles swung to the danger. Rosa screamed. She had an unformed face, a teenage bride with puppy fat and acne. She caught another breath through a mouth that was a big black blob and screamed again. Beatriz was laying the baby on the ground. The face was flushed, exploding with blood. Beatriz still had a hand clamped over its mouth and nose. That hand had been rivetted in place for an hour and a half. The baby was long dead.

# 18

I was struck through.

Beatriz, how could . . .

Words wouldn't come. I was struck dumb. Struck with despair.

Murderers, exploiters, fascists she called the army and the government. The Brigada was committed to creating a new order where peace and social justice flourished. One or two stumbles along the way. Unfortunate but necessary.

There would be stumbles for ever and ever. The brave new world was to be built with the bad old humans. Keep the revolution rolling. Be strong. Be resolute. Social progress cannot pause for weaklings. Broken eggs, omelette, that argument.

It's just that, after cracking eggs in the Soviet Union for seventy years, where's the bloody omelette? That's what they want to know in the psychiatric hospitals and the prison camps of the Gulag.

The cries from Rosa lifted up to the hills.

'Shut up!' Beatriz yelled. 'It was going to give away the *tatu*. They army would have shot us all.'

'They killed Maximo,' Rosa screamed back at her. 'Now you've murdered Cristina. She was all I had left of him.'

'*We* are what you've got left of him. The Brigada. Your comrades.'

Rosa knelt by her baby and laid her cheek on its body. It was a doll, small and still. The last of the Brigada were crawling out of the *tatu*. They stood up, blinking in the sunshine and joining the group that stared at Beatriz and Rosa.

'Murderer.' Rosa's voice had dropped. The word struggled out through sobs.

'*We* are your family. We fight together. We share pain and hardship for the cause. We live together. We are prepared to die for each other. You must accept that, Rosa, or you are not one of us.'

'You killed Cristina.' Rosa got to her feet with the bundle hugged to her chest. 'I gave her to you to comfort and you smothered her. Cristina means nothing to you. She was mine, she was my love, she was my life. You don't care.'

And Beatriz found that everybody's eyes were on her. They were waiting. She stared round the faces, even at mine. She was puzzled. I think she saw this as a supreme test of character. There was a choice. She could be the iron leader, insisting that sacrifices had to be made for the common good. Or she could be a sister to the bereaved mother, and risk losing her authority.

'You're not sorry, are you?'

Everybody waited. Three men had gone part way to fetch the body of Hector, and had hesitated, and now began to walk back. Nobody else moved. Nobody spoke.

'It is to be regretted,' Beatriz began.

We waited. What was she going to say? I wanted to know. But it wasn't a beginning. That was all there was. She couldn't say she was sorry. That would be to admit she was wrong. Beatriz was never wrong. Her belief in herself was absolute. It was the steel rod that gave her strength.

I hated Major Portillo and his torture chamber. I hated the drug pushers. And Beatriz – I didn't hate; I pitied her.

I had had enough. I wanted to get far away. Rosa still stared at Beatriz, not realizing she had spoken her last words. I kissed Rosa on the cheek and moved away towards Darcy. He was the last one to come out of the *tatu*. He stood at the entrance zipping his blouson. His eyes were roaming the sky, enchanted by its blueness, and then his head snapped down. What I remember vividly is the instant his expression changed. One moment his face showed delight at being free. The next moment amazement flashed into his eyes.

The gunshot wasn't loud. Out here in the open it was no

more than a door slamming. Something was happening I couldn't understand. That lightning change on Darcy's face – surprise, fright – why was someone shooting at him? Not at him. Idiot. Brain swamped by exhaustion.

I turned as Beatriz staggered sideways, sank to one knee, got up. Rosa, with the baby clasped to her, held the little pistol in her right hand. The gun was following Beatriz, waiting for her to stay still. Most murders are within the family. Rosa, with a blood-debt to avenge, was going to kill the head of the family.

She shot again and missed. She wasn't aiming, just pointing. Dirt kicked up behind Beatriz. Rosa moved her gun hand but she never got to fire again. The second shot broke the spell. There was a surge towards Rosa, shouts, people pulling and pushing, hands snatching at her hand. The gun was taken from her. But when someone tried to take the baby, she clutched it tighter.

She used her last weapon on Beatriz. She spat.

People were screaming. Alonzo was threatening to kill the stupid slut. The voices were muddled in my head as if I was the one shot. Beatriz looked round. There was no chair or bench so she sat on the ground. It was her right shoulder that had been shot. She must have ducked round at the last moment. She reached behind with her left hand and inspected her fingers. She blinked as if the sight wasn't real. At that stage she felt no pain. The shock had numbed her and pain would creep in later.

The sun was bright, the blood was fresh and red, what had happened was beyond her. Why did the fingers look like this? Why had they got nail varnish on the wrong side?

'Jesus,' Darcy muttered. 'Let's get out of here. They're as crazy as spaghetti.'

The whole world is mad. Why should this twisted little patch be different?

I knelt in front of Beatriz and she met my gaze. Yes, her eyes showed she was in shock.

'It doesn't hurt,' she said. She tipped her hand towards

me, offering her bloody fingers. 'I felt a blow, that's all. Something hit me, went inside me.'

'How many peasant boys have you done that to?' I asked. 'How many soldiers in that helicopter?'

I got a knee in the back and was sent sprawling and when I scrambled up it was to find Alonzo raising his rifle. I moved and sensed people scattering behind me. Who wants to be a human sandbag if the target is missed? The rifle had centred on my chest. Like Rosa, he was simply pointing. But he couldn't miss with a rifle at that distance.

He was three long strides away. I couldn't knock the gun aside.

I wasn't kneeling. There was no dirt I could scoop into his eyes.

If I went into a forward roll and he was surprised enough to miss, there was the rest of the Brigada to contend with. A dozen bullets would end my move.

I said: 'Is one of you a doctor?'

Alonzo had his finger inside the trigger guard. I kept my eyes on his eyes. At the edge of my vision I saw the brown skin of that finger going white at the knuckle. The pressure on the trigger was increasing. A sudden movement, a sharp noise, anything could stimulate the reflex in his finger and the trigger would come all the way back and in a fraction of a second my life would be blown away. *Something hit me, went inside me.* No, something would be going out of me. Rosa's pop-gun was primarily for show; this rifle was meant for killing.

'Beatriz must have a doctor immediately. Do any of you have medical training?'

Alonzo swallowed. 'She says it doesn't hurt.'

'I can begin to feel something,' Beatriz said. 'Hot and sharp. Angry as if it wanted to get out.'

'The bullet is inside,' I said.

'How do you know?' Alonzo asked.

It seemed safe to move my eyes from his. Slowly I looked over to Beatriz. He followed my gaze.

'There's blood on her back where the bullet went

211

in. There's no blood in front. The bullet never came out.'

'You can't be sure –'

'Oh for God's sake.' I lost patience with him. 'That's a little pistol Rosa used, not a rifle. The bullet entered Beatriz's back where that bloodstain is and ploughed through muscle and was stopped by the shoulder blade. It's a strong bone, certainly capable of stopping a low-power small diameter bullet. It's possible the bone is fractured. A doctor would establish that. More important, he would take the bullet out.'

'There is no doctor here,' Alonzo said.

'Then take her to a town where there is.'

'Señorita Cody,' Beatriz said, 'you understand very little of our struggle. Major Portillo has a simple rule for when the army captures one of us: if they cannot rape a prisoner, they shoot him. If the prisoner is wounded and can fight no more, they still shoot him. If one of us is wounded and goes to hospital, he is taken out at night and shot. Sometimes it is just possible for a comrade to pretend he was wounded while heroically resisting communist *terroristas* and then he will be treated and can slip back to continue the revolution. But I do not have that option. I am known.'

She lifted a hand and swept the shock of white hair away from her face.

'You must have the bullet removed,' I said. 'It's not a question of pain. If the bullet stays lodged there, it will poison the wound.' What was the word for *gangrene* in Spanish? It was not a word I'd ever had to use before. 'The flesh round the wound dies and infects your blood. The infection passes through your blood stream. You will sink into a fever and die.'

'Are you a doctor?' she asked.

'No.' My father had been. I hadn't wanted to live my life in a world of suffering, as if we can ever escape.

'But you have medical training?'

'I'm telling you what everyone knows. These are simple facts. The revolution doesn't alter them.'

'You were never a nurse?'

212

'No.'

'This gift of Rosa's is stirring. I can feel fingers exploring my shoulder.'

'It will get worse,' I said, 'much worse.'

'Yes,' she agreed. 'It will get worse.'

She looked round the faces. No one had a suggestion. These were people of the land. She was the leader.

'If the bullet must come out . . .' she began, and gave an experimental lift to her shoulder. That hurt. She looked at me, her mind made up. 'I want you to take the bullet out.'


'You guys call me Doc,' he said. He had a sniff, as if a cold was starting. But it was simply distaste for us. 'And I'll call you whatever seems fitting. Now my time is valuable. I don't want to waste it on any repeats. So listen to what I say, watch what my hands do, and keep your pants clean. If you can't stomach this, now is the time to get out. Lost one guy from your intake already, so the story goes.'

That had been Abe Juul who'd jumped from a window the week before. Juul couldn't take any more. It seemed his suicide had tainted the remaining eight of us the Agency was training for SIS. We'd begun as Limeys; after Juul, we were SISSIES. That was what it said on the card we found pinned to the social noticeboard.

This section of training had been termed Body Emergency. Shortly after lunch we reached the messy part.

'These little beauties are scalpels.' Doc sniffed. 'They've gotten various names for various functions but I don't want to burden your brains with too much lumber. So far as Body Emergency goes, these are plain old scalpels.'

Body Emergency, I'd thought, wasn't that typical? It could have been called First Aid or Medical but that didn't sound important enough to satisfy Doc's ego.

'Feels good in the hand. Like a steak knife.'

He dug it into the thigh.

'Of course, if you're vegetarian you won't know what the hell I mean.'

His eyes searched for hints of nut cutlets amongst us. I stared him out. I decided Doc's name was Butcher. Or possibly de Sade, the way he lingered over our queasy faces. He drew the scalpel out slowly. Not much marking on it. A corpse from the chiller drawer doesn't bleed much. Dedicate your body to science and it can end up in some damn funny places.

'Let's assume you're in a hostile environment – an attic room in Warsaw for instance – and you've gotten a bullet lodged in a limb and hospitalization is out of the question. What you're going to do is isolate the limb with a tourniquet for two reasons . . .'

I'd gone on listening because it was important. But another part of my mind kept nagging: What if it's not a limb? What if I stop a bullet in my belly? I'd waited for that vital trick to be explained but it never came. No Body Emergency tip. Don't scare the SISSIES with out-of-control situations.

'Alonzo,' I said, 'I want you to light a fire over there.'

This wasn't Warsaw. Nor was it a training session in that windowless classroom in the compound in Virginia.

'Bring her into the hut,' I said to anyone who was listening. My mind was already skipping ahead to what had to be done.

'Leave me alone. I can walk.'

She could too. She limped. Nothing wrong with her leg but the pain was starting to spread from the shoulder all down the right side of her body. Anyone else would have accepted an arm. Not Beatriz. Core of steel. People were watching.

She would have to lie on the bed. There would be nothing else that could remotely double as an operating table. I was first through the door into the hut and there was no bed. There was a hammock. A hammock for two? Had Rosa and her man slept together in it, conceived the baby in it? No sofa either. There was a square table but it was too small to be of any use. It was going to have to be down on the floor. The windows gaped. Instead of glass there was plastic sheeting to keep the rain out. I'd seen sheeting like that a few hours ago. It had Major Portillo's endorsement for

214

blood spillage. I tore a piece down and laid it on the floor.

'There?' Beatriz asked.

Nothing that Doc had demonstrated was going to help. There was no limb I could isolate, no painkillers, no forceps, no antiseptic, no bandages. I looked round. There were two chairs beside the wooden table, a rolling pin, a jar with forks and spoons, plastic beakers, a family photo in a wooden frame, a coloured picture of the Madonna, a bowl, a tin tray spread with dry beans, a coat hanging on a nail, a small mattress on the floor with a coverlet and a rag doll. A cardboard carton held basic foods. Another carton had a jumble of clothes. A spade and a machete stood against the wall. This was Rosa's life. The baby had been the richest thing in it.

'Rosa,' I called out.

Men were crowding the hut. No one would be parted from his gun. I couldn't move, I couldn't think, until I'd cleared them outside. Rosa was brought with a man gripping her arm. She was crying without making a sound, tears slipping down her cheeks. I wanted to join her.

'Let her go.' The man hesitated. He was one I recognized. 'Mauricio, she's not going to run away. Where would she run to?'

There were potatoes and onions in the carton. A cut papaya showed black seeds. One of the seeds moved and turned into a fly.

'Rosa, I can't see any knife.'

'I hid it away because of Cristina.'

The baby hadn't been old enough to crawl never mind pick up a knife. But she had been precious and no risk must be run. Rosa gave me a knife from a shelf. It had a pink plastic handle and a serrated edge. This? I might as well hack with the machete.

'Have you any scissors?'

She kept scissors in the box of clothes. They were long, thin and rusted.

'What are you going to do?' Rosa asked.

Beatriz and I looked at each other.

'First,' I said, 'I'm going to cut the shirt away from the wound. You can help me.'

'Why me?'

'I need help.'

And Rosa needed to help, an act of service to the person she had tried to kill.

Beatriz was stretched out flat, with her head to one side so she could watch me. I cut the material of her shirt. Rosa gave a sob as she pulled it away from the wound. I didn't want to look. But I was going to have to look very closely indeed.

See it as something else.

It is a painting done in a kindergarten. Pretty red paint has been splashed about by an exuberant toddler. Here is a flowerbed of poppies. There a red river waters the poppies. The source of the river is up this slope. It's a spring. See how above the spring the slope is brown like sandy earth. Mottled purple and white surround the spring. From the centre of the technicolor fantasy the red flows out.

I touched Beatriz because I didn't want to. I was having to force myself at every stage not to get up and walk away. These are not my people, Beatriz is not my friend, this wound is not of my making. I am not responsible for every sick dog in the world.

But once you know a person, you are involved. Walk away and it is yourself you walk away from.

'Do you have any spirits? Any rum, for instance?'

'No,' Rosa said.

I would have used some on the wound, given the rest to Beatriz to drink. Rum would have helped. There was no anaesthetic.

'Put a bowl of water to heat on the fire. You've got salt? Add a handful.' I got to my feet and said to Beatriz: 'I won't be long.'

What had the scissors been used for last? Trimming hair, cutting toenails, slitting a rabbit's throat? I went outside where Alonzo had rebuilt the fire he had kicked out. He'd used dry branches that gave a good flame. Rosa was balancing a pan of water between two stones. Alonzo watched as Rosa leant over. They were well matched, I thought, better than Alonzo and Beatriz. He could give Rosa a new baby. Let Beatriz get on with the revolution – that was her child. If she lived. There were no antibiotics, no antiseptics.

I did the best I could. I held the blades of the scissors in the flames. At first the cold metal was streaked with soot. This burnt away. Fire cleanses. The metal was still stained but sterile. Rosa followed back into the hut.

'Do you have a clean cloth?'

She frowned and went to the box of clothing.

'Will this do?'

It was a dress, all white. It was tiny, about right for a baptism.

'Keep that. You'll need it again some day.'

In the end it was my own bra I handed to Rosa. She was to dab at the blood, I explained, so I could see what I was doing. Rosa and I knelt side by side, like communicants. Beatriz's face was twisted towards us, her eyes dark and serious. How could I begin while she watched? I wanted to tell her to look away. She was concentrating on me, taking strength from me.

'Where is the rest of your Brigada?'

'Elsewhere.'

That was a hell of an answer. Yesterday there'd been other women and children. Also there were men who were missing from here. I remembered the two boys smoking in the jeep.

'How many of you are there in the Brigada?'

'Why do you ask these questions? What will you do with the information?'

My wild sister didn't trust me.

'I want you to talk. I know nothing about you except you are fighting the army. That is why I ask these questions. I want you to talk because it will occupy your mind a little. It will distract you from what I have to do.'

'Like a man who recites the twelve-times table to himself while he makes love, so he will not be premature?' There was a memory passing through her and the ghost of a smile. 'I am not afraid of the pain.'

'It is I who am afraid.'

'No,' she said. 'Not you. I know you.'

'Beatriz,' Alonzo said from the door, 'there is a plane coming.'

'Everybody must take shelter.'

Some came into the hut, some retreated into the *tatu*, others made for the trees. The sound grew. It wasn't a helicopter. It wasn't a jet fighter. Possibly it was a spotter aircraft. It passed a little way off, its course north-north-east. I watched it out of sight from the window. It was a light aircraft. The time was now 10.24. Was it my Rolls-Royce heading for Guazatan? My chauffeur was early.

I knelt beside Beatriz again. I picked up the scissors. Now Doc, don't dismiss me as a sissy, just tell me the correct procedure for this particular body emergency.

'In our Brigada,' Beatriz said, 'there are six companies. The company I lead is the smallest. We must move a lot to keep the initiative. Sometimes towards the river, sometimes near Guazatan, sometimes right up by the border. It's a different world up there. We camp among pine trees. You wouldn't think it was the same country at all. The other companies keep on the move too. We join forces for a big operation but we are less noticeable when we are few. Sometimes the children are with us, sometimes not. They are in La Palma at present where there is a proper teacher. Why don't you begin?'

'Go on,' I said, 'tell me about La Palma.'

'It is better than Guazatan. People live in the houses. You can get food. The road goes through to Honduras but nobody uses it. La Palma is where President Duarte met with some of our leaders. From the very start I rejected Duarte. He came to power as a man of peace but for that you have to control the army, not be its puppet. Why wasn't the Queza-catl Battalion disbanded? Why was Portillo permitted to keep his uniform and his medals . . .'

At first the flesh offered no resistance. I opened the scissors

218

wide and probed with the thinner blade. The path a bullet makes is called the permanent track and I had to establish just where the bullet was lodged. I would let the permanent track guide me. The thing was to be receptive to tiny changes. I needed a sensitive touch, lock-picker's fingers, to judge when I was going wrong. The point of the blade slipped further in and a few drops of blood spurted out.

'*Madre de Dios*,' Rosa whispered.

Beatriz's eyes flicked across to her face. 'Women are not afraid of blood. It is part of our lives. We give our blood every month.'

Rosa nodded. She touched the bra against Beatriz's skin and the material drank the drops and turned red.

'And blood is part of our country. The land is soaked in it. It is the necessary part of the revolution, which is why our flag is red. Blood flows when the army slaughters our people. It is in every struggle we have ever fought for our freedom from poverty. It was part of the Spanish conquest. It was part of everyday life before the Spanish came. Have you heard of the cult of Xipe Totec?'

'Tell me,' I said.

She had been turning as the shot was fired. If her back had been at right angles to Rosa's pistol, then the bullet would have been almost visible – the muscle covering this part of the scapula is not thick. As it was the bullet had penetrated obliquely a couple of centimetres. It hid in a *tatu* of Beatriz's flesh. I had found it now, tapped the end.

'Have you finished?' Beatriz couldn't see what I was doing. She had felt the blade withdrawing. She didn't flinch.

'Not yet.'

Now I had located the bullet I had to close the scissors before reinserting them. The scissors were my forceps for drawing the bullet out. There was no other way. Doubled in size, the scissors no longer slipped easily through the permanent track. As I pushed in I felt the resistance of her flesh. Bleeding became more profuse. I had a hand on her shoulder to steady it and red trickled between my fingers.

Rosa wanted to clean it away but I stopped her. She obscured my view.

'Speak,' I said. 'Say something. Talk.'

'It was a religious cult of six hundred years ago.' Beatriz stopped. She didn't like the sound of her voice and started again much lower. 'The cult of Xipe Totec had an important ritual. A prisoner was taken to the place of sacrifice and was skinned alive. The priest began with the scalp and went on to the rest of the body. The prisoner was completely flayed, right down to his feet. He was conscious. At least he was at the beginning. At some point he must have died.'

'No, no, no.' Rosa was sobbing and shaking her head. I don't know whether it was at Xipe Totec or at the scissors forcing their way along the path her bullet had taken. I was pressing the muscle apart. Nerves would be sending urgent signals to Beatriz's brain. The pain would be screaming. She swallowed. She spoke again, slowly, one word built on another. It was an act of will.

'Then the priest put on the skin like a suit of clothes. They did it in the spring to help the crops grow.'

She stopped speaking. I looked in her face and saw her eyes were very wide and the muscles of her jaw clenched. I had reached the bullet and this was the worst part. Gradually I forced the scissors apart until I could trap the end of the bullet. It slipped out of the pincer grip, and slipped a second time.

'Rosa,' I said, 'there is a trickle of sweat coming down into my left eye. Wipe it away.'

She used the bra. Did I have blood smeared on my forehead?

Sweat ran on Beatriz's face too. Her skin had paled and the sweat spread like a mould. Her mouth was open and her breath came in pants. She would look this way when she made love. Pleasure is pain. What do you say to that, Doc?

'You must succeed,' Beatriz said in a whisper. 'You must.'

I tried angling the scissors a fraction to one side. The grip seemed firmer. She was watching my eyes. She was too intent on my progress in her body.

'I must have missed something,' I said. 'How did torture and killing make the crops grow?'

It was moving. I felt the bullet shift. Had she?

'Do you understand the *escuadrones de la muerte*? Do you understand Major Portillo? Does their killing make the crops grow?'

I'd lost it again. I closed my eyes a moment. No, I didn't understand the death squads or Portillo. Nothing had changed in six hundred years. Sacrifices were still demanded.

Come on, concentrate. I can do it. It is only a tiny distance to haul a tiny burden.

'What you must understand . . .'

She broke off as I went to work once more, gripping the bullet, easing it backwards through the flesh it had grooved. Beatriz swallowed and spoke in spasms.

'. . . this has always been . . . a land of cruelty . . . Once socialism has triumphed, it will be different.'

The bullet came suddenly free as if Beatriz's body had expelled it with the violence it had entered. A miniature rivulet of blood gushed with it. I dragged the bullet across her skin, leaving a snail's trail of red. Then the scissors slipped for the last time and the bullet rolled down the slope of Beatriz's back and plopped onto the plastic sheeting. Its nose was flattened on one side, distorted by the force of its encounter with her shoulder blade.

My hand began to tremble.

Beatriz expelled all the breath in her lungs.

Rosa turned aside and threw up.

Warm salt water was all there was to clean the wound. Blood oozed out again and I could think of no way of preventing it. The bleeding would stop in time. Whether the wound healed or poisoned her body was in the hands of the gods. She had a rich choice to pray to: Christ, Xipe Totec, Lenin. I had done everything I could.

'Stay with us,' Beatriz said. Her voice was tired, exhausted by pain. 'Together we can win. The future belongs to us.'

She was lying against a wall. The crucifix was above her.

I shook my head.

'If you won't join us, why do you help us? Why did you take the bullet out?'

To show the difference between the two of us? Compassion? It was impossible to explain. Everything about this country was alien. Beatriz was just a twentieth century version of that priest, putting on her violent politics like someone else's skin, certain the crops would grow.

'It is time we went,' I said. 'It'll be too dangerous to try and go back past the army now, so we'll make for the border.'

'Come here a moment.'

She pulled me down with a hand and kissed me.

'You must come back when we have triumphed.'

I nodded. You can give what meaning you like to a nod.

'Take care of her,' I told Rosa. 'Make her rest.'

'You expect *me* . . .' Her voice trailed off. It was rough from vomiting.

I went outside. A dozen of the Brigada sat on the ground. It seemed their lives were spent waiting for something to happen. Two others were digging a grave at the edge of the field.

'Where's Darcy?' I asked.

'He's not here,' Alonzo said. 'He's gone.'

'Gone?' I swung round and looked at Alonzo in amazement. 'What do you mean he's gone?'

He stared a few seconds. It was the same look he gave Beatriz: I was another woman trying to boss him.

'When that plane came and we went under cover, that is when he must have left.'

'And you let –'

'We were looking at the plane. Can't you get that into your head, woman? Sometimes the planes come and bomb us or radio our position to the army. It is necessary to watch the planes. That is what Beatriz orders: watch the sky. After the sky was clear, we noticed your friend was no longer here. Your lover, you said? Well, your lover didn't wait for you.'

There was an edge to Alonzo's voice. He had scored off me.

'Which way did he go?'

'We were watching the sky. I've told you. So are you running after him?'

The hell with Alonzo. Then my anger shifted to Darcy. The bastard, after what I'd done for him. I knew where he'd gone: rushing off to meet Crevecoeur, leaving me to play Florence Nightingale.

# 19

The sun swayed in the sky. I was on a small boat in a rough sea and the deck tilted and lurched back and above me the sun swung in a wide arc.

I stopped and closed my eyes and still saw the sun swinging over my head. The blood thudded in my ears. With each pulse a band of pain tightened across my forehead. How had Beatriz stood the pain as I probed for the bullet? No crying out, no flinching, no pleas. Core of steel. I needed something of it now.

11.53.

There was no more running in me. A day, a night and another day I had been running and my reserves of strength had gone. There was only willpower left. Willpower is what had brought Beatriz through. It would get me through to Guazatan. But I wouldn't arrive in time.

11.55.

Crevecoeur's midday deadline would pass and the plane would leave without me. That was bad enough. More bitter was the thought that the plane would be carrying Darcy. I didn't for one moment imagine he'd tell Crevecoeur to wait. She's enlisted with the guerrillas, he'd say, so let's get the hell out of here. I didn't like Darcy. I didn't like Crevecoeur either because he was cynical and ruthless and used you and threw you to the dogs afterwards. In other words he was good at his job. Just couldn't stand the skeleton sight of him, couldn't bear the way he stood too close.

But Darcy was something else. He was an enigma, beyond me. Crevecoeur said he was 'very good' but his talents were hidden. Relationships in the Sûreté were like marriages: no outsider could appreciate the subtleties and the pressures. It was nine hours since I'd met Darcy and I still knew nothing of him. Or rather only negatives. I had helped him escape torture and he wasn't grateful. He'd tried to overwhelm me sexually. He despised his boss as a *pète-sec*. He was frightened as we walked into the guerrilla ambush. He displayed no initiative in getting out of danger. Though he'd got away from the *tatu* unobserved, run out on me without a word.

11.59.

Black thoughts of Darcy vanished. There were shouts to the left. On the wooded slope of a hill I caught glimpses of movement. They were just shapes, five or six of them. You'd swear they were nothing more worrying than tree trunks until they disappeared among shadows. They weren't wood-cutters: no sound of sawing. They weren't cowboys: no cattle. Also they were strung in a line, materializing, vanishing, but definitely a line. The army flushing out *terroristas*? Guerrillas tracking down an isolated soldier? Then they shouldn't be shouting. They were like hunters, hoping enough noise would put up game birds. Crazy country.

In any case they weren't friends. I turned away and walked down the ravine, slipping from tree to rock to bush. A black bird with a long tail hopped up and down, squawking *Co-Co-Co*. Shut up, stupid bird, you're no buddy of mine. The ground was rough, tripping my clumsy feet. Stopping to take my bearings I saw the range of hills on the horizon. Above were clouds like muscles. They weren't far away. They were an afternoon's hike if you were in good shape. I was a wreck with blood soaking my socks and with legs as unsteady as a foal's.

12.08.

I was going to have to talk to those hills. Honduras began there.

A thought was pushing up in my mind, a memory. Walk to freedom, walk to save your life. The memory was of walking a week in the Sahara with my body drying out. My mouth had the beginning of that feeling.

The ravine broadened and flattened into a plain. I passed a hump of grey basalt and came onto the dirt road that ran to Guazatan. Somewhere a look-out would keep watch on this road. He wouldn't be a soldier. The army would only come in force. A guerrilla would see a lone woman limping along the road and do what? Shout a challenge? Fire a shot? If I kept to the hills and ravines it would take me longer, tire me more and still expose me to some watcher's eyes.

I studied the surface of the road. A jumble of tyre tracks. I went to the curve where drivers are more individual, some swinging wide, some hugging the inside. Rough-patterned prints of army trucks, narrower prints of a jeep. I'd driven both ways down this road but my tracks didn't show. There was something that might be a heelprint. Darcy? It was just one print, like Man Friday's on the sand.

Doves cooed. A flicker in some rocks was an iguana. Good food if you're fast enough to catch one. Round a corner a lake lay some way off. Go and drink? Put it off until Guazatan? I stayed on the road. I'd drink later if the water seemed safe. There was a rise and over the top I saw the sprawl of the village.

12.45.

I halted. Deep weariness swept over me now that the place was within sight. I'd run through a lifetime in twenty-four hours and I'd got here too late. Come on, get going, move. My body was like a mule that wouldn't budge.

This time in the village I went the rounds of the shacks looking for secret watchers. The place was deserted. People had been born here, scratched a living, and vanished. They left emptiness behind. I could feel it. You could be swallowed up by such a place and no one would suspect you'd ever existed.

It had been about the same time yesterday that I'd climbed the rise outside the village, reading the tyre tracks in the dirt of the road. The army convoy had added a fresh chapter of prints. The heat of the sun was solid on my cheeks. At a bend I stopped to look out. The flat plain ran into small hills where you could hide several armies. I searched and it wasn't completely deserted. Two horsemen plodded. Smoke rose from a hidden fire. A breeze brought a hint of the stink of rotting flesh. You hunger after life and get a reminder of death. On, upwards.

The *hacienda* worried me. It was the building of a lost civilization. In a day it seemed to have crumbled further into ruins. Another season would see weeds taking root in the rafters. Vines would climb the walls. In five years the jungle would swallow it. I picked my way across the terrace over smashed roof tiles and plaster. I called out for Crevecoeur and Darcy. Nothing. What did I expect? An open door was an invitation. I hesitated, listening and smelling. Don't go in, instinct warned me, the house is demanding one more death. From the doorway I couldn't spot a booby trap. But I saw enough to ring alarm bells: a cigarette packet on a table, a tattered copy of Playboy, an orange. Anything might be spiked with poison or explosive.

At the back of the house nothing moved except sparrows squabbling in the dirt. I kept calling out. I peered into sheds, a woodstore, a dairy, a granary where rats had chewed the sacks. There was no logic to looking. I was tired and nervy, that's all. I was lonely. Everything was desolate. Humans had fled from this scene of disaster.

'Crevecoeur.'

My voice was a little girl's voice. Try again, loud enough to wake the dead.

It wasn't shouting. It was croaking. I was moving away from the house now. A barn, a dormitory with wooden bunks and slashed mattresses. Darcy would never have camped so close to the guerrillas for ten days. Therefore Crevecoeur wouldn't be looking for tapes and films here. But I went on searching.

'Crevecoeur! Where are you?'

Why did I call out for him? He wasn't hiding from me. He'd gone. I'd been abandoned.

Stables with stalls for a dozen horses. An old pony-trap with a wheel off, a mildewed saddle astride a stall door. The heat, the exhaustion, the closeness of death, the blood, the fierceness of Beatriz's eyes, everything was coming down to crush me. I was going mad, though who'd notice in this

227

country? It was Crevecoeur who'd got me into this and I hated him and called out his name. I backed out of the stables.

'Come on, Crevecoeur!'

I shouted into a plantation of citrus and bananas. A line of papayas formed a tall boundary. I shook a gangling trunk and a ripe fruit crashed by my feet, splitting open. I sank my teeth into orange flesh and felt juices cool on my tongue. I was a monkey, holding the fruit in two hands and tearing at it until I noticed my fingers. There was blood under the nails, the blood of Beatriz dried black. I hurled away the fruit.

Crevecoeur wasn't here, was he? Nor was Darcy. Nobody was here. I was going to have to walk through the fruit trees, across·ground chewed up by the army, through scrub, over the airstrip, across the plain, into the hills, climbing up through the trees until I reached freedom. Provided that the guerrillas didn't shoot me, the army didn't capture me, Honduran soldiers didn't turn me back, American planes didn't machine-gun me.

I started.

I walked through the fruit trees, across the ground chewed up by the army, through the scrub, through a gap in the wall of agaves, right onto the airstrip and I stopped. Crevecoeur hadn't taken off. At the end of the airstrip by the kerosene drums was a Beechcraft. It was a Sundowner, with the low wing profile, useful for air-taxi work, nifty as an executive runaround. The plane was deserted. It was like the *hacienda* and the village below – all humans had been wiped out by a plague.

But somebody had been here a short while ago. A hose connected one of the barrels to the fuel intake on the plane. Someone had been topping up the tanks and left in a hurry. The smell of kerosene tainted the air and as I drew close I saw where it dripped from a fault in the pump.

The skin at the back of my neck was crawling. It's a primitive response, tightening the skin so the hair stands up to present a bigger and more frightening aspect to an enemy. But I could see no enemy. I opened a door and looked in the plane. A map and dark glasses had been laid aside. Jammed between the two front seats was a half-drunk bottle of Sprite.

Why not take the plane?

One minute the thought wasn't there. The next it had popped into my brain. You can't unthink a thought.

I couldn't steal it. Could I?

The thing to do was to look round first, see if the plane had been abandoned. Ease my conscience. Then return to that thought.

I closed the door and looked back at that drum. The pump always dripped. A tin bowl was kept handy to catch it. The pilot Serpollet was refuelling. That's what the dribble meant. Perhaps there'd been no time at San Salvador before take-off. Or Crevecoeur had just sprung a new destination on him and he needed extra fuel. Anyway he'd stopped in mid-barrel and gone away. Crevecoeur had called him. He'd been a couple of hours searching the area and must have found where Darcy camped. Why would he need the pilot's help?

The answer came at once. Voices rose on the side of the airstrip away from the house. Crevecoeur and another man came in sight. Between them they carried a body. It wasn't the body of Darcy because Darcy hadn't been wearing blue jeans and a denim jacket. Crevecoeur had his hands hooked under the body's armpits. The other man shuffled between the legs with his arms looped under its knees. They staggered crabwise across the airstrip, Crevecoeur leading, the body's head masked by his hips. They could have seen me if they'd lifted their eyes. But a corpse has a terrible fascination. They stared at it. They were half way to the aircraft when I stepped out.

It had to be Serpollet who shared the carrying. He had a puffed and ruddy face, as if he enjoyed a bottle or so. At first sight you'd say he was a good one for fun until you recalled he'd been a terrorist himself in France in his young

229

days. Movement caught his eye and he stopped, simply letting go of the knees.

'There she is,' he said in French. 'There's your English-woman.'

Heels dragging along the ground brought Crevecoeur to a halt. He glanced over his shoulder and grunted when he saw me. He turned back to Serpollet.

'Okay. You go and collect the stuff and don't dawdle.'

'Are you kidding?'

Serpollet ran his eyes over my body and turned to walk back. Crevecoeur hauled his burden a little closer before giving up. He kneeled to lay down its head. He handled it with care, even gentleness, whereas Serpollet had dumped the legs like so much trash. He mumbled something and I said I couldn't hear. So he shouted at me.

'I said you took your bloody time.'

What do you say to a *pète-sec* like Crevecoeur? Answer back or argue or deny something and he takes it as a sign of weakness.

'We'd have flown out already if it wasn't for . . .'

He nodded to the body.

'And I'd have taken the first flight out to Miami this morning,' I said finally, 'if it wasn't for getting your man out of that army camp. Or have you forgotten? Are all your department as useless as he is?'

'What the hell are you talking about?'

'Your man Darcy.'

Crevecoeur got slowly to his feet. He wanted to hit me. His eyes hated me. They were exploding with loathing. This was a new Crevecoeur whose emotions had melted the ice in him.

'You got a strong stomach, Cody? Come and feast your eyes on this.' He stepped aside from the body. 'This is Paul Darcy. At a guess he's been dead for two days.'

I like watching a man sleep. His face gives hints of what he was as a boy. He used to play on his own, I would decide, or play with his schoolmates, or play with a puppy, or play football. That was before he played with girls and began to struggle with life.

I watched Crevecoeur's face. I didn't let my eyes stray to what was on the ground. He dug out a pack of Gitanes and his lighter and pulled furiously at the cigarette. Even in the tropical sunlight I could see the end glow. He filled his lungs until they would hold no more. The smoke was drowning his anger. I watched his face change. You want to be very careful not to have a man like Crevecoeur for an enemy. Hatred had reddened his cheeks. The heat retreated in him and I noticed the grey of his eyes once more. No more hatred, just anger and contempt.

Then I looked down.

Vomit rose and I swallowed and swallowed. Nothing in my twenty-eight years had prepared me for this. Nothing could have hardened me.

The face was turned up to the sky. The eyes saw nothing – there were no eyes. The sockets gaped. The exposed flesh was red and rust and black. There were no lips. The mouth was a hole, a scream. The soft flesh under the chin was ploughed. The throat was a rotting sponge.

The world boiled in front of my eyes. I reached out a hand to the wing in support.

'Crows.' Crevecoeur spat out the word. 'Crows and shrikes and rodents. Paul is nothing more than lunch. Have you ever seen more crows in your life? They prosper in this country. It's one big restaurant for crows. See – they only bother with the delicacies, the softest . . .'

'Stop it.'

He stopped. He took puffs from his cigarette, letting the smoke mask the smell. In tropical heat, the flesh is quick to putrefy. He was staring at me with the beginning of a scowl.

'What's that garbage about getting my man out?'

'He said his name was Darcy.'

Crevecoeur looked down at the corpse and opened his mouth to say something.

'No,' I corrected myself. 'I thought he was Darcy. I called him Darcy. He never denied it.'

'How could you be so . . .'

Crevecoeur didn't finish. Gullible? Stupid? But I'd heard Major Portillo boast on television of capturing a foreigner. Crevecoeur insisted the prisoner was Darcy. Whoever he actually was he hadn't corrected me. With hindsight I realized how strange he'd been. Odd scraps of behaviour floated through my mind.

'Then who did I get out of the army camp?'

Crevecoeur took his time, frowning as he concentrated. 'It has to be the man who did this.' He jabbed a foot towards the body. 'Monsieur X. Paul has been dead for a couple of days and for his own reasons the mystery man hung round until the army scooped him up. Perhaps he knew Paul by sight or knew what he was doing here. Anyway he watched and waited. Couldn't rush Paul because he was armed. Monxieur X chose his moment. Paul was preparing to use his radio. He still had the headphones on when I found him. That's why he has ears – the crows couldn't get to them. Monsieur X crept up behind him and used a knife. He didn't stab Paul in the back. He leant over and slashed his windpipe.'

I had to close my eyes again. There was the memory of that knife pricking the back of my neck.

'I hate the ones who use knives,' Crevecoeur said. 'They're the quiet ones. They're sly and treacherous. They like killing. They like the feel of the knife in a body.'

'He knows you,' I said. 'When I spoke your name he reacted. Even at the time the way he behaved puzzled –'

I broke off. Crevecoeur was wearing a cotton jacket. It was Mediterranean blue and would have wowed them in Nice in 1928. Dirt and blood had marked it. The thin material gave hints of the shoulder holster underneath. He gave no warning, simply dropped his cigarette and snatched under the jacket. He jerked out a Browning automatic, the policeman's pal, brother to the gun I'd once lifted from him in East Berlin. His hand was a blur. He was like a Mississippi gambler, snake-fast and whirling to meet danger. There'd been no sound. But he'd caught sight of a movement that the plane had hidden from me. He was sidestepping and swinging his gun round.

A voice snapped out: 'Drop it!'

Crevecoeur froze, his gun half raised.

'Loustau,' he said. 'So you're the bastard.'

'Drop the gun.'

Crevecoeur swallowed. I heard his throat contracting, a small choking sound as he forced down his fear. But he kept his grip on the automatic. It must have been the hardest thing he ever did in his life. But by keeping the gun, even if it wasn't pointing at the other man, he was half way to setting up a stalemate situation. The longer he kept the gun, the stronger his position, and so he talked.

'Loustau works for one of the Paris gangs. They're the mob who plan on taking over the Snowline.'

'I'm warning you,' Loustau said. 'Drop your gun right now.'

Crevecoeur took a breath. He was staring at the other man's face, at the bruises and contusions, wanting to add some of his own.

'He's known as "Le Philo". You see, he's the intellectual of the gang, at least by comparison with the others. His one fault is he has an un-Platonic love of money. We had him in our hands once for smuggling arms to his fellow Basques in Spain but he got free. He had a smart lawyer. Or he bought some high-powered protection.'

'There were no guns,' Loustau said. 'It doesn't take a smart lawyer to point that out.'

'There were guns in the van when you were stopped at Ainhoa. Rifles and grenades were itemized on the charge sheet at Pau police headquarters. The examining magistrate also inspected them.'

'No guns were produced in evidence. You couldn't even provide the original charge sheet in court.'

'We couldn't even produce the examining magistrate. Victim of a hit-and-run accident. That was convenient, wasn't

233

it, Philo? Two years ago. Perhaps you read about his case in the papers.'

'Something,' I said. The Spanish government had been furious that gunrunners to ETA had been freed.

'Where's your knife?' Crevecoeur asked.

Loustau smiled. 'I thought this might come in useful.' The pistol was still on Crevecoeur's chest and he made the slightest of movements with it. 'I picked it up in the *tatu*.'

'You picked it up where?'

'Just drop your gun,' Loustau said. But he'd lost the initiative. If he intended to shoot Crevecoeur he'd have done it already. Instead he took a step forward as if that threatened a violent attack. It was the opposite. He hobbled. It was why I'd arrived before he did.

That thought opened up a chain of other possibilities. If he had that moment arrived, he didn't know about Serpollet. Loustau saw a light aircraft and Crevecoeur apparently interrupted during refuelling by my arrival. Loustau wasn't going to shoot Crevecoeur, except as a last desperate measure. He believed Crevecoeur was the pilot and needed him to fly the plane out. His feet, as the saying goes, were killing him.

Loustau's eyes never flickered from Crevecoeur's face but he gave a nod in my direction. 'Get away from the plane.'

Crevecoeur still held his gun. How long would it take him to swing it up, target it on Loustau and squeeze the trigger? Would he be quicker? Would he be certain of a disabling shot? The equations must be running through Crevecoeur's mind. They certainly were in Loustau's mind. Sweat had sprung up on his forehead and trickled like a tear past one of his eyes. He could snap at any moment, decide Crevecoeur who refused to drop his gun was an unacceptable risk and would be better dead.

'What are you going to do with me?' I asked.

'Nothing.'

'Liar,' Crevecoeur said. 'Don't believe him.'

'I want her out in the open where she can't be a danger. I've seen how she operates.'

'I meant, what happens to me when Crevecoeur flies you out to Honduras?' Had Crevecoeur grasped his importance to Loustau? I spelled it out. 'You need him as a pilot, don't you. So what happens to me?'

'That's a good question,' Crevecoeur said, 'and I'll provide the answer. If I'm going to pilot this plane over those hills, I'll need her as navigator.'

Yes, he'd picked it up and was telling me in return he understood. Crevecoeur had never flown a plane in his life. We were using a simple speech code, like married people do. It occurred to me we'd work well as a team except for one problem: I couldn't stand the sight of the man. Together Cody and Crevecoeur make the world safe for democracy. The bone tiredness, the beating sun, the stench of death, the danger – and still I had this thought. I should be planning a move, *anything*, because Loustau had an edgy excitement to his eyes. It was a look that said: there's a death hovering in the air. A knife, a gun, both were a thrill to him. He needed Crevecoeur, so he'd kill me instead. If only I'd be so good as to step forward.

'The woman stays behind,' Loustau said.

People of his kind always talk of me as 'the woman', like they say 'the dog'.

'I must –' Crevecoeur started.

'I'm not being cooped up with her in that little plane. She's too full of trickery.'

'I cannot fly and navigate at the same time.'

'You can,' Loustau said, 'if I tell you to.'

Out beyond the airstrip there was a clamour like raucous shouting. Above the line of agaves half a dozen well nourished crows flapped into the air. Loustau's eyes wavered a fraction and snapped back on Crevecoeur. How was he going to solve the problem of Crevecoeur's gun? Come and wrestle it away from him? Shoot him in the leg? The crows were sinking out of sight.

'You're not coming.' Loustau was talking to me again. 'Sorry, gorgeous.'

The crows were up in the air a second time, calling out in alarm or anger.

'You should have been a little sweeter to me up on the hill. You're not going home.'

Across the airstrip Serpollet appeared, took a couple of steps and halted. Given the angle, he wouldn't be able to see the gun in Loustau's hand. But he could suspect it. There was the Browning that Crevecoeur held towards the ground. There was our rock-like immobility. Above all there was the tension. He must sense that. It was as bad as a courtroom in the moments before a judge pronounces sentence of death.

'For the moment,' Crevecoeur said, 'forget about Cody. What happens to me? Perhaps I won't cooperate.'

'You'll do what I tell you.' Loustau's eyes were furious. 'I'm giving the orders.'

The pistol was levelled at Crevecoeur's chest. That made Loustau the boss, unless Crevecoeur could prove his will was stronger.

I could see the crows. They stood like mourners at a funeral, dressed in black. You'd swear they were waiting.

'You and I are going out in that plane. We're not flying to Honduras. We're going to Guatemala City.'

'Why Guatemala? Who's your contact there?'

'This is not Paris. This is not an interrogation. You're not the boss.'

'And when we get to Guatemala, what happens then? What happens to me?'

Loustau didn't answer that question. He stared and said: 'You're to drop your gun. Do it before I count five. One.'

Crevecoeur swallowed. I saw the bob of his Adam's apple. Across the airstrip Serpollet had dumped everything he was carrying. I couldn't look directly at him but he seemed to have tape cassettes, an aluminium camera box, an attaché case. He picked out a pistol and began to walk.

'Two. I mean it: drop your gun. Three.'

236

'Loustau, answer me this: suppose I don't, what happens then?'

'I'll shoot you. You're going to be in the way.'

'Then you'll shoot me anyway.' Crevecoeur swallowed again. 'I fly you to some field in Guatemala and you'll jam your pistol in my ear and pull the trigger. You'll already have killed Cody so it's only logical you should kill me. In your view that means no witnesses who have seen what you did to Darcy. Speaking frankly, Philo, that's a lousy bargain. What's in it for me? Nothing.'

'Put your gun down. Four.'

'Don't rush, Philo. Listen to me. If you shoot me, you'll be dead in two seconds. That's the truth, Philo. There's a man with a gun pointing at your back coming up behind you.'

Serpollet was still thirty metres away, too far to be certain with a pistol. But what choice did Crevecoeur have? Loustau's hand was shaking but at that range he couldn't miss. There was nothing I could do. If I moved now – even if I moved away from the plane as ordered – I had the conviction Loustau's nerve would crack and he'd squeeze the trigger in a reflex action.

'Wonderful. Where did they teach you that trick? Nursery school?'

Loustau gave his meaningless smile. It died and the look in his face hardened. The decision to act was taken. This was the last second of Crevecoeur's life and I yelled at the top of my voice.

'Serpollet, now!'

What happened was simple. What is difficult is sorting it out in my mind. It was violent and over so quickly. It was unreal, hinting at magic powers.

In the end Loustau had an instant's doubt. Perhaps he wasn't falling for the oldest trick in the book. Perhaps some assassin really was creeping closer. His eyes abruptly widened as he squeezed the trigger. Crevecoeur, diving to his left, gave a cry as he was hit. He tumbled on the ground, losing his Browning. At the same moment Serpollet fired and shot wild. Loustau swung round and was aiming across the airstrip

237

as Serpollet shot a second time. He hit Loustau. There was no doubt of it. Loustau staggered back a couple of paces, bent over as if kicked in the stomach. He straightened upright and where was the blood? A stomach wound gives a generous rush of red and he was unscathed. The bullet had no effect on him. He should be screaming. A stomach wound is agony. Instead there was a half smile on his lips.

This smile had a meaning. He was going to make a kill.

Loustau didn't rush at it. He was going to make damn certain he hit his target. He stood with the gun gripped in his right hand and his left hand steadying his aim. He was lining up his shot like a champion when Crevecoeur crawled to his gun and picked it up in his left hand and shot Loustau in the back.

'*Maman!*'

Loustau stumbled forward onto his knees, dropping the gun. He reached over his shoulder as if he could brush away the burning pain. There was no problem in seeing this wound. A dark red stain was spreading across his blouson. From his mouth entirely different blood came, pink and frothy. He wiped it away with the back of his hand and it bubbled out more strongly. He twisted his head towards Crevecoeur and there was a look of disbelief on his face.

'You old *pète-sec*, you've . . .'

He coughed through the blood and pitched forward. He jerked on the ground and gave a convulsive heave and was still. He lay in the grotesque twisted position of the violently killed.

# 20

‘*Bon Dieu de bon Dieu.*’

Crevecoeur gave a shout of frustration and anger. His arm hurt but it was more than that.

‘I wanted him alive. I truly did.’ He clamped a hand on his sleeve just above the wound.

‘Shooting someone in the back is the wrong way to go about it.’

‘You’re a fool, Cody. Do you know that?’

Maybe. But it was a slaughterhouse on the airstrip and it sickened me. It’s always the men who carry guns who end up dead. Why do they never learn? Why do men want to shoot their way out? Why don’t they use their brains?

The crows had been disturbed by the shooting and wheeled above the airstrip. They weren’t going away. From up in the air they could look down and see there was work for them to do.

‘Paul is dead so I cannot have his testimony. I wanted Loustau back in Paris and under the bright lights. Instead of which . . .’ He prodded with his shoe at a shoulder and the body eased over. ‘Some philosopher.’

Serpollet walked up with his pistol still threatening Loustau. He was frowning, puzzled.

‘I hit him. My second shot got him in the guts. You saw it too. Look, there’s the hole in his blouson. He went back like a boxer on the ropes and came forward fighting. It’s like his body ate the bullet and it did him no harm at all.’

The two men stared down at the corpse. I pictured surgeons wondering what had gone wrong with an operation. Crevecoeur got out his pack of Gitanes and gave one to Serpollet. Serpollet did the Chief Inspector a favour in return and lit the cigarettes. Real buddies now. He flicked the match over his shoulder as if the leaking fuel pump didn't matter.

'Forget the post mortem,' I said. 'Can't we get away from here?'

'Nothing to wait for,' Crevecoeur agreed.

'You want to take this butcher's meat along too?' Serpollet asked.

Crevecoeur shook his head. 'Paul Darcy murdered by gangsters is a hero. Loustau shot down by the Sûreté is revenge. We can do without complications.'

He knelt beside Loustau and felt in his blouson pocket. He came out with a sheet of paper and brightened.

'Couple of useful names and phone numbers.'

He patted the blouson all over and took a fistful of the material covering Loustau's stomach. He unzipped the blouson and pulled up a tee shirt.

'Bulletproof vest?' Serpollet suggested. 'Never seen one like it.'

Crevecoeur was undoing straps. He jerked the vest off and held it up. A bullet rolled free and dropped to the ground with hardly a sound. It was a very special vest, very expensive. It was the moneybelt, fashioned out of Erica's pillowcase, plump with dollar bills. I had last seen it dumped for safe-keeping on a wooden table in the *tatu*. Loustau had been last out of the *tatu*, hadn't he, helping himself to artillery and booty and armour-plating, and look where it got him.

'There's a hundred thousand dollars in there,' I said. 'It's the cash I brought in as a pay-off.'

Serpollet took the moneybelt from Crevecoeur. It had a bullethole on one side, unbroken cloth on the other. The Bible has saved men's lives in battle: carried in a breast pocket it has stopped an enemy bullet. Mammon does as well as God, until you get one in the back.

'It's still good, isn't it?' Serpollet had a fistful of dollars. He stuck a finger through a hole. 'Okay, maybe you don't pay your restaurant bill with them but the bank will exchange them for new ones.'

'What do you suppose the guerrillas will do when they

find the money's gone?' Crevecoeur asked. 'Hijack another plane?' The prospect pleased him.

'Don't ask me.'

I walked away. I was sick of Crevecoeur and drugs and guerrillas and killing. I wanted home. I wanted Paris with the hint of spring in the air and a certain look in men's eyes and a certain smile on girls' lips. I wanted Madame Boyer's sniff of disapproval that told me a man was waiting in my apartment. I wanted that particularly. Philippe was gone and memories of him were buried under the landslide of the last couple of days. I wanted a new lover, a man I trusted enough to give a key. I wanted a man to unlock me.

I lay on the ground. I should have moved further away. Voices drifted like puffs of hot air on a summer afternoon.

'It doesn't belong to anyone,' Serpollet said.

'It came from Jules Debilly originally,' Crevecoeur said.

'You're joking. The old queen who made tough-guy movies? Is he involved?'

'Damned if I'm returning a drug pusher's money to him.'

'You're overlooking the vital fact: we're the ones who physically hold it. The money is ours. One hundred thousand she said?'

'Well, certainly Loustau had no legal title to it. His widow – assuming there is a Madame L – has no claim.'

'Frankly, *mon vieux*, you are being too legalistic about this. The man tried to kill you. You shot in self-defence. Perhaps it's yours.'

'As an officer of the Sûreté Nationale I cannot –'

'Though of course I shot before you did. That's the hole my bullet made. That should be taken into account. In a sense I got there before you.'

'Come to think of it, the last person who legally handled the money was the woman.'

'What? Some peasant terrorist extracts a ransom and it's legal?'

'Not that woman,' Crevecoeur said. 'Her.'

241

There was silence. When I opened my eyes and turned my head, both men were staring in my direction.

'Welcome to the Free Democratic Republic of El Salvador.'

It was Beatriz. Her voice had lost its firmness. She faded and came back.

'Put your hands on your head. Come forward very slowly.'

'What the fuck's going on?' That was in English. Then in Spanish: 'Get that crazy fool off my back.'

It was a dream. I opened my eyes and blinked at the sun.

'You won't get hurt provided you do exactly what you're told,' Beatriz said. 'Don't try any tricks.'

It wasn't a dream. Crevecoeur had a cassette player in his good hand. Darcy must have lain hidden by the agaves and used a directional microphone. Crevecoeur looked pleased. He was salvaging some evidence from the wreckage of his operation.

'*Brigada 24 de marzo,*' the man said. I recognized the voice: it was the American who'd refuelled here. 'Son-of-a-bitch, the comrades.'

I struggled to my feet with my head reeling. I'd dozed five minutes and a throbbing pain split my brain down the middle.

'Let's go. Listen to your tapes when we're out of here.'

'Your Spanish is better than mine. Tell me –'

He broke off as a pistol cracked beyond the agaves. Crows rose in alarm.

'Where's Serpollet?'

'He went to fetch Darcy's night glasses,' Crevecoeur said. 'A souvenir.'

'You don't shoot your souvenirs.'

'Maybe he hates crows.'

A short burst of automatic fire and a scream put that theory out of our heads. Crevecoeur abandoned the cassette player and began to run for cover. I went to the far side of the plane with some thought of getting inside. I wanted a flight to freedom and the first stage was boarding the Beechcraft.

'Stop!'

Crevecoeur didn't. He loped like a wolf. Another short burst of gunfire sent me diving to the ground. I raised myself and wondered if Crevecoeur had been cut down. Then his head lifted. His cheeks were thin and his eyes black-ringed. He was a small animal on the prairie on the look-out for danger.

I had ended up close to the barrels. The stink of dripping kerosene was rank in my nose. Perhaps I could snake my way to safety behind the barrels. I looked across the airstrip at the man who'd shot at us and went still. Safety was an illusion.

I recognized Major Portillo from his book-lover's glasses and his hungry cheeks. On television he'd worn a beret slanted over one ear. He'd swapped that for a floppy sunhat in camouflage colours. A curl was licked by sweat. He was on horseback, an army pony that didn't rear up at the sound of gunfire. He swung a leg over the saddle and jumped to the ground. I'd expected someone bigger but he was no more than another peasant boy puffed up by power.

It's the United States that's armed the Salvadorian army. But not Major Portillo. He cradled an Uzi, an Israeli sub-machine-gun with a lightweight stock. Grenades bounced at his belt as he came forward. He walked with something of a swagger, or it could be stiffness from the saddle.

'Don't do anything sudden. Keep your hands where I can see them.'

Crevecoeur stayed silent. For the second time in half an hour he was under a gun. This was more dangerous.

'That's smart of you. Okay, now get up. Slowly.'

Portillo spoke Spanish but there was no mistaking the meaning of the gun barrel urging Crevecoeur to his feet. The Major stepped back to give him room and walked round Crevecoeur to search him from behind. Portillo patted his legs and his back and under his arms and removed the Browning and slipped it into a pocket of his combat jacket.

'What is your name?'

'Crevecoeur.'

'Been holding a party?'

Portillo jerked his head in the direction of the bodies by the plane.

'What are you?'

Crevecoeur didn't reply.

'Do you speak English?'

'Yes.'

'Perhaps you prefer that. I speak English. No, I speak American. The United States Army taught me. I was at their school down in Panama before it got closed. Wonderful place. You looked round at all these future leaders of their countries and you thought how smart of Uncle Sam to teach them to respect the Stars and Stripes. Yes sir, real smart.'

Portillo kept his mouth open when he finished speaking. It was like a safety catch left off. His mouth was ready to talk or spit or bite.

'You okay, mister? Not hurt too bad?'

'I'm okay.'

'The *Yanquis* don't like me just now.' Portillo's forehead wrinkled. He wasn't angry but perplexed. 'It's kind of a compliment maybe that they've heard of me but it's still crazy. They figure there's going to be peace and I'm the wrong kind of guy to have in a peaceful country. Well mister, they don't understand my country. Our peasants are poor. The point is they'll always be poor. There's not enough land for them. So there'll always be trouble. The communists will see to it. Bombings, murders, strikes, we'll always have them. Now it could be this year, it could be next year, it could be later, but the time will come when the US needs me. Suddenly they'll remember Major Portillo is a friend. Only by then there'll be serious trouble and they'll need me as a colonel, maybe as a general. You sure you're okay? You don't say much for yourself.'

'I'm okay.'

'Well, that's fine. If you're feeling comfortable, why don't you tell me some things. How did you say you were called again?'

'Crevecoeur.'

'Crevecoeur. You bet.' Portillo nodded. He hadn't forgotten. He was just checking Crevecoeur kept to his story. 'Well now, you're not American. You're surely not Salvadorian. What are you? Hold on. You're not . . .'

Portillo broke off. He raised the Uzi to his eye and sighted down the barrel. He aimed directly in Crevecoeur's face. Crevecoeur froze.

'You're not Russian by any chance? What sort of name is Crevecoeur?'

'French.'

'French, eh? You know, I have an excellent view of your face. I'm centred just between your eyes but I can see your forehead and your cheeks and your mouth. You look . . . concerned. Tell me frankly – are you frightened?'

Crevecoeur didn't answer.

'It's all right to breathe if you want to. I shan't pull the trigger because of a breath or two. In fact, it's safer to breathe than stop. Don't you agree?'

Crevecoeur still kept dumb. He was a toy. Portillo enjoyed playing with him. Crevecoeur knew this and wasn't going to slip into the expected role of terrified prisoner.

'What kind of French are you?'

'Chief Inspector in the Sûreté Nationale. Your nearest equivalent, so I'm told, is the Treasury Police.'

'So.'

Portillo lowered his gun. He went for a little walk round Crevecoeur and ended up in front. He inspected his face.

'You know, I've never admired those soldiers who are . . . What is the expression the Americans use? Gung-ho, that's it. Give me a man who knows fear but controls it. That is a brave man. Do you know who I am?'

'You command the forward camp of the Quezacatl Battalion.'

'You mean I'm famous even in France?'

'You were on the news last night.'

'And you watched because you had an interest in me?'

Crevecoeur didn't think that needed an answer. What was going through his mind? Was he making a plan? Just trying

245

to stay alive from one moment to the next? Because it was obvious this teasing by Portillo would come to a climax very soon and there had to be *some* way of escape or the ending would be violent.

'This is my country, Chief Inspector. It is not your country. You have no damn right to be interested in me.'

For a moment anger flashed out of Portillo's spectacles. Some small cog had slipped inside him and it was like this that he turned into a torturer and killer. With a visible effort he controlled his temper. I lay watching between the wheels of the plane as Portillo prodded Crevecoeur into movement. They ambled, they strolled. They should have been arm in arm, old friends, except for the Uzi. Portillo got out a cigar. It was short and stumpy, a long way from a Corona. He didn't light it. It was just a macho prop.

'Too many French,' Portillo said. 'That's what I'm beginning to think. When Chief Inspectors carry on their business here, it starts to feel like a French colony. I don't like that.' He stopped and swung round on Crevecoeur, his mouth open, ready to bite. 'I don't like it one little bit. Do you know El Salvador once applied to join the United States? No, why should you. Last century that was. There are times when the United States treats us as their colony. Do this, their ambassador orders. Or stop doing that. We are a proud people, you know. We don't like foreigners who poke their noses into our affairs. That's why the terrorists will never win. Our people see the Cubans and Russians over their shoulders. Now it seems we have French tripping over each other and killing themselves.'

My view was distorted. Black rubber tyres filled my eyes. Beyond were legs stretched on the ground. Approaching legs were upright. In the distance was the pony, a roan, neck bowed as it cropped grass. I was the lowest of the low, a worm with a view. Slowly I turned my face towards the fuel drums. I would stay where I was, not moving. My eyes smarted from the kerosene in the bowl beside me. If Portillo noticed me, he might just take me to be another corpse.

'You should understand why I'm here, Major.'

Crevecoeur said it as an opening statement. Portillo stopped him going further.

'Believe it or not, Chief Inspector, I already do.' His voice was surprisingly American. The Army School in Panama – the one its critics called Dictators College – had done a good job and somewhere in the Carolinas or Virginia the accent had been given its final polish. He sounded sincere; he could be selling insurance or a place in heaven. This was no time for shouting. He was a schizophrenic and it showed in his face and his voice. 'You're here to get evidence on the Snowline. This man you shot in the back was in my hands during the night. I'd hardly begun my questioning when he came out with a truly amazing story of how there were new people taking over in Paris. He made a *very* interesting offer for my wholehearted cooperation. Well, naturally, to show I appreciated his offer, I stopped questioning him. It's true he'd been hurt a little bit but that was before he understood who I was. It shows the importance of introductions.'

I heard the scuff of shoes and felt the power of the sun and was heady with kerosene fumes.

'Once I knew the offer I tried to contact my old friend and colleague Ernesto in San Salvador. Ernesto Blum, that is. Have you made his acquaintance? No? Well, he wasn't at home, they said he was at his office. His people assured me of this even though he didn't answer the office telephone. So I made use of our helicopter and found him locked in his office and mad as hell. Only natural. When he was able to use his own phone, he made some enquiries in Paris. The old French connection paid well. The new French connection will pay even better. But I confess at this precise moment things are a mess. The old firm's plane hijacked for ten days. Ten days, I ask you! The new firm sends someone to negotiate and you shoot him. It won't do. This kind of thing seems unprofessional to people in the States and Europe. I'm here to put a stop to it. That means you, Chief Inspector.'

They were close to the other side of the plane now.

'Jeez, what happened to this one?'

'Your new friend slit his throat. Vermin did the rest.'

'Loustau never told me.'

'Loustau was out of his depth,' Crevecoeur said. 'His kind always thinks a murder or two turns things their way.'

'I have to tell you frankly that killing one or two people can make a difference. That has been my experience. I regret, Chief Inspector, but I must protect this facility from international exposure. Only in that way can I continue to provide –'

He stopped.

He'd seen me. He must have looked over to gesture at the fuel barrels. A clink of metal, such as a gun makes, was in my ears.


'Well, well, well.'

Portillo's voice had a new tone, a freshening of interest. Crevecoeur had just been an inconvenience to be removed in order to protect his 'facility'. I was something else, appealing to a darker side of him.

'Move over there and sit on the ground.'

It wasn't me he was talking to. I couldn't be any closer to the ground. It was an order to Crevecoeur, who wasn't fast enough. There was the solid thump of a gun on a body and a cry as Crevecoeur was sent sprawling.

'Sit cross-legged so you can't make a run for it. Or do I shoot you now and get it over with? No? Life is sweet, Chief Inspector. Even when the last few minutes are bitter, they are sweeter than dying. Put your hands on your head. Okay, don't bother with the wounded arm. See how human I am. Now . . .'

I heard footsteps. Portillo's voice was brisk and vigorous. The footsteps were slow. I knew why. He was a soldier on patrol now, each step bringing a changing perspective and new angles to check. Seeing me on the ground had been a surprise. He had to be sure there were no more surprises. He stopped.

'Ernesto warned me about you. "That sweets is a real bitch," he said. "If you catch her, give her one for me."

248

Okay? You did something to upset Mister Ernesto Blum. You hurt his pride.'

Lie still. Don't breathe. Act dead. I'm another corpse. As long as he doesn't put a bullet into me to see if it's just make-believe.

'So, sweets, get up and say Hi. Let's see what you're made of. But don't rush it.'

The stink of kerosene flooded my nose and throat. My lungs hated it. I was going to convulse with coughing. *No.* A corpse doesn't cough. Crevecoeur, say something to take Portillo's attention away.

'I'm talking to you. Get on your feet. Do I have to make you?'

Major Ballbreaker they called him. He didn't earn that nickname dealing with women. What would he do with me? Crevecoeur said he favoured the blowtorch. Major Blowtorch. Yes, that was it! If . . .

'She's unconscious. Can't you tell? Leave her alone.'

'Chief Inspector, you amaze me.' The voice was different. He'd turned round to speak to Crevecoeur. Now was my chance. I got on one elbow and leant over. 'People do not fall unconscious round here. They drop dead. But that woman was trying to hide behind the plane. She wants to play possum. Don't be stupid.'

Could Crevecoeur see me? He went on: 'Major Portillo, this is your country. I have no power here, even over French citizens. And I certainly have no authority over a man with a sub-machine-gun. But if you kill us you'll find you've got three French and one English corpse to explain away. That's a big international dimension. The media –'

'You know what I say to that?' Portillo cut in. 'Ess-aitch-eye-tee. What does that spell in your language, Frenchy?'

Yes, there was a chance for Crevecoeur and me. The slimmest chance. The one per center. But infinitely better than the zero per center.

Portillo was moving again, coming round the front of the plane. His voice sounded closer and harsher. 'Sweets, up on your feet.'

Don't call me that. I'd warned Blum. I couldn't tell Portillo. But warnings were useless anyhow. He was a torturing, murdering son-of-a-bitch. In only quarter of an hour he'd shown himself. He was a sadist, a killer. Hold on to that. Sadist, killer.

I got up and faced him.

'Hey, Ernesto was damn right. You're quite something. You fill your clothes well.'

Blum only knew the half of it. Major Portillo, you're going to know the other half.

He'd stopped at a point where he could watch me as well as check Crevecoeur didn't make a move. He held the Uzi across his chest like a man at ease with it.

'Come closer.'

I took a step.

'Closer, sweets.'

Another step, another. I was so near he must smell me. He didn't raise the Uzi as a threat. No need. I was only a woman, no use except for one thing.

'Come on, what's with the sour face? I bet you're a real scorcher between the sheets. How about a kiss?'

Couldn't help the sour face. As for kissing him . . . He was disgusting. Remember how he tortured and killed.

'What's wrong, sweets?'

Nothing. I was going to vomit or faint. Nothing else.

'You going to give me that kiss? Lost your tongue? Nothing to say for yourself?'

He stuck the cigar in his mouth. He rolled it from side to side. That's another trick I've always hated. I was aware of Crevecoeur without looking in his direction. He was frowning, wondering what was happening. Nothing yet. I was just face to face with a piece of garbage who had a superficial resemblance to a human being.

'You could say: Please spare me, I'll do anything. That kind of stuff.'

He smiled and it turned into a sneer. The cigar jiggled up and down. He dug out his lighter. A nice gold job. Could afford it, couldn't he, with the money rolling in from the

Snowline. He thumbed it and got a spark and thumbed it again and got a flame.

'Be nice to me and it could be your passport out of here. You're not French, after all. This isn't your business. No? It's your only chance.'

He was right. This was my only chance.

He put the lighter to the cigar and drew and the tip glowed bright in the flame and I convinced myself: he's a psychopath, a killer for pleasure. He has the gun. He's killed Serpollet. He's going to shoot Crevecoeur. If I witness that killing, he'll never let me live. This was the jungle. Him or me.

And I leant forward with my lips pursed for a kiss and exploded my mouthful of kerosene full in his face.

There was a flash. His head was a fireball. His face dissolved and reformed in waves of yellow and blue flame. His eyebrows, cotton hat, hair were ablaze. He opened his mouth and took in a breath to scream and sucked flames down his windpipe and gagged and had to suck in again. Fire was scorching his lungs. At the moment of blowing out the kerosene I'd thrown myself sideways. Where I'd been standing he blasted with the Uzi, seeing nothing, his finger jerking, his whole body shuddering.

Major Blowtorch.

I saw him from the ground. A human blowtorch beating at fire. No longer human. Flames behind his glasses, devils dancing in his eyes. There was a compulsion to scream and he sucked in more fire, and crashed to his knees, flailing. Then he fell on his face and rolled away out of my sight.

I could still hear him. His screams had got inside my head. They were trapped inside my skull and couldn't escape. They echoed, louder and louder, driving me mad.

'Shut up! Shut up! Shut up!'

The screams had stopped, but not inside my head.

# 21

'Are you okay?'

'No.'

'I meant,' Crevecoeur said, 'are you all right to walk?'

I nodded.

'He was going to kill us both.'

But it was I who had killed him. I was no better than the men with guns.

'Help me,' Crevecoeur said. 'I can't do it on my own.'

Together we slung the body of Darcy over the pony. I'd refused point blank to take the plane up. Why not, Crevecoeur demanded, you can do it. Yes I could do it, I'd finally got round to getting a private pilot's licence. But no, I couldn't do it. I was too drained, my nerves too shot to hell. There was a saddlebag which Crevecoeur filled with tapes and papers and rolls of film. He'd also taken photos, using Darcy's camera, of Major Portillo's body with kerosene drums at his back.

'How long do you reckon?'

'For ever,' I said.

'Snap out of it, Cody. How long to the border?'

The border between innocence and corruption seemed hazy.

'You've got to remember he took money from drug runners, he was a torturer and a killer.'

'I'll remember,' I said. I'll remember Loustau killed Darcy and Crevecoeur killed Loustau and Portillo killed Serpollet and I killed Portillo. I would never forget. There was a terrible taste in my mouth and no spitting would get rid of it. What man would ever want to kiss my mouth again?

'This refuelling facility is finished,' Crevecoeur said. He

sounded cheerful, not affected by the killings in the least. 'When certain evidence . . .'

I heard his voice droning on: a general in Colombia, Blum, Air France crew, customs and police and pushers. He was really cleaning up. I cut him short.

'Crevecoeur, when we get back to Paris . . .'

'Yes?' he prompted.

'For a change you can do something for me. You're still holding Debilly?'

'Oh yes. He hired himself a smart lawyer, but we've got him locked up.'

'Then find out who gave Debilly my name. I want to settle with the bastard.'

'Don't get involved any more. Just leave it. Bit of advice for nothing.'

Crevecoeur was flipping through a notebook. It was Darcy's and perhaps had something important. But there was something about his watchfulness that held me. An idea sparked in my brain and grew and wouldn't go away.

'Crevecoeur, it was *you* who got Debilly to hire me. I don't know how – you couldn't have seen him direct. You used some crooked go-between when you heard Debilly needed a courier.'

He went on looking through the notebook. His voice was languid. 'Don't be absurd. You've already accused me of that. Back in the hotel.'

And he hadn't given an answer. No more than he was now. There was no evidence. It was just a feeling in my guts that somehow I had been a pawn in a dirty game of his.

'What possible reason could I have had for getting Debilly to hire you? You messed everything up, remember.'

Then I had it. I knew the reason.

'I didn't mess it up, Crevecoeur. Loustau did when he shot your man. Darcy was meant to photograph me handing money over to the guerrillas. I was to be part of your evidence.'

Crevecoeur looked up at me. There was some emotion I

couldn't make out at the back of his eyes. Hatred, fear, contempt – one of those.

'You're mad. You've had too much sun and seen too much blood. Cody, I would never do that, involve an innocent citizen.'

'I'm not a French citizen.'

'And you haven't any proof, not a scrap.'

'No, but I'm right, aren't I?'

His temper suddenly snapped and he opened his lungs and bawled at me: 'You stupid woman, you're obsessed by me.'

Obsessed? By that man?

I could take no more and wanted to put distance between myself and him. I started to walk towards the hills and the border. There was no pain in my feet. It was elsewhere, in my head, in my heart. Behind me I heard Crevecoeur encouraging the pony with clicks of his tongue. A raucous chorus saw us off.

'Bloody crows,' Crevecoeur shouted.

# DAVID BRIERLEY

## SKORPION'S DEATH

Cody is unique, recruited by the SIS, trained by the CIA, and now she hunts on her own. Very much on her own.

Her quarry is a pilot, Borries. Hired by an unknown organisation for an undercover job in Tunisia, he's gone missing and his wife wants him back.

Cody finds Borries, at an army garrison deep in the Sahara, but by then it is almost too late. By then the organisation has a name: Skorpion. And Skorpion has a secret, a secret so deadly it will torture and kill to protect it. And Skorpion has Cody in its pincers . . .

'Tough, staccato, sardonically witty'

*The New Yorker*

'Fine unflagging stuff'

*The Observer*

# Post·A·Book

A Royal Mail service in association with the Book Marketing Council & The Booksellers Association.

Post-A-Book is a Post Office trademark.

## ALSO AVAILABLE FROM CORONET